Mythical Ireland

About the Author

Anthony Murphy is a journalist, photographer and the author of *Island of the Setting Sun: In Search of Ireland's Ancient Astronomers* (with Richard Moore), *Newgrange: Monument to Immortality, Land of the Ever-Living Ones* and *The Cry of the Sebac*. He lives in Drogheda and manages the website www.mythicalireland.com.

Mythical Ireland

New Light on the Ancient Past

Text and Photographs by
Anthony Murphy

The Liffey Press

the liffey press

Published by
The Liffey Press Ltd
'Clareville'
307 Clontarf Road
Dublin D03 PO46, Ireland
www.theliffeypress.com

© 2017 Anthony Murphy
Reprinted 2019

A catalogue record of this book is
available from the British Library.

ISBN 978-0-9957927-2-2

Printed in Spain by GraphyCems.

Contents

6. The Meaning of Myth

7. Cosmology

Acknowledgements

It is incumbent upon me to say a few words of gratitude to people who helped in some way towards the completion of this book. The most vital supporters are, of course, my lovely family. To my wife Ann, I'd like to give thanks and love for her unstinting support and for constant patience and understanding, especially when I've out at some ungodly hour of the late night or early morning taking photographs! And to my children Amy, Luke, Josh, Tara and Finn, likewise. I love you all. Thank you also to my parents and family who have always supported my work.

I would like to also say thanks and acknowledge the assistance and support of the following, all of whom contributed, helped or supported in various different ways:

Clare Tuffy, Leontia Lenehan and all the wonderful and helpful guides, OPW staff and bus drivers at Brú na Bóinne and indeed the guides at Loughcrew; Jack Roberts and Judith Nilan; Lar Dooley; Ken Williams; Noel Meehan; Treacy O'Connor; the Heise family at Rosnaree; Richard Moore; Ollie Fitzpatrick; Martin Byrne; Courtney Davis; the Naper family; Kerem Gogus; Sharon Oddie Brown; Ronald Hicks; David Redhouse of Newgrange Farm; Robert Hensey; Steve Davis; the Francis Ledwidge Museum committee; Owen Brennan; Helen Stanton; Martin O'Donoghue; Padraig Flynn; Niall Shortt and Sarah Farrell; Brendan Matthews; Declan Craig; Seamus Counihan; Richie

Acknowledgements

Hatch; Colin Bell; Roisin Fitzpatrick; Derek Ryan; Patrick Casey; Roisín Marsh; Mary McKenna; Una Sheehan; Fintan and Margaret White.

To all the custodians who have looked after our most precious monuments throughout the years and centuries, and to all those who cherish our myths and folklore. Keep the flame burning. Thank you.

Abundant gratitude to all my patrons – those who support my work. If you would like to help, visit https://www.patreon.com/mythicalireland.

Dedicated to the memory of Fiona Fay

Prologue

Arrive magically; descend in a mist

It appears to be the purpose of the myth, as in the case with the dream, to keep alive in our memory our psychological prehistory, right down to the most primitive instincts, and the assimilation of the meaning of myths has the effect of broadening and modifying consciousness in such a way as to bring about a heightened aliveness.[1]

… before the Christian Church existed there were the antique mysteries, and these reach back into the grey mists of neolithic prehistory.[2]

For this is the call of our ancestors, the call of the Tuatha Dé, the Divine Tribe, and if we listen for it, the call of our soul.[3]

A thought sometimes comes to me when I consider the convoluted history of my homeland. In the stillness of the evening, standing alone at some monument of antiquity, I wonder if it was the beauty of the place that made my ancestors remain here – those who were the first to arrive after the ice retreated, and those who later survived imperialism and starvation. The world is a big place, and the human race is a migratory species. There were other places these ancestors could have gone to. But they held on.

The forces and factors that kept them here may be the same ones that make me a captive of this wondrous island. Ireland's landscape is lush and fertile. It is beautiful and enrapturing. Many places have an otherworldly placidity about them, even today. The climate is such that, as the saying suggests, you can experience four seasons in one day. This makes for a great variety in how that beautiful landscape is presented to the beholder. It changes with every passing day. In fact, it changes by the hour.

In earlier days of our history, the 'great mistiness ... so consonant with the moisture of the Irish climate ... was ascribed rather to magic than to natural causes'.[4] In modern times, there is a tendency to over-rationalise and analyse, such that a landscape that has always been seen as somewhat magical and austere is reduced to something functional and banal. It becomes stripped of its numinous function. I refuse to occupy that space. My previous work has opened up to a mystical vista. Having become detached from the religious institutions that we trusted when we were younger, as a people we now seem to have set ourselves upon an atheistic course, perhaps to some degree as an over-reaction to the extent and depth of that detachment. In losing our religion, have we also lost all account of the concept of the meta-

physical, the mystical, the miraculous, and of the search for any trace of the divine and the eternal in our lives and in the greater cosmos? Because religion has failed us, do we now regard spirituality as defunct?

There are so many places in Ireland that are liminal and seemingly enchanted that it's easy to see why the landscape of this island has often been described as magical. It is possible to stand at one of countless special or sacred places in Ireland and feel that you are standing on the edge of forever. If you don't believe me, or if you think that's a load of old tosh, then go to the cliffs at Dun Aonghasa on Inis Mór in the Aran Islands and watch the rolling waves of the vast Atlantic stretch out before you and imagine 'next stop – Brazil' (or Hy Brasil, whichever takes your fancy); climb to the summit of Croagh Patrick and view the innumerable islands of Clew Bay, where it is said there is an island for every day of the year; stand on the shore of some isolated beach in the late summer evening and watch the stars in the midnight twilight glow and think about your ancestors who did the same thing, many moons

Scenes like this, looking out towards Lough Sheelin from Loughcrew, make it easy to see why Ireland is often described as a magical land.

ago. Over the past few years in particular, I've spent a lot of time at Newgrange, the place most associated with the Tuatha Dé Danann in mythology, known variously as Brugh na Bóinne, Síd in Broga, Síd Mac Ind Oc and the Palace of the Boyne. It's lovely spending time out there on my own. I find it such a pleasurable and peaceful and intro-spective experience. I expect that plenty of other people have spent time alone in the evening at Newgrange, but I hardly ever see anyone out there at night. I like it that way. I've really come to feel that the place is my own. I share it with people through my writing, my photos and my films, but I like to think that it is mine, something that I can share at will.

What an idiotic notion. What a thoroughly Milesian notion.

'I like it, so I'll make it mine.'

That's the sort of thinking that got us fighting all those years ago, when we left the forests and started erecting buildings and making shiny jewellery and deadly weapons. We wanted to possess the land-scape – again, a very Milesian notion. The Tuatha Dé Danann were happy to leave it to us – they had found somewhere entirely different and much more wonderful.

'Have it,' they said. 'We're going somewhere else.'

And they disappeared into the mounds. They gave up fighting over Ireland. They were happy to leave it. Or were they? Apart from gaining paradise, was there another reason for their willing departure? They had come here from distant shores. Perhaps they felt that they didn't really own it, or that possession of Ireland simply wasn't possi-ble. You come here as a visitor, no matter how long ago your ancestors arrived here. It is an island. We all came here, from across the sea.

We say that we are Irish. We belong to it. But it does not belong to us. And nor can it. The Tuatha Dé Danann realised this. Or at least, the people for whom the Tuatha Dé Danann were omnipresent realised it. They loved it, and it loved them. But they could not own it. It is no one's to own.

The Tuatha Dé Danann, mythical original owners of Newgrange,
were said to have arrived into Ireland in a mist.

And here, on this island nation today, her story is much the same as it has always been. It is a story of comings and goings, of arrivals and departures. Dublin Airport is a great metaphor for Irish mythology and history. There are always people arriving, and always people departing.

How we arrive into Ireland is central to the nature of our belonging here. This is something the late John Moriarty realised and wrote about.[5] Do we descend upon this island from a cloud, wrapped in a mist, like the Dananns? Or do we sail across the rough seas, like the Milesians, with their flotilla of ships – a Spanish Armada of the prehistoric world – to take Ireland, partly due to jealous longing, and partly for vengeance?

If we do that, we will never belong here, and we might end up like one of those voyagers of old, setting sail into the perilous ocean of the west, chasing dreams and shadows in the far-off turmoil of a tumul-tuous Atlantic. Maybe we might come to Hy Brasil, where perchance we might have arrived in heaven. More likely, we will sail forever on barren seas or have our ships smashed on the rocks of some desolate island.

I'd much prefer to descend into Ireland in a mist, from the stars, and set my foot gently upon her soil, wrapped up in the *Féth Fiada* with Manannán by my side. That way, my arrival might take place unknown, so that I could gently tiptoe across dew-covered grasses into some otherworldly copse, and there enchant my every thought with the newfound joy of arrival into an earthly paradise.

A halo around the moon over the Bend of the Boyne.

I would much prefer this to a Milesian arrival. From a distance of nine waves, as a Milesian you come in sturdy ships, beating drums of battle, and unfurl your banner of war, your standard of conquest.

But no nation ever conquested in spite or by subjugation or force could afterwards live a peaceful existence.

So I urge you to come like the Tuatha Dé Danann. Come in a mist. Arrive magically. And ask Eriú, gently, if perchance you can stay awhile, and dance and sing upon her carpet of tender green, and write joyous words and sing merry songs about netherworlds concealed in the ditches and vales of her beautiful quarters.

Find your Danann voice. Call into the *sídhe*. Invoke the sleeping warriors of your better nature. Find that point of light in the dim shaded corners of the world and transform it into a blade of pure gold. Go not as the meek neophyte into the dark interior of the Brug. Rather, venture into the darkness as a keeper of the light, called to action in the twilight of the world, ready to draw the sword from the stone and to rouse the Danann gods of your subjugated fears forth to show themselves in this realm once more.

Folklore says that the Tuatha Dé Danann live on, and that they will come back, at a time of great need, to restore Ireland to glory. Despite repeated imperial offensives against them, the Tuatha Dé Danann have not been defeated. Nor have they been diminished. In fact, unquestionably, they are returning as prophesised. They are returning, in you and I. Despite all the invasions, they live on. They are waiting to be called when needed.

Introduction

Mythical Ireland emerged as an entity on the 16th of March in the year 2000 with the creation of a brand new website, from which this book borrows its title – *Mythical Ireland: New Light on the Ancient Past.* Those were earlier days of the internet, when connection was established via a convoluted dial-up routine, and before digital photography. Countless hours of typing and scanning photographic prints were required for this website to be born.

The new site had as its aim the dissemination of information and photography relating to the ancient monuments of the Boyne Valley region and their associated myths and astronomy. Just over a year earlier, I had met Richard Moore and we had initiated an investigation of the megalithic sites of the Boyne that would eventually lead, in 2006, to the publication of *Island of the Setting Sun: In Search of Ireland's Ancient Astronomers.*

But while we were still carrying out research, I felt it would be good to have a website where articles and photographs could be published, giving people some insights into the discoveries we were making. It turned out to be a good idea. Within a few years, www. mythicalireland.com was attracting significant traffic. Visitors liked the infusion of myth, megaliths and astronomy, and there was particular interest in the photography. The site continued to expand beyond the initial confines of sections about ancient sites, mythology and astronomy, and, by the time ten years had passed it was a huge resource. Now, it contains hundreds of pages of material, hundreds of photographs and many videos. The improvements in computer hardware and software, coupled with advancing digital photography technology, now make it possible for a truly rich and immersive web experience.

As I write this, www.mythicalireland.com is receiving a major overhaul. A brand new version of the Mythical Ireland website will hopefully be unveiled as this book is printed. The main reason for the upgrade is because the old site was designed around the coding and technology of the old internet. Things have changed dramatically and the website needs to catch up. Mythical Ireland has also now branched out into social media, where there is a significant following on Facebook, YouTube, Twitter and Flickr.

The idea for this book stemmed from the Mythical Ireland website. There was so much material that had either been published as blog

The Mythical Ireland journey, in words, photographs, videos and film, has been going on for over 17 years.

*Winter sunset over the River Boyne and the Boyne Canal
viewed from Roughgrange.*

posts or articles on the site, and so much more that I had written that remained unpublished (as draft chapters for planned books or for future posting on the website), that I felt bringing it all together in book form would be a great idea.

There is also a part of me that likes the apparent permanence of printed matter. Text and images that only have a digital presence are, I feel, somewhat transitory. One cannot be certain what changes in technology will affect the way we access information. The internet has evolved and continues to evolve. Mythical Ireland the website might be irrelevant in five years' time. The printed book, it might be said, has a longer shelf life! In the spirit of the people of the Neolithic, who undoubtedly passed on a great deal of their knowledge orally, I will also graft my words onto paper (something a little less permanent maybe than their megalithic engravings) in the hope that these words, and photographs, might endure in a more permanent medium.

And so I present to you *Mythical Ireland* – the book – a collection of work that I have written over the past three or four years. Some of the chapters are quite scholarly or academic. In others, I find my poetic voice. It strays from the scientific into the metaphysical and back again. The work has been grouped into sections and themes, which I hope will make it a convenient and interesting read for you.

I sincerely hope you enjoy the journey, as I have done.

Anthony Murphy
Drogheda
September 2017

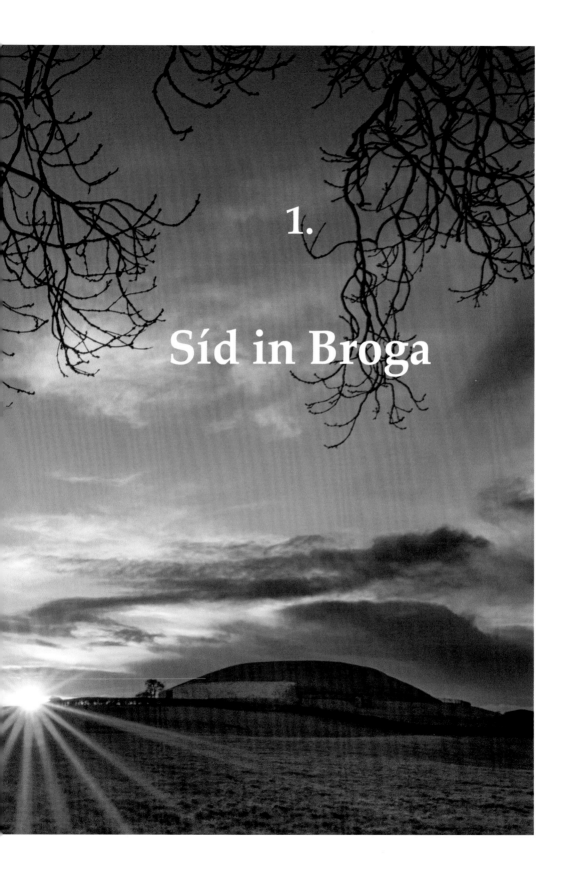

1.

Síd in Broga

Sunrise at Newgrange around summer solstice, viewed from the air.

1.1

Summer solstice sunrise at Newgrange

For a moment of the year,
the sun stops its run,
and stays awhile in the
northeast at dawn.
But, like everything in nature
the spiral will wind down once
more towards winter, when the sun
will come home again.

The world comes to Newgrange on the shortest days of the year. Hundreds of people gather at the ancient monument. The media congregates for the spectacle. An ancient ritual lives on in the modern age.

But the substantial crowds that come to Síd in Broga[1] on winter solstice are completely absent for summer solstice. And I am very glad for that! On the longest days of the year, around June 21, the sun rises at an angle that is perpendicular to the alignment of the Newgrange passage. It comes up from the side, illuminating the quartz front of the ancient mound beautifully. With the sun rising at 5.00 am on summer solstice, it's probably no surprise to find the place devoid of human activity, but sometimes it's nice to be the only human presence walking among these magnificent remains.

1.2

Science and mysticism:
The genius of the Stone Age

The more insignificant modern man becomes – on his shrinking earth, hardly a cosmic speck – the more arrogant he is. He feels far less humility toward the ever-vaster unknown than his forefathers did toward what was thought to be known in a flat, God-ruled, man-centred universe. Science does not seem to touch man's emotions at all: he loses his religious awe and acquires in its place only a boastful complacency about himself. His intelligence grows, but not his genius.[1]

The photo on the next page shows a symbol carved into the stone at the very rear of the chamber of Cairn T, Loughcrew, Ireland. It was likely carved there more than 5,000 years ago, by a society of people for whom, I believe, science and spirituality were not considered as separate things. Our ancient ancestors expressed their genius by grafting huge edifices in stone, lasting memorials to a time in the story of humanity when people had what Freund refers to as 'inventive mind, poetic aspiration, and awe-filled heart' – and yet they watched and measured the movements of the sun, moon and stars. They were equally adherents to empiricism, metaphysics, philosophy and mysticism. They were farmers, engineers and astronomers, but they were most likely also poets, diviners and shamans, as suggested in mythology. They were scientists and mystics.

I believe that they saw themselves as one with a cosmos that was vast beyond comprehension. They were neither atheistic nor agnostic,

Solar symbol on the 'Equinox Stone' at the rear of Cairn T (The Hag's Cairn) at Loughcrew. This symbol, along with others, is illuminated by the light of the sun on the equinoxes.

but held a deep hope and belief in the existence of an afterlife. The great mounds of the New Stone Age are the best physical exemplifications of this belief. At the end of life, the burnt or unburnt fragments of the individual were lovingly and delicately placed in the chambers of these sacred spaces, from which (as is implied by the construction and alignment of these monuments towards the rising and setting places of the heavenly bodies) the soul of the deceased was magically transported to the next realm.

The people who built the temples of stone that are Cairn T and its sisters on the ancient hills of Loughcrew, and indeed the vast monuments of the Boyne, which mark a zenith in the achievements of that society, did so, I believe, in unity and zeal towards a shared belief.

Sunset at Síd in Broga. Newgrange represents a zenith in the achievements of Irish Neolithic culture.

Joseph Campbell said that the 'awakening of awe, that awakening of zeal' is what pulls people together.[2]

In relation to the great cathedrals of Europe, Campbell said 'you mustn't think of slave drivers; that isn't what built the cathedrals. It was a community seizure, a mythic zeal.'[3]

The same is probably true for the mound builders.

So what happened to the culture that dedicated itself to fervently building these innumerable mounds and cairns across ancient Ireland?

In the words of Campbell, 'this zeal has disappeared'.

Our sense of the cosmic, and the awesome, and the everlasting, and the transcendental, became diminished when we became fascinated with the material, and the corporeal, the earthly, the ephemeral. When bronze arrived, and later iron, we perceived that we need not dream of otherworlds to empower our beings and enrich our lives. We could fashion gleaming possessions – decorative and combative – and this gave us a sense of our own authority over nature. We could transform the murky raw materials of the earth magically into jewellery and weapons. We became alchemists and metalworkers. The need to divine our place in the cosmos and in the frantic and at times incongruous schemes of life was no longer so urgent. We could, we believed, impose our own will upon it. Spirit moved aside a little – or was pushed – and ego took centre-stage. This conflict of spirit and ego is perhaps best epitomised in the battle between the Tuatha Dé Danann, the owners of the *sídhe*[4] – and the Milesians, who came from Spain to take Ireland from them, driven by mixture of revenge and a jealous longing for a country that they beheld as being so beautiful it looked like the clouds of heaven.

Instead of the Dé Danann magician Elcmar, who stood at Newgrange at Samhain with a fork of white hazel, the archetypal mystic – a diviner, a druidic wise man – we became the Milesian Eremon, who wished to take ancient Tara and impose the domination of a new force upon the land. The symbol of that imposition would become the Lia Fáil, the phallic stone of kingship that would scream when the rightful king placed his foot upon it. And thus at Tara even today it is possible to discern the transformation that occurred after this battle between spirit and ego. The old ways are represented by Duma na nGiall, the Mound of the Hostages that rises out of the earth like a pregnant belly, the mother who is at once part of both world and cosmos. The new ways are represented by the Lia Fáil, the phallic stone placed there in an act of imposition, declaration, and perhaps banishment. We shouldn't be surprised to think that the Neolithic culture was a matriarchal one – its stone chambers are somewhat uterine in design – although we get the distinct sense of a polytheistic society when we take account of mythology which may or may not date to that remote time. But the cultures that followed, in the Bronze

Sunset over Duma na nGiall, the Mound of the Hostages, on the Hill of Tara.

*The Newgrange family ... do Síd in Broga and the other mounds symbolise
a sense of emergence from the earth and cosmos?*

Age and Iron Age, created enclosures and ramparts encircling the
sacred hill that I believe attempted to make a statement that, instead
of considering the monuments to be an extension of the earth, saw
the earth as being enclosed within a new system of ownership and
dominance. We were no longer an emergence from cosmos. We were
an imposition upon it.

The Lia Fáil, the phallus, is another icon of imposition, and the pa-
triarchal nature of that imposition. We planted it there as a symbol of
our wish to claim ownership, dominance and control over the land. We
did similarly when we planted a flag on the moon. We went there at
considerable expense in the greatest single achievement of our era, but
we did so as much as an act of imposition and ownership as we did as
an act of scientific exploration or altruistic humanity. We cannot own
the moon. At what point will we realise that we cannot own the earth
either?

1.3

Do the myths about the mounds offer an insight into their function?

A historian once told me, very matter-of-factly, that 'myths are just stories'. As far as he was concerned, they were stories that were made only up for entertainment. In that mindset, myths are not metaphors, and they certainly don't contain detail about real history, or any information such as astronomical data.

However, students of mythology know the truth is much more complex. Many myths are metaphorical. Some do refer to actual events. And there are stories that appear, in certain interpretations, to contain astronomical information.

My own view is that myths should never be dismissed as mere stories. However, the truth is that in most cases we can only travel so far along the road of hypothesis and speculation, no matter how well grounded it might seem, because often we are unable to discern the true age of a myth, or how it might have been altered by the voices of time. A further difficulty is that many of the myths in the medieval manuscripts were written by Christian monks, who in their zest for their own beliefs may have altered or enhanced the texts:

> Much of the pagan mythology found in the Lebor Gabála, for example, had passed through a biblical filter that did everything it could to link the ancient Irish with the Hebrews short of turning them into a lost tribe.[1]

In *Archaeology and Celtic Myth,* Emeritus Professor of Archaeology at the National University of Ireland Galway John Waddell said that his book was 'an exploration' and that its 'central premise is that elements of pre-Christian Celtic myth preserved in medieval Irish literature shed light on older traditions not just in Ireland but elsewhere in Europe as well'.[2]

In the case of Newgrange, Dowth and Knowth (the former two in particular), there are myths and folk tales that appear to offer a tantalising possibility – that they contain information about these sites and the function of these monuments that might go all the way back into deep prehistory. I will discuss some of these myths and folk beliefs in the context of possibility only – without drawing any definitive conclusions.

Winter full moon setting behind Newgrange.

*A storm approaching Síd in Broga. Newgrange's passage
and chamber were hidden for four millennia.*

I've written in several publications about the Venus connection at Newgrange.[3] Joseph Campbell, writing in *The Masks of God: Primitive Mythology*,[4] referred to a local story that suggested that at sunrise on one day in eight years, the morning star rises and casts its beam into the chamber. This story was recounted, it would appear, before the excavation and restoration of Newgrange in the 1960s, work which resulted in the leading archaeologist Michael O'Kelly witnessing, in 1967, the light from the winter solstice sun entering the chamber. Prior to the restoration, neither sun nor Venus (nor any heavenly body for that matter) could be seen from the chamber because of the subsidence of the passage cap stones during the five millennia since Newgrange was constructed.

Of particular intrigue is the fact that archaeologists maintain that Newgrange was 'sealed up' within a few centuries of being built after cairn material slipped off the top and covered the kerb and entrance,[5] and that its passage and chamber lay concealed for about four millennia until local landowner Charles Campbell rediscovered the entrance in AD1699.

Another folk belief in the 1930s[6] told how the Tuatha Dé Danann brought stones from the Mourne Mountains for the building of the mounds. During the excavations in the 1960s, it was indeed discovered that there were water-rolled granite cobbles at Newgrange, which had previously been hidden beneath the cairn slip. These, it was revealed, came from the Cooley Peninsula, but have their origin in the Mournes.

In his 1990 paper, *Time, Memory, and the Boyne Necropolis,*[7] John Carey examined aspects of two stories – one about Newgrange and one about Dowth. The Newgrange story, *Tochmarc Étaíne* ('The Wooing of Étaín'), tells of how the Dagda sent Elcmar away so that he might have illicit relations with Elcmar's wife, Bóinn. The Dagda worked a magic

'Command him not to come (again) to the house from which he departs until ogam *and* achu *are mingled together, until heaven and earth are mingled together, and until the sun and moon are mingled together.'*

spell, so that Elcmar would think that he was only away for a single day, when in fact he had been away for nine months. Dagda lay with Bóinn and the child Oengus Óg was conceived and born. The Dowth story, from the Dindshenchas, told how the king, Bresal, had brought the men of Ireland to build him a tower to reach heaven. The king's sister cast a spell on the sun to make it stand still, so there would be endless day to allow the tower to be built.

Carey makes a very interesting observation: 'I am aware of no Irish legends associating the control or construction of sacred sites with the manipulation of time other than those which concern the tumuli of the Boyne valley.'[8]

In the tale *Altram Tighe Dá Mheadar* ('The Fosterage of the House of Two Drinking Vessels'), Manannán advises Oengus on how to take Newgrange from Elcmar: 'Command him not to come (again) to the house from which he departs until *ogam* and *achu* are mingled together, until heaven and earth are mingled together, and until the sun and moon are mingled together.'[9] The mingling of heaven and earth could imply the mating of sky with the earth-mound Newgrange during winter solstice, while the latter reference to sun and moon being mingled might refer to an eclipse, something that I think is implied in the story about Dowth, in which the magic spell on the sun is broken when Bresal commits incest with his sister and a sudden darkness comes upon the land.[10] I have discussed at length the idea that the mound builders were competent astronomers, whose knowledge of the complex movements of the moon (and by extension the predictable patterns of eclipses) were recorded in stone, and inherent in the design of the monuments.[11]

Writing in 2009, Ronald Hicks of Ball State University suggested, in a paper entitled *Cosmography in Tochmarc Étaíne*, that the story of *The Wooing of Étaín* was 'meant as an allegory about lunar cycles in which Étaín represents the moon'. These lunar cycles, wrote Hicks, include the 19-year Metonic Cycle, which was 'likely to have been of interest to the ancient Irish'.[12]

In one part of *The Wooing of Étaín*, Midir's wife Fuamnach became jealous of her husband's new wife, Étaín. By magic, Fuamnach turned Étaín into a butterfly (some versions say a fly) and raised a storm that buffeted the butterfly around Ireland for seven years.

> At last, however, a chance gust of wind blew her through a window of the fairy palace of Angus on the Boyne. The immortals cannot be hidden from each other, and Angus knew what she was. Unable to release her altogether from the spell of Fuamnach, he made a sunny bower for her, and planted round it all manner of choice and honey-laden flowers, on which she lived as long as she was with him, while in the secrecy of the night he restored her to her own form and enjoyed her love.[13]

Ronald Hicks suggests that Étaín might represent the moon.

There is only one 'window' at Newgrange – the sky window, or roof box, as it is more commonly known. This aperture allows the sun to shine into the chamber on winter solstice. Perhaps the 'sunny bower' is the chamber of Newgrange, illuminated by the rays of the rising sun on winter solstice? Hicks raises a further interesting possibility:

> … two elements appear significant, that he drapes a scarlet or purple cloak about her and that her color returns to her at night. This sounds rather as though she—or at least her crystal bower—may be the moon when it appears in the sky during daylight hours. The comment about her color returning to her certainly fits the moon's appearance at nightfall when it has been in the sky during daylight hours.[14]

Étaín sometimes carries the epithet *Echraide,* meaning 'horse-rider'.[15] Hicks draws attention to the fact that in Irish tradition, the moon is sometimes called *an lair bhán,* meaning 'the white mare'.[16] This is especially fascinating in light of some of the folklore surrounding the Milky Way, and how it associates with the moon, which we will discuss later.

1.4

Folk memory: 1938 knowledge foreshadowed excavation findings

Time and again, I've written about the apparent curious persistence of local folk memory. You might recall one of the most famous examples – the fact that local people said Venus (the Morning Star) shines into Newgrange on one morning every eight years. This had been recorded by Joseph Campbell and written about in 1959, prior to Professor Michael O'Kelly's excavations and restoration of the roof-box, before which time any such phenomenon could not be observed within the chamber. Of course, there's always the possibility that the alignment was observed indirectly, from outside the tomb entrance, and thus deduced by locals. But the thing about folklore is that it cannot always be easily dismissed as just some fanciful story.

Between 1937 and 1938, the Schools' Collection was being gathered around Ireland by the Irish Folklore Commission. It was an initiative which sought to involve senior primary schoolchildren in the collection of the oral traditions of the Irish people, which were fast dying out. The total amount of written information gathered for the School's Collection is estimated to be 'far in excess' of half a million manuscript pages.[1] At Monknewtown School, which was one of the closest schools to the great monuments of Newgrange, Knowth and Dowth, a man called Gerald Duggan from Dowth recalled some local lore about fairy forts to one of the school pupils. Here are Mr. Duggan's recollections about these great monuments:

There are three very important tumulus in this district. They are Newgrange, Knowth and Dowth. They are within view of each other. There is supposed to be a cave running under ground from Newgrange to Dowth.

Fog rolls in towards Síd in Broga at twilight.

This latter claim about a cave connecting two ancient sites is very commonplace in Irish folklore. Many places, including old mounds, forts and even ecclesiastical sites such as monasteries, were said to have been connected by underground tunnels. Perhaps this supposition is

Folklore suggests the basin stones in Newgrange were used for burials.

The great granite basin stone in the right-hand recess of the chamber of Newgrange.

based upon the observation of souterrains, of which there is a remark-able proliferation in this northeastern part of Ireland.[2] Mr. Duggan, speaking about Newgrange, says (the spelling is reproduced here ex-actly from the manuscript):

> Outside the entrance there is a large stone with spiral writing on it. Inside in the fort there are two large stones in the shape of a basin. It was the custom long ago for the bodies of pagan kings that died to be buried in these baisins and the ashes used to be burned.

The long-standing association of Newgrange and the other great mon-uments of the Boyne with the Tuatha Dé Danann is reaffirmed:

> It is said that it was the Tuatha De Dannans that built those forts. It is said that they brought the stones from the Mourn Mountains to build them.

It is now postulated by geologists that stones for the construction of Newgrange came from three, and possibly four sites, as follows: (1) The large kerb stones, orthostats and structural stones, which are of grey-wacke, were brought along the coast from Clogherhead; (2) the milky white quartz stones which form the front wall of Newgrange came from the Wicklow Mountains (although the exact site has never been conclusively located), with a possibility, recently suggested, that this quartz came alternatively from Rockabill Island off the coast at Skerries;[3] (3) the rounded water-rolled granite and granodiorite cobbles which were interspersed with the quartz came from the beach at Rathcor/Temple-town, which is on the southern shore of the Cooley Peninsula. It is said that these stones originated in the Mourne Mountains.[4]

In 1938, when the Schools' Collection was being gathered, the granite cobbles which originated in the Mournes were all buried under the cairn spill – material which had, over time, slipped down from the top of the cairn over the kerb stones and buried the white quartz and rounded cobbles under several feet of stones. When Professor O'Kelly excavated Newgrange, he found this layer of quartz and granite/granodiorite cobbles at the very bottom of the cairn slip. Through experimentation, he postulated that the quartz and water-rolled cobbles had originally formed an almost-vertical facing on the mound, and thus Newgrange was reconstructed in this manner.

The question that arises from all this is this – how did a local man, speaking in 1938, three decades before the excavation of Newgrange, possibly know or have any indication that stones for the construction of Newgrange might have been brought from the Mournes?

Is it possible that some of these cobbles had indeed been found, especially outside the entrance to the tomb, where, in 1699, the landowner Charles Campbell's servants had quarried stone for the construction of his house?

There could be a more prosaic explanation. Perhaps Mr. Duggan was an educated man, who had become aware of the writings of

Local folklore suggests a giant went into the cave of Newgrange and when he died his body was placed in a 'stone cup' where it was burned.

George Wilkinson. Writing in 1845, Wilkinson had suggested that a large stone basin in the chamber of Newgrange was made from granite which originated in the Mournes.[5] Writing in 1912, George Coffey quotes a Mr. R. Clark of the Geological Survey as suggesting that the stone from which this basin was constructed had 'more resemblance to some of the granites of the Wicklow series than to those of the Mourne district'.[6]

Another story which is interesting was told by a Patrick Walsh of Rushwee, Stackallen, about a giant who lived in a cave near the Boyne:

> The giant lived in the cave at the river Boyne for a long time until an army came and hunted him out of it. It is said that after that he went to the cave at Newgrange and he stayed there until he died and it is said that the people put his body into a stone cup and burned it. The cup that the giant's body was burned in is in the cave at Newgrange yet.

One presumes the 'stone cup' referred to is one of the stone basins inside Newgrange. It is interesting that Mr. Walsh's story hints at a funerary use of the ceremonial basins. It is implied by many experts on the great passage-tombs that the interment of the fragmented remains of the deceased were placed carefully in these ritual basins.

I will later discuss the possible means and methods by which human remains might have been defleshed and cremated such that there were only small fragments left to inter. There is still the tantalising possibility, though, that Mr. Walsh's story is a folk memory of an ancient custom going back deep into prehistory, of burning the corpses of the dead, and placing their fragmented remains in stone basins or urns.

Newgrange (Síd in Broga) at sunset on a summer evening.

1.5

The archaeologist who unwisely dismissed Newgrange folklore

The earliest antiquarians who visited, documented, sketched and spoke about Newgrange after its 'rediscovery' in 1699 sometimes get a hard time from the modern academic establishment. The writings of Lhwyd and Molyneux and Pownall and Vallancey are all criticised for one reason or another (poor Charles Vallancey is largely ridiculed, perhaps because he referred to Newgrange as a Mithraic temple). All of the early antiquarian accounts of the monument are valuable for one reason or another. Some of them have captured aspects of New-grange that have disappeared since they wrote. Without the tools and techniques of modern archaeology, all of them were poking around in the dark, so to speak. They couldn't have known the true age of Newgrange, nor could they have appreciated the skills of the artists and builders who created it, those whom they all too often referred to as barbarous.

However, Dr. Glyn Daniel, lecturer in archaeology at Cambridge University and editor of the academic journal *Antiquity*, perhaps should have known better. In 1964, Daniel's book *New Grange and the Bend of the Boyne* was published.[1] It had been a collaborative effort with University College Cork professor of archaeology, Sean P. Ó Ríordáin. Sadly, Ó Ríordáin had passed away in 1957 in his early fifties, when the pair were only half way through completion of the book. Daniel was the General Editor of the *Ancient Peoples and Places* series of books, under which the *New Grange* title was published. It was to become the largest single study of the Newgrange monument since George Coffey's 1912 book, and would be the last before Professor Michael J. O'Kelly's excavations at Newgrange revealed so many of its secrets.

One of the shortcomings of the Daniel/Ó Ríordáin book is that it fails to deal in any substantial terms with the mythical history of the New-grange monument or indeed its counterparts in the Bend of the Boyne. Except for one passage in which he relates that New Grange might be an English corruption of *An Uamh Greinè*[2] (the cave of Gráinne), Daniel does not discuss the ancient names of Newgrange, or its import in the early texts, as O'Kelly later did in his own work on Newgrange. Failing to acknowledge the earlier Irish names of Newgrange, and its mythology and associated stories, Daniel falls into a trap – he assumes the folklore about the site to be utter fantasy, and dismisses it as such:

Newgrange (Síd in Broga) and Mound B near the Boyne
on a misty autumn evening.

It is natural that impressive monuments like New Grange and Stonehenge should be visited a great deal by the general public and should themselves have attracted a folklore based on imagination, half-forgotten history, unappreciated archaeology and the sort of nonsense that luxuriates in the lunatic fringes of serious archaeology.[3]

And in that foregoing paragraph, Daniel was just setting himself up for a fall.

The visitor to New Grange and Dowth will not be surprised to be told that these monuments were built by and were the homes of 'the little people' or to be asked their connection with the Druids.[4]

One should always be careful about dismissing the fairy folk – even if one is a leading archaeologist and 'expert' of the times!

But the following is perhaps indicative of the excessively arrogant attitude of Daniel in dealing with a monument such as Newgrange. In his impetuous haste to dismiss the folklore, he dismissed also notions about the site that would later transpire to be based in truth:

A coloured calendar current in Ireland in 1960 had in it a good photograph of the decorated stone at the entrance to New Grange; this was accompanied by an account which needs quoting almost in toto as an example of the jumble of nonsense and wishful thinking indulged in by those who prefer the pleasures of the irrational and the joys of unreason to the hard thinking that archaeology demands. 'The entrance in the east was originally triangular,' says this description, 'but is now changed for easy entrance, formerly it was necessary to crawl in and progress was retarded by interference, stones compelling the neophyte to stoop and stumble. The rays of the rising sun at certain times of the year penetrate the opening and rest on a remarkable triple spiral carving in the central chamber. Like the Great Pyramid of Gizeh in Egypt the New

Grange Temple was originally covered with a layer of white quartz and was a brilliant object of Light for a considerable distance. Nuda, first king of Tuatha de Danann in Ireland, and his Master Magician, are said to have officiated here in the very, very old days. Artemidoros the Ephesian stated: 'To Sacred Ierne of the Hibernians men go to learn more of the Mysteries of Samothrace.'[5]

Two very important statements in this 1960 calendar demonstrate that there were enduring traditions about Newgrange that were fascinating and even compelling (and certainly worthy of at least some investigation) – one that the sun shone into the chamber during the year and the other that the monument may once have been covered with white quartz. Understandably, Daniel could not have known about the existence of quartz, given that the O'Kelly excavations at Newgrange had just begun when the Daniel/Ó Ríordáin book was published, but there was at least one possible reference to this feature in mythology –

The pre-excavation folklore suggested the rising sun shone into Newgrange and illuminated the triskele in the chamber.

the 'white-topped brugh' was said to have been 'brilliant to approach'.[6] Furthermore, he was doubtless aware that the westernmost of the hills of Loughcrew, with its smattering of ancient chambered cairns, was Carnbawn[7] – meaning the 'white cairn'. If he had been a bit more familiar with some of the mythology of Newgrange, he might not have been so quick to dismiss it.

But Daniel certainly should not have been so dismissive in relation to the solar alignment – especially as it had been previously suggested by the likes of Solar Physics Observatory director Sir Norman Lockyer in 1909, and W.Y. Evans-Wentz in *The Fairy-Faith in Celtic Countries* in 1911.[8]

Within three years or so of the publication of the Daniel/Ó Ríordáin book, Professor Michael O'Kelly would stand in the chamber of Newgrange and become the first person in the modern era (and perhaps since the Bronze Age) to witness the winter solstice sunlight streaming into its inner chamber, illuminating (by reflected light) the triskele or triple spiral in the chamber. During his excavations at the famous monument, O'Kelly would uncover a significant layer of quartz beneath the

A beautiful winter evening red sky at Newgrange. Long before the excavations, it had been suggested that Newgrange was once covered with white quartz.

cairn spill material – quartz that he would later demonstrate through repeated experiment that actually fronted the monument. In other words, at the very least Newgrange had a white quartz façade, and it is not such a huge leap of imagination that the cairn was once covered with this bright stone.

One wonders what Daniel made of O'Kelly's revelations, and how it might have altered his thinking in relation to folklore. Folk memory is a very powerful thing. This might have been demonstrated in the case of the story in the locality of Newgrange suggesting that the Morning Star (Venus) shone into the chamber of the monument once every eight years, as recorded by Joseph Campbell.[9] Then there was the folklore collected in 1938 that suggested the Tuatha Dé Danann had built Newgrange using stones brought from the Mourne Mountains, another apparently wild and imaginative claim that had some basis in reality.

Even in the claim that 'Nuda' officiated at Newgrange, the calendar was not too far off the mark. In the early texts, Newgrange is associated in particular with Elcmar, Dagda and Oengus. Dagda was chief of the gods, a kind of Tuatha Dé king, so to speak, and Elcmar was described as a 'magician' and 'original master of Brug na Bóinne'.[10] The 'Nuda' mentioned in the calendar is undoubtedly Nuadu, the king of the Tuatha Dé Danann who led them into Ireland. Nuadu was, according to the late Dáithí Ó hÓgáin, Associate Professor of Irish Folklore at University College Dublin, one and the same deity as Elcmar:

> In early Irish tradition, Nuadhu was associated with the Boyne, being married to the eponymous goddess of the river, Bóinn. He was displaced through a trick from his residence at Brugh na Bóinne (the Newgrange tumulus) by the Mac Óg (i.e. Aonghus) and went to live at the nearby place called Sídh Chleitigh.[11]

Unfortunately, I can only challenge Mr. Daniel posthumously. As he is not here to defend himself, I must not take undue licence in criticising him for his sweeping dismissal of the folk beliefs as related in the 1960 calendar, only to say that almost everything related by that calendar turned out to have a basis in truth.

I am glad that this diminution of folklore is not ubiquitous among modern archaeologists. As mentioned above, Michael O'Kelly outlined the mythical importance of Newgrange, and seemed to have a great reverence for the site, and acknowledged the possibility that it was 'a house of the dead and ... an abode of spirits' which, he said, was a concept not contradicted by the findings of the excavation. O'Kelly felt that a connection between the archaeological evidence and the early literature was to be found in the older and 'more genuine tradition'.[12]

Daniel allowed only one statement in the 1960 calendar to stand: 'It is at least true in this strange wild-cat account we have just quoted, that New Grange might well be described as belonging to 'the very, very old days'.'[13]

'It is our object in this book,' he continued, 'not only to describe the great tombs in the Bend of the Boyne but to set them in what appears to us their true prehistoric context, as far as the limitations of archaeology allow, eschewing the little people and Artemidoros.'

The O'Kelly excavations came at the end of the 60-year custodianship of the monument by local woman Anne Hickey. Interviewed by RTÉ television in 1962, at the age of 90, she said that the old people considered Newgrange a 'place for fairies, and you dream about them'.[14] She added that people were quite terrified of them, and that if anyone was seen walking around the mound at night, it was a sign that 'something was going to happen to us'. The fairies were a very real presence up until the time of the excavations.

One eschews the *daoine sídhe* at one's peril.

1.6

The collapse of Mellifont and the renaming of Síd in Broga

Idreamt I could see an old wall, or a portion of an old building. There was a storm, and the wind was very strong. As I watched, I could tell that this structure was going to collapse. And collapse it did. It came crashing down. I was greatly moved by this, and a sense of urgent duty compelled me to reach for my mobile phone, to call for help. I'm not sure who I was supposed to ring for help, but the words were there, on the tip of my tongue, ready to be shouted into the phone to anyone who answered: 'Mellifont Abbey has collapsed.'

The location of my dream was not Mellifont Abbey. It was set in another tranquil and scenic location, a place with which I am familiar, overlooking the River Boyne. However, there was no doubt in the dream that it was Mellifont Abbey that had collapsed. Its strange appearance and obvious dislocation may also have meaning, but for the moment I am concentrating on what seems to me to be the central import of the dream.

For those of you unfamiliar with Ireland and its history, Mellifont Abbey is one of those places that occupies a reasonably prominent and influential role in our past. A Cistercian monastery, it was founded in 1142 by Saint Malachy of Armagh and went on to become the largest Cistercian abbey in Ireland.[1] It is located on the banks of the River Mattock, a tributary of the Boyne, and is located just over five kilometres (3.3 miles) north of Newgrange.

The lavabo at Mellifont Abbey.

Mellifont's importance to my own work is largely through the fact that after its establishment, the Cistercians came into ownership of a lot of the land in the area, including lands at Brú na Bóinne. They established farms, known as granges, with the purpose of supplying the monastic order with enough food to make them self-sufficient, and established exclusive fishing rights along the River Boyne. Several of their granges have, it is believed, left their names in the landscape today. They include Newgrange, Sheepgrange, Roughgrange and Little-grange.[2]

Donnchadh Ó Cearbhaill, king of Airghialla, granted the monks the site for their abbey and the lands with which it was endowed, in the twelfth century. It was around that time that the monument we know today as Newgrange assumed the name by which most people now know it. The 'New Grange' of the Cistercian monks contained this most auspicious monument of ancient Ireland, the one previously known by several different names and variations thereof. Today, it is simply known as Newgrange, but I wonder how many visitors to Newgrange know any of its pre-Medieval names.

In the Dindshenchas (lore of place names), it is called *Tech Mic ind Óc* (the house of the son of the young, viz. Oengus/Aonghus). In *Tochmarc Étaine,* 'The Wooing of Étain', it is known as *Síd in Broga* – *síd* being commonly translated as a 'fairy hill or mound'[3] and Broga being from *bruig,* meaning 'abode, house, mansion, etc.'[4] The *áes síde* were the supernatural beings, or fairies, who inhabited these mysterious mounds and hills. Many believe the fairies represented a later folk survival of the Tuatha Dé Danann, the gods who were said to have owned the mounds and lived in them. Dagda, the chief of the gods, is described as the original owner of Síd in Broga, but later his son Oengus took possession of it.[5] Newgrange was also previously known by variants such as Brug Oengusa and Brug mac ind Óc.[6]

Some time ago, I watched a beautiful documentary on the Irish language station TG4, called *Fís na Fuiseoige* ('The Lark's View'). It was an exploration of the deep connection between Irish people and their places. In it, one scholar suggested that the anglicisation of many Irish place names had helped to undermine this sense of connection, and, by extension, we could propose that a sort of disempowerment had taken place.

> Still today, the land comes alive through its placenames, in a way that a non-Irish speaker cannot perceive… Tim Robinson captured this withering of geographical insight in his profound and elegant way in *Connemara: Listening to the Wind* (Penguin, 2006) where he writes, 'Irish placenames dry out when anglicised, like twigs snapped off from the tree.'[7]

A view from inside the lavabo at Mellifont Abbey looking towards the sky above.

Did the same thing happen when Síd in Broga became Newgrange? Did it lose some, or all, of its power for people? I believe that something of its importance was diminished by that renaming.

The Cistercians experienced their own disempowerment with the dissolution of the monasteries in the sixteenth century. Mellifont was dissolved in 1539 and today it lies largely ruined, although small but impressive remnants survive, including the much-photographed and documented Lavabo, or wash room. In terms of a direct, literal portent, the dream could hardly refer to a physical collapse of Mellifont, for there is not much left to collapse. The Cistercian order does survive, to this day, at the nearby New Mellifont Abbey, in the nearby village of

Collon (on land which was part of the original Cistercian grant), which was founded in the 1930s by the surviving Cistercians from Mount Melleray Abbey in Co. Waterford.[8]

Fascinatingly, although long renamed, the 'New Grange' of the Cistercians had not altogether relegated nor eradicated the older names of the monument, even in the late nineteenth century, when William Borlase mentioned that the place name Bro/Broe, presumably a survival of Brug/Brugh/Brú, still existed in the vicinity of Newgrange and the Bend of the Boyne. There was (and still is today) a Broe House near the river beneath Newgrange. Borlase quotes a Mr. O'Laverty, writing in the *Journal of the Royal Society of Antiquaries of Ireland*, who had spoken to a Mr. Maguire and his son, of Newgrange, who told him that 'the field in which Newgrange tumulus stands is called Bro Park' and that in the immediate vicinity of Newgrange are the Bro Farm, Bro Mill and Bro Cottage.[9] It appears that some things are not easily forgotten.

I'm not entirely sure how the connection was made in my mind, but since I had the dream I've been thinking that it is, at least in part, related to the renaming of Síd in Broga to Newgrange. And I cannot help entertaining the thought that the renaming was not necessarily a deliberately sinister or suppressive act on the part of the Cistercians, but that it was merely coincidental to the long and slow degradation of the mythic and sacred importance of this monument or *sídhe* that we have come to know as Newgrange. For Síd in Broga slumbered in the shade for great ages of this world, and through many times of turbulence and transformation the *áes sídhe* kept a quiet watch on the comings and goings of kings and chieftains and monks and abbots from the unknown hidden realms beyond its doorway.

The Tuatha Dé Danann encountered many 'invaders', according to the *Lebor Gabala* (Book of Takings), and it was the Milesians, arriving from Spain, who finally dispossessed them of Ireland. But it was an incomplete dispossession, because in their armistice with the Dé Dananns, the Milesians empowered the ancient deities for eternity when

A beam of sunlight points to Síd in Broga.

they granted them possession of the *sídhe*. Failing to understand the gravity of this lack of foresight, the Milesians guaranteed the undying Dananns a special immortality. They may have been removed from the physical landscape of the invaders, but in the realms of dream and song and netherworld, they assumed a transcendent elevation of extraordinary proportions – something that legitimised and prolonged them and ensured their vitality for countless generations of people for whom they remained (and still remain) a very real presence.

And so, in the dying light of an apparently vanquished Dé Danann world, the *sídhe* which had kept hushed for centuries its remarkable secret of hidden realms and banished gods had even been made to suffer the ignominy of the loss of its name. And thus, through deliberate act or unwitting insult, the Cistercians became another in the long line of 'arrivers', or invaders, or takers, to attempt by guile or gullibility to degrade and dispossess the stony vault of Síd in Broga of its divine and sacred import.

And what is that import? That there survives in people, even today, a light, a sacred essence, a revered and inviolate aspect, which derives originally from the very best facets of humanity. This aspect preserves the wish to initiate oneself into divine realms, with the express aim that one can be of service to one's greater community. The sacrifice of the Dé Dananns was immense. They yielded ownership of the beautiful Éire, the land we are so blessed to call our home, in order to avoid another war. They were weary of their encounters with the Fir Bolg and the Fomorians. With their blessing, the Milesians would become the new caretakers. But they were only custodians. Their time would come and go with the waning of the years.

In the past century, Newgrange has been unearthed and restored. Given a facelift, it has emerged from the rubble of its forlorn and dormant state. After five millennia, its secret crystal bower receives the golden sunlight once again on the winter solstice. The great *sídhe* has experienced a resurrection of sorts. The Fir Bolgs and the Fomorians were vanquished. Cessair and the Partholonians perished. The Vikings and the English came and went. And the Cistercians changed the sacred name of Síd in Broga to the newfangled Newgrange. But the Dé Dananns never died. Even in the hushed ages of their belittlement, they emerged as the diminutive fairies, the 'good people', and danced and sang with unrestrained merriment around their ancient hollow hill in the midnight moonlight.

Is it too bold a proposition to suggest that Newgrange be given back its old name? If we call it Síd in Broga once again, perhaps those diminutive fairies will arise in us as the unvanquished gods of our better nature, ready to bring light back to a somewhat darkened world.

1.7

Newgrange and the return
of the Tuatha Dé Danann

What journey did humans embark upon when we left the forests and turned away from the hunter-gatherer lifestyle towards organised agriculture and monument construction? It was the beginning of modern civilisation, and perhaps the beginning of conflict between humans. It was a brave but perilous step, emerging from the woods, and clearing land so that we could state in stone and earth something of our cosmology and our spirituality and of our meagre understanding of the great metaphysical mysteries. These questions do not have a time frame. They are relevant today just as much as they were in ancient prehistory:

Who are we?

Where did we come from?

Why are we here?

Where is here?

What is out there?

Why do people die?

What happens to us when we die?

It could be said that the stone monuments of the Neolithic embody those questions. Their construction was an attempt at understanding – or at least attuning to – some of these mysteries. The mythology of the great monuments of Newgrange and Dowth speaks of the desire to control time on behalf of the gods or kings. If you could measure time, and elucidate some of the complex patterns of the sky, perhaps you could open a vista into deeper mysteries.

There has been a lot of speculation – some of it valid – around the idea of monuments as portals. Do passage-tombs such as Newgrange offer access to hidden realms – realms of consciousness or spirit? Realms of the gods? Detached from the sense world, in the darkness of the interior of Newgrange, do you hallucinate, seeing the geometric shapes that are carved on to the stones of the monument?[1] Trance-like, do you meet the ancestors?

In ancient times, people brought the fragmented remains of their ancestors into these chambers and carefully, lovingly, placed them there in the obvious hope that out of their remains would spring new life – perhaps a life eternal, in other realms. These realms are spoken of in mythology.

In the myths, the gods wage war against each other. There are two battles of Moytura. Eventually, in the second battle, the 'good guys',

Winter sunlight in the passage of Newgrange (composite image).
Did the sídhe offer access to hidden realms?

the Tuatha Dé Danann, win out against the 'bad guys', the Fomorians. When you witness the magic of the winter solstice light in Newgrange – as I have done – and you see that beam of sunlight piercing the darkness, you awaken to the possibility that that was what the journey of the ancient world was all about – the defeat of darkness by light.

But the light of the Tuatha Dé Danann waned when the Milesians came from Spain. The Tuatha Dé Danann went underground, so to speak, agreeing to occupy the *sídhe* while the Milesians took sway over Ireland.[2] They weren't defeated as such. They made an accord with the Milesians and vanished into the *sídhe*. But this was not their defeat, nor their end. In accessing the *sídhe,* those portals to other realms, they were guaranteeing their survival. And the lasting folklore of the Tuatha Dé Danann is that they will return. In fact, some folk prophecy states that they will re-emerge for one last great battle, some end-of-the-world scenario, some apocalypse, and that they will be victorious.[3]

So what does all this mean in practical terms, if anything? Were the rumours of a coming return of the Tuatha Dé Danann (and sometimes other great mythical and historical figureheads, such as Fionn Mac Cumhaill or Gearóid Iarla) founded upon the wishes of a repressed and depressed people – an Irish population that had been beaten, downtrodden and starved by centuries of cruel occupation? It is likely that that is part of the tale.

However, there is something about these people of light that makes them endure and endear.[4] They represent our hopes for a better world, those unquenchable hopes that, out of darkness, light will spring. We imagine the return of Lugh Samildánach to Tara, or we envision Oengus Óg emerging from the great *sídhe* of Brugh na Bóinne, to reveal himself once more to the world. We should not lightly discard mythology as mere fairy tale. Joseph Campbell is reported to have said that 'Myth is much more important and true than history'. Myth offers a window into the human spirit, our core nature. We venerate the Tuatha Dé Danann[5] as manifestations of our light and compassionate aspects,

There are just three heavily decorated kerb stones at Newgrange. Kerb 52 (top) features an array of designs which might be centred upon the belt stars of Orion and the Dog Star, Sirius, which shone into the chamber when the monument was built. Kerb 1, the entrance stone (bottom), has the famous triple spiral carved beautifully among other patterns.

those facets of our being with which we would bring about a peaceful, harmonious and just world, where the very best aspects of humanity would be allowed to flourish. Equally, we acknowledge the presence of the Fomorians, as manifestations of our tyrannous and malevolent aspects, those facets of humanity that would see the world destroyed and allow human suffering to endure. In world myths, the conquest of darkness by light is a recurring theme. This is unsurprising. The myth with light versus darkness at its core is an enduring myth of hope – hope that we will vanquish the dark side of our nature once and for all, or in the Jungian analysis, that we may integrate our shadow with our ego-consciousness.

Newgrange slept for four millennia, its kerb and entrance concealed by the stones which slipped down off the cairn and sealed it shut. It was 'reawakened' in 1699 when the entrance to its passage was rediscovered, and more significantly in the 1960s when it was excavated and its solstice alignment and illumination revealed to the world. Now, hundreds of thousands of people visit the monument every year. The Tuatha Dé Danann are reawakening.

But let us not make the mistake of creating a religion out of the Tuatha Dé Danann. Let us not make them gods or messiahs. Rather, let us make them symbols or metaphors for the reawakening of our own best aspects. In the constant turmoil of a sometimes baffling human existence, where we do the most horrendous things to one another, let us acknowledge that the power to bring about positive change lies entirely within. To create gods of the Tuatha Dé Danann is to engage in a circumvention of our own power, a cop-out in which we declare that the gods have the power, and that they control our destiny.

The truth of the mytho-prescient folk belief in the future return of the Tuatha Dé Danann is that we should not wait at the doorways of the *sídhe* for the unlikely emergence of some spectral forms in our desire to prevent a cataclysm. Joseph Campbell also said, in *The Power of Myth*:

Heaven and hell are within us, and all the gods are within us. This is the great realization of the Upanishads of India in the ninth Century B.C. All the gods, all the heavens, all the world, are within us. They are magnified dreams, and dreams are manifestations in image form of the energies of the body in conflict with each other. That is what myth is. Myth is a manifestation in symbolic images, in metaphorical images, of the energies of the organs of the body in conflict with each other.[6]

In choosing to allow the Tuatha Dé Danann to manifest within us, we are saying yes to heaven and no to hell. We are inviting the metaphorical image of light to transform into a practical reality, a living embodiment of our own goodness, so that we might prevent the Fomorian forces of darkness from bringing us to the brink of destruction.[7]

Aurora Borealis (northern lights) at Newgrange.

The prophecy of the re-emergence of the Tuatha Dé from the *sídhe* should come as no surprise. In a world where darkness often appears to get the upper hand, we need Newgrange to serve as a reminder that the light can and will return – gloriously – and that the darkness is not un-ending. Imagine that for centuries and more likely millennia, the winter solstice light was unable to enter Newgrange because its structural stones had slowly subsided under the weight of the cairn, and the light was cut off. And yet, 5,000 years after it was first constructed, a miracle happened – the light began to shine brilliantly in the cold interior of the monument once again. So too will a miracle happen with the Tuatha Dé Danann. Countless centuries after they retreated to the *sídhe*, they will re-emerge. This is a metaphorical miracle – our own good nature must re-emerge, and as a species we must find a way to get along with one another. What other choice do we have? In a world constantly under threat from the forces of darkness, should we just retreat to hidden realms and allow the darkness to abide without challenge?

With Newgrange reconstructed, the portal is now open. It is up to us to call the Tuatha Dé Danann from the *sídhe*, to make them manifest within us, to ensure that, as the prophecy states, they will be victorious.

Kerb stone 67.

1.8

Lecc Benn: The stone on which the monster was killed

In the old place name lore about the monuments of the Bend of the Boyne, written down beginning around the twelfth century, there is reference to a very mysterious stone called the Lecc Benn.

The stone is mentioned in an equally mysterious tale about a giant monster (sometimes described as a tortoise[1]) called the Mata, which is said to have been killed at Newgrange and torn to pieces before being thrown limb by limb into the River Boyne.[2] As we will see later,[3] there is no doubt that the story of the Mata is a very ancient creation myth, with similarities to other origin myths from different parts of the world.

The Mata is described as a 'strange beast' in the Dindshenchas.[4] It was said to have had 'seven score feet' and four heads.[5] Elsewhere, it is described as a tortoise[6] or a 'Sea-Turtle that could suck down a man in armour'.[7] Whatever its form, the Mata appears to have been slow-moving: he is described as the 'sluggish Matha' in the Metrical Dindshenchas.[8] The whole episode of the killing of the Mata is wrapped in mystery and arcane language:

> … long since had the seer foretold
> the beast that was on Lecc Benn.
> The beast that was on Lecc Benn
> had seven score feet, four heads;
> its shank and its toe reached to here,

> it licked up the Boyne till it became a valley.
> … the strange beast, it found rest:
> it was slain on Brug maic ind Óc.[9]

So the strange beast that was called the Mata licked up the Boyne, moving sluggishly. It was killed at Newgrange, or rather 'on' Newgrange (Brug maic ind Óc), as the story implies. So who killed it?

> It was slain after the skilled hosts battled with it
> Causing much havoc.[10]

But who were these hosts?

> You will have heard of the mighty Ulstermen
> From Conn's half of the country,
> To strive with the strength of the slow moving Mátha
> So his limbs were broken on Lecc Bend.[11]

These Ulstermen are elsewhere described merely as 'the men of Erin', whose task was not just to kill the great beast, but apparently to dismember it and throw its limbs into the Boyne. This aspect of the story suggests that it is an indigenous version of a creation myth found in other parts of Europe (and indeed the world) whereupon 'the creation is preceded by an act of dismemberment'.[12] The task is an unpleasant one, but apparently necessary for the creation of new parts of the landscape to occur:

> When the men of Erin broke the limbs of the Matae, the monster that was slain on the Liacc Benn in the Brug maic ind Óc, they threw it limb by limb into the Boyne, and its shinbone (*colptha*) got to Inber Colptha (the estuary of the Boyne), whence *Inber Colptha* is said, and the hurdle of its frame (i.e. its breast) went along the sea coasting Ireland till it reached yon ford (áth); whence Áth Cliath is said.[13]

*A ribbed stone at the threshold between the passage and chamber of Newgrange.
The ribs of the Mata, perhaps?*

Writing in the early part of the twentieth century, but without indicating his source, Charles Squire gave complete credit for the destruction of the Mata to the greatest of the gods (and the first owner of Newgrange), the Dagda:

> He [Dagda] did great deeds in the battle between the gods and the Fomors, and, on one occasion, is even said to have captured single-handed a hundred-legged and four-headed monster called Mata, dragged him to the 'Stone of Benn', near the Boyne, and killed him there.[14]

In the *Tochmarc Emire*, 'The Wooing of Emer', there is mention of the plain of Muirthemne, which covered what is mostly County Louth today and would have included the great monuments of Brú na Bóinne, reaching as far south of the Boyne. Muirthemne, we are told, is 'from the Cover of the Sea' and:

> ... it is from this it got its name; there was at one time a magic sea on it, with a sea turtle in it that was used to suck men down, until the Dagda came with his club of anger and sang these words, so that it ebbed away on the moment:
>
> 'Silence on your hollow head;
> Silence on your dark body;
> Silence on your dark brow.'[15]

What is the mysterious Liacc Benn or Lecc Bend upon which the beast was slain? It is described in the *Dindgnai in Broga,* a listing of the monuments of the Bend of the Boyne contained in the Rennes Dindshenchas, simply as 'the stone of Benn'. R.A.S. Macalister describes the Lecc Benn as 'the stone on which the Mata was slain'.[16] Its name, Lecc Benn, possibly means the 'grave stone on the summit'. *Lecc* can infer a slab or rock or stone, or a flagstone, and even a tombstone or altar-stone.[17] *Benn* means a little point, a peak, a crest or summit, a pinnacle or even the horn of an animal.[18]

There are several other monuments and landscape features at Brug na Bóinne that are connected with the beast:

> Among the remarkable places of Brug na Bóinne, *Dind-shenchas* Érenn enumerates Lecht in Matae (the grave of the Mata); Glend in Matae (the valley of the Mata); Lecc Bend, 'the stone on which the Mata was slain'; and Duma na Cnám, 'the mound of [the Mata's] bones'.[19]

It seems that, after Mata was killed and dismembered and his limbs and ribcage tossed into the Boyne, the rest of his bones were buried:

> A solid barrow was built by them
> for a rampart over the bones of the beast.[20]

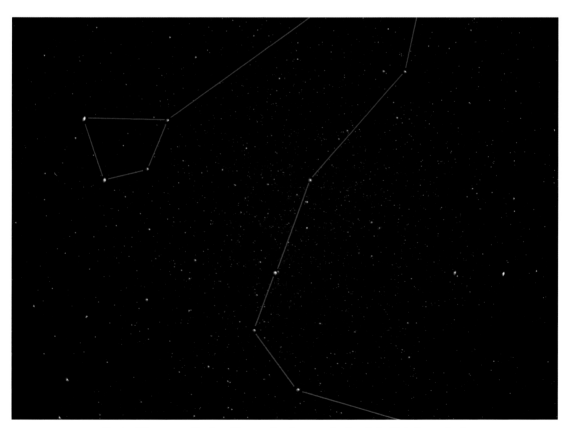

Part of the constellation Draco, the dragon. Its head (left) is formed of a trapezium of four stars – the four heads of the Mata?

A bizarre and fascinating ritual takes place:

> Afterwards came – everyone knows this story –
> The kings from all the fertile lands around,
> To view the vast Mátha,
> Each marked the killing-ground with a stone.[21]

The kings from fertile lands come to place a stone on the 'killing-ground'. Who are these kings? Are these lands in the vicinity of Brug na Bóinne or further afield, perhaps even overseas? We are not told. Gwynn's translation says the kings were from 'a pleasant land'.[22]

We find echoes of the story of the mound of the Mata's bones in China, where the great serpent Pa lurked in the waters of Grotto Court Lake. A hero called Archer I (Yi) killed the serpent and a small hill at the side of the lake is known as the Pa Mound:

Three hundred years ago Newgrange had a stone on its summit.
Perhaps this was the Lecc Benn, the stone on which the Mata was killed.

It is where the bones of this gigantic Pa serpent were supposed
to have been piled up after Archer I had killed the monster.[23]

What is not immediately clear from the literature about the Mata
is why there are apparently two different monuments related to his
death – one the Lecht in Matae (grave of the Mata), the other the Duma
na Cnam (mound of the bones).

Archaeologist Geraldine Stout has attempted to identify several of
the monuments of the Bend of the Boyne from the Dindshenchas passages. She has linked a partly destroyed passage-tomb, known as Site
U, to the east of Newgrange, with the grave of the Mata.[24] Stout suggests that the Lecc Benn, the stone upon which Mata was killed, is one
known as standing stone D, not far from Newgrange in the townland
of Dowth.[25]

However, there is another fascinating and intriguing possibility.
There was, in fact, a standing stone on the top of Newgrange. It was
seen and written about at the end of the seventeenth century, around
the time local landowner Charles Campbell and his labourers rediscovered the entrance to the passage of the great monument which had
been hidden under the cairn slippage material for centuries and perhaps millennia.

Edward Lhwyd, a Welsh scholar who was the first antiquarian to
visit and study Newgrange in the wake of Campbell's discovery,[26] 'described a standing stone on the summit as being visible from the area
around the monument'.[27] It seems to have been somewhat smaller than
the large standing stones or monoliths which surround Newgrange
(these are collectively known as the Great Circle). Newgrange was described by Lhwyd as 'having a number of huge stones pitched on end
about it, and a single one on the top'.[28]

The stone is actually shown in a somewhat crude drawing by
John Anstis, who made copies of Lhwyd's original drawings of Newgrange.[29]

Sadly, the stone disappeared in the years following the reopening of Newgrange. 'Thomas Molyneaux, writing in 1725, did not mention the stone ... nor does it appear on Vallancey's or in Beranger's watercolour of the mound'.[30] It does appear in an 1844 sketch of Newgrange by W.P. Newenham. However, there is a note adjacent to the sketch which says:

> This stone was undermined and thrown down the mound by men seeking for hidden money. Gold ornaments &c were found at the base.[31]

The loss of this stone undermines a full archaeological evaluation of Newgrange, and unfortunately deprives us of something that might have been unique in the design of Irish passage-tombs. The fact that

Megalithic art on a standing stone in front of Newgrange. The stone on the summit of the mound was removed some time after the entrance to the passage was rediscovered in 1699.

there was a stone mentioned in the manuscripts as being on top of Newgrange adds to the intrigue, but also to the sense of loss.

Was the stone perhaps supposed to function as a sort of *axis mundi*, a cosmic and world axis? Certainly Newgrange occupies a central and prominent position among the Bend of the Boyne monuments. The monument occupies a similar prominence in the myths. It is, so to speak, the centre of the ancient Irish world.

Furthermore, there is the possibility of a cosmological significance for the Lecc Benn. Could it have been possible that the stone mimicked the pole of the sky, and the star known as N'iatha (that which does not turn)?[32] In this cosmological world view, the Lecc Benn might have been seen as a terrestrial equivalent of the sacred axis around which the entire sky revolved. Fascinatingly, around the time Newgrange was built, the star we know today as Alpha Draconis, or Thuban, in the constellation Draco (The Dragon), was close to the position in the pole of the sky.[33] Was Draco, perhaps, known in ancient Ireland as Mata, the monster? The head of the Draco constellation is formed of a trapezium of four stars – the four heads, perhaps, of the Mata?

The 'beast that was on Lecc Benn' was 'slain on Brug maic ind Óc'. This is Newgrange, the Brug of Oengus Óg, also known as Síd in Broga, and the Lecc Benn appears to have been on top of it. Its disappearance, along with others such as the destruction of Ireland's Stonehenge, is one of the great losses of Irish archaeology.

2.

Cnogba agus Dubad

The sandstone pillar outside the entrance of the western passage at Knowth.

2.1

What is the meaning of Knowth's pillar stones?

A large sandstone pillar stands outside the entrance to the western passage at Knowth. The exact purpose or meaning of this pillar, and a similar but smaller one on the eastern side, is not known. They appear to be somewhat phallic in nature, and both are accompanied at a short distance by two large 'testes' stones.

At Knowth, the white quartz has been left in situ, on the ground, where it was found during excavations, which is contrary to the reconstruction of Newgrange, where the white quartz found on the ground beneath the cairn slip was once thought to have been on the front of the mound, forming a near-vertical wall, and thus Newgrange has been reconstructed that way. The quartz at Knowth is interspersed with water-rolled granite cobbles identical to those found at Newgrange. The interpretations are different. Perhaps the two monuments were built differently?

There is no easy explanation for the presence of the pillar stones at opposite entrances. Martin Brennan has noted the interplay of the shadow from the stone at the western side with a vertical line on the centre of the stone immediately outside the entrance to the passage around the time of the equinoxes, when the sun's light illuminates the passageway.[1] (I witnessed and photographed this in September 2000, but the maximum reach of the sun into the passage does not occur for another 18 days after this, around October 10th).

*A view of the eastern entrance at Knowth from the pedestrian foot bridge,
showing the stone settings and the pillar stone.*

The stone pillar outside the eastern entrance is much smaller, and is made of a different type of stone. Unfortunately, alterations to the outer portion of the eastern passage in medieval times due to souterrain construction have meant the outer section of this passage has a bend in it, precluding light from travelling into the eastern passage/chamber around the equinoxes. The addition in recent times of a bridge and a concrete door surround have further exacerbated this problem. Is there an argument, I wonder, for the removal of part of the souterrains in order that any possible alignment with the sun be investigated? Could we once again (for the first time possibly in thousands of years) witness the sun illuminating the cruciform eastern chamber of Knowth, in a way similar to the solstice illumination of Newgrange? I live in hope.

It might still be possible to witness and record any interplay between the shadow of the pillar stone (which might be described as a gnomon) at Knowth's eastern entrance around the time of the equinoxes. In fact, OPW staff recently witnessed this occurring at sunrise on

Knowth's eastern passage. At some time in the past, the light of the rising sun would have shone in here around the time of the equinoxes.

autumn equinox 2017. Studies of both east and west entrances could prove very valuable in revealing any subtle astronomical functions of these entrance settings. These stones undoubtedly had a purpose and a reason for being there in the minds of the builders.

Another interesting facet of the sandstone pillar outside the western entrance is that it is quite polished on the side facing the mound – as if it had been rubbed smooth over a period of time. One wonders if there might have been some ritual involving the touching of this stone over a prolonged span of time in antiquity. The story about the Lia Fáil (another phallic or pillar stone) at Tara and how it screamed when the rightful king touched it brings to mind the idea of perhaps many people rubbing a stone to receive some sort of blessing or luck from it. Perhaps neophytes or pilgrims kissed the Knowth pillar stone, like kissing the modern-day Blarney stone?

Yet another interesting aspect of the Knowth entrances is that, with the preponderance of stones carefully placed and set out in front of

(top) An aerial view of Cnogba (Knowth) and its satellite mounds, with the River Boyne in the background. (bottom) The sandstone pillar and another curious rock outside the entrance to Knowth's western passage.

these portals, it must be assumed that access into the passageways was not easy, and was perhaps undertaken only by the chosen few. Indeed at Newgrange the only reason tourists can access the passage and chamber today is because (a) the entrance area was widened, and set back from the kerb to accommodate people and (b) wooden steps were installed so that people don't have to clamber over the entrance kerb stones, thereby slowly eroding and damaging them.

A shallow basin-type feature outside Knowth east, replicated on a smaller scale at Knowth west, may have perhaps held water for some sort of ceremony. Unfortunately, a similar circular-shaped stone setting outside the entrance of Newgrange, in which a stone phallus artefact was found, was removed during excavations and not reinstated afterwards. Perhaps there were more similarities between these sacred entrances than we might have considered.

One thing that seems clear is that there was an intentional liminal aspect of the entrances. These are boundaries, thresholds. The kerb stones outside Newgrange as well as Knowth East and West are all lavishly designed. Settings of stone on the ground were perhaps associated with rituals held outside the entrances in ancient times. One wonders if the builders of these magnificent structures were to somehow magically venture forward in time to today, would they be delighted, or horrified, to see so many people entering these sacred womb-tombs?

2.2

Dowth and the story of hunger

I was at Dowth on the summer solstice. It was nice to be at Dowth on the longest day of the year, and quite fitting because of an ancient myth about the site. I was with a small group, talking about the mythology of the Tuatha Dé Danann, and the sun was beating down from its height at the very apex of its circuit through the zodiac. We could not see it, but at that moment the sun was being carried across the sky by the great constellation Orion.

There is a myth about how and why Dowth was constructed, contained in the Metrical Dindshenchas, the oldest versions of which are found in the twelfth century *Lebor na Nuachongbala* (known as the Book of Leinster).[1] As I sat there in the sunshine at Dowth, I wondered about the sudden darkness that is described in the Dindshenchas story about Dubthach/Dowth, the darkness that broke a powerful spell.

The king at the time, according to the story, was Bressal Bódibad (the second part of his name means 'lacking in cattle',[2] for reasons that will become obvious). He wished to build a 'solid hill', in the likeness of the tower of Nimrod, 'so that from it he might pass to heaven'.[3] It is said that 'the men of all Erin came to make for him that hill' and that they came to do it all in one day.[4]

The king's sister cast a spell on the sun, so that 'there should be no night but bright day till the work reached completion'.[5] I have stated previously that I think this is a reference to the summer solstice,[6] when the daylight is pretty much continuous, and when the sun's rising and

Dubad (Darkness) under the light of a winter full moon.

setting positions appear to halt on the horizon, that is, the sun stands still. At this latitude, even in the middle of the night we get a constant twilight, giving enough light to enable us to see in the dark.

The king's sister is not named in the surviving Dindshenchas verse about Dowth. However, as the work progresses, the king commits incest with her, and the spell is broken. Night falls suddenly. The men abandon the construction project. 'Since darkness has fallen upon our work, and night has come on and the day is gone, let each depart to his place'.[7]

One of the most interesting aspects of this grand project, which seems such an extraneous venture orchestrated by an egotistical and megalomaniacal king, is that the legend says it was built during the time of a great famine: 'In his time a murrain came upon the kine of Erin, until there was left in it but seven cows and a bull.'[8]

At the height of this famine, the king gathered all the men of Erin to this place to build him a tower so that he could reach heaven. Is this a description of slave labour? If there is any real substance to the myth as a record of actual historical events, it must be pointed out that surely the worst time to ask human beings to indulge in heavy physical work is when they are famished. However, that's what the story says. They built it during a murrain, with only eight cattle left on the whole island of Ireland to sustain its population. This aspect of the story is, we gather, allegorical. But it is interesting in light of a strange coincidence between myth and reality that has always been obvious to me but which I only came to realise the true significance of on the summer solstice of 2016.

That coincidence is this – Dowth was said to have been built during a famine, and it was almost destroyed during one too.

Moving from myth into factual, recorded history, we skip forward in time to the 1840s AD. In the years 1847-1848, R.H. Firth, at the behest of the Committee of Antiquities of the Royal Irish Academy, carried out a disastrous excavation of the Dowth monument which caused it considerable damage.[9] A commentary in the *Drogheda Conservative* newspaper in 1856 describes the damage:

...we find that beautiful tumulus literally torn to pieces.[10]

The crater in the top of the Dowth cairn is a result
of the disastrous Firth excavations.

A view of the kerb stones at Dowth and its giant sycamore tree.

Large amounts of cairn material were removed, and tossed over the sides, in an ill-fated attempt to find some treasure, or central chamber containing perhaps trinkets that might make men rich. But as I always say, the true treasures of Newgrange, Knowth and Dowth are not any material goods that might be found within them. Their true treasures are much, much deeper.

I wonder too whether a discovery a few years previously at Newgrange had provided some motive for Firth's catastrophic foray at Dowth. In the early 1840s, a labourer digging near the entrance of Newgrange found 'two ancient gold torques and a golden chain and two rings',[11] called the Conyngham find, 'since it was Lord Conyngham who brought the objects to the notice of the Society of Antiquaries of London'.[12]

Indeed, this find did not escape the notice of the Royal Irish Academy. The Newgrange gold objects found their way to the British Museum, something that caused consternation with Royal Irish Academy Vice-President William Wilde, who wrote:

Summer solstice sunset at Dowth.

Where are these? Are they in the great national collection of the Royal Irish Academy? Have they been recorded in the proceedings of that, or any other learned body in the kingdom? No, we regret to say that they were carried out of this country by an Irish nobleman, to exhibit at a learned society on the other side of the channel, in the transactions of which they will be found figured, together with a letter from their present owner, which, as he is our countryman, we will not quote![13]

An even greater tragedy about the Firth excavation is the fact that this rich men's treasure hunt occurred during the Great Famine, when the failure of the potato crop due to blight caused death and starvation for hundreds of thousands of people.

It is interesting to note that, in the middle of the Great Famine, during which a million Irish people died and another million emigrated, the esteemed gentlemen of the privileged class had nothing better to occupy their thoughts than an ill-conceived and unsuccessful 'treasure hunt' at Dowth, for which a special subscription had to be raised, while the population was suffering one of the worst calamities in Irish history.[14]

Fascinatingly, there is perhaps a hint in the Dindshenchas myth about its future fate at the hands of Firth and his colleagues. Is this an example of the prescience of myth?

From that day forth the hill remains
without addition to its height:
it shall not grow greater from this time onward
till the Doom of destruction and judgement.[15]

Notwithstanding the obvious Christian intrusion into this verse, with its mention of judgement, the story suggests that no more would be added to Dowth's height. Could this be taken to suggest, perhaps, that something would in fact be taken from its height? Today, there is a large crater in the cairn, and its height is much diminished as a result of this reckless excavation of the nineteenth century, if we could dare to call it an excavation. In essence, the myth's prophetical aspect has been substantiated through real events.

The synchronism of events, mythical and real, leads us to consider the Dindshenchas verse as not mere poetry for amusement, but as a mytho-prescient work with far-reaching vision through the long and sometimes tortuous history of this island. It is not alone in that regard, and I am especially drawn to the *Lebor Gabala* – the 'Book of Invasions' – and how that presaged a series of real invasions, as if forecasting a dire series of raids before they ever happened. But that's for another day.

2.3

Heaven's mirror:
As above, so below at Knowth

The interpretation of megalithic art is a highly subjective area. Martin Brennan's comprehensive account of the megalithic art in an astronomical context is impressive and persuasive.[1] He puts forward a compelling interpretation of what he calls the 'Calendar Stone', kerb 52. This does not mean we should be absolute converts to the notion that all of the Neolithic symbolism carved on stones in the Boyne Valley is cosmic or astronomical in nature. I like to observe and to admire the art, and in some cases to interpret it in the context of astronomy. But what works for the interpretation of one stone does not necessarily transfer to other stones. There's so much art, particularly at Knowth, where one is constantly impressed by the sheer amount of petroglyphs that one wonders how many different people were responsible, and over what span of time. I've been going there for years, and I still stand in awe at this massive megalithic art gallery, crafted carefully and lovingly all those millennia ago.

The kerb stone opposite is kerb number 86 (according to the archaeologist's numbering convention, which we'll use for convenience). It is located on the western side of the kerb, a short distance north of the dramatic and cryptic entrance to the western passage.

So what do I see? Do I see the C? The opposed Cs, as the archaeologists call them?

Well, kind of. But I don't think like an archaeologist. So I dislike the simplicity and arbitrary nature of labels like 'opposed Cs'. I don't think the people who carved them thought of it that way at all.

> In the extensive literature on old Irish art and culture a certain attitude that seeks to simplify symbolism is frequently encountered. The cause may be that there is no authoritative interpretation of these phenomena or that all features of mythic religion are generally thrust aside from fear of being unable to handle them. In their place are irrelevant aesthetic consideration of themes and 'ornaments,' which are judged solely as decoration and considered as entirely external forms.[2]

Heaven's mirror... 'opposed C' engravings on kerb stone 86 at Knowth.

So what do I see? Do I see what I want to see? Perhaps.

As an astronomer, I might see crescents; crescent moons. And I believe the moon is everywhere in megalithic art. But no, in this stone I see more than that. Here follows my (very subjective) interpretation – and remember that the tour guides at Newgrange tell you that you can all have your own theory, and that everyone's theory is as valid as anyone else's. So here is my just-as-equal-as-yours theory about kerbstone 86 at Knowth.

I might see the arc of heaven. I might see the Milky Way, in all its glory, stretched in a spectacular arch across the ceiling of night, in the beautiful ancient Boyne Valley under the darkest of skies, unpolluted by the choking fumes of modern industry and transport, and unhindered by the artificial light with which we so alienate ourselves from the cosmos today. And I might see this milky road of the stars, this

A red sky at Cnogba (Knowth) around Samhain.

bright way of the heavens, reflected on earth by the Boyne river, which loops magnificently around the great monuments of Brú na Bóinne. Did the ancients think this way? Did they think cosmically? Did the monuments somehow proclaim their tiny place of presence and permanence in a vast cosmos?

In olden times, one of the Irish names for the Milky Way was *Bealach/ Bóthar na Bó Finne* – the Way/Road of the White Cow. The Boyne river is from *Bóinn* – *Bó Finne* – the river of the White Cow. The names of the river on earth and the 'river' in the sky had a similar derivation.

Do these carvings on kerbstone 86 at Knowth represent the idea of Heaven's Mirror – As Above, So Below? Is the sky reflected on the ground? Is the line in the middle representative of the demarcation, the liminal boundary between heaven and earth? All of the symbols are enclosed in a great cartouche of sorts, perhaps an indication of the cosmos as an entity with limits – something that ends where the stars are fixed, where the souls go after we gently place their remains in the stone chambers.

Or is this stone's symbolism representative of opposed worlds (or even mingling worlds) rather than opposed Cs? The *sídhe* (mounds) were considered access points through which the Tuatha Dé Danann could pass between worlds – between this world and the otherworld:

> And as to Angus Og, son of the Dagda, sometimes he would come from Brugh na Boinn and let himself be seen upon the earth.[3]

Underworld, overworld. This world, the otherworld. Earth, heaven. Ground, sky. Conscious realm, unconscious realm. Reality, fantasy. Fact, theory. Objective, subjective. Tourist, tour guide. Tomb, womb. Decoration, language.

Say what you C. You are unlikely to be proven wrong. But have a go at interpreting it. Because if you don't, someone else will. Someone else will C what you don't C ...

2.4

Winter sunlight at Dowth

Last winter, in the weeks leading up to the winter solstice, I was lucky to be able to spend a few mornings at Dowth. It is one of three great monuments of Brú na Bóinne, but is the least visited of the trio. Personally, I'm glad that Dowth retains this almost-forgotten status. It is not on the official tour. It is wild and overgrown, and many of its secrets are in the deep slumber of the centuries. I like it that way. It's a lovely place to spend time. There are no tour guides, no buses, and visitors are generally few and far between. This makes it unique. One gets no such peace in proximity to Knowth and Newgrange, where visitors are constantly milling about.

In keeping with the fact that it is named after darkness (the Irish name is *Dubhadh*), Dowth presents a very interesting notion – the belief that we must experience the darkness of the longest night before the new year dawns.

While its near neighbour Newgrange is famous for its winter solstice sunrise alignment, Dowth's alignment to the sunset on the shortest day is less well known. Discovered (rediscovered actually) in 1980 by Martin Brennan and Jack Roberts, it was studied in detail over the course of a number of winters by Anne Marie Moroney, who published a lovely little book about it featuring lots of colour photographs.[1]

While the focus at Dowth is undoubtedly centred around winter sunset, there is something really beautiful that happens just after the sunrise on these short days of midwinter. The very well-known kerb

The Seven Suns lit up by the low sun at dawn around winter solstice.

stone 51 at Dowth, more famously referred to as the Stone of the Seven Suns (so named by Martin Brennan),[2] is gloriously lit up by the warm lustre of the midwinter sun. For about an hour after sunrise, these ancient solar symbols are highlighted in a dramatic fashion by the acute angle of the low sun. As a photographer who has spent many years taking pictures of this stone under various lighting conditions, I can safely say that I have never seen them so impressively and dramatically in relief. It's quite striking.

The Stone of the Seven Suns is on the eastern side of the great mound of Dowth. Curiously, over on the southwestern side, the entrance stone to the southern chamber is also lit up by the morning sun in winter time. This is due to the alignment of the stone, which is orientated roughly northwest-southeast. There are two large cup holes on the stone, referred to by some as Lucy's Eyes. There is also some worn megalithic art, which appears to be part of a spiral. A sizeable portion of the stone is still buried beneath the ground – only the top third or quarter is visible above the surface.

The myth of Dowth is all about light and darkness. The mound is built at the time of endless day (summer solstice) but the work is cut short by a sudden darkness (a total eclipse):

> Dubad, whence the name? Not hard to say. A king held sway over Erin, Bressal *bó-dibad* by name. In his time a murrain came upon the kine of Erin, until there was left in it but seven cows and a bull. All the men of Erin were gathered from every quarter to Bressal, to build them a tower after the likeness of the Tower of Nimrod, that they might go by it to Heaven. His sister came to him, and told him that she would stay the sun's course in the vault of heaven, so that they might have an endless day to accomplish their task. The maiden went apart to work her magic. Bressal followed her and had union with her: so that place is called Ferta Cuile from the incest that was committed there. Night came upon them then, for the maiden's magic was spolit. 'Let us go hence,' say the men of Erin, 'for we only pledged ourselves to spend one day a-making this hill, and since darkness has fallen upon our work, and night has come on and the day is gone, let each depart to his place.' 'Dubad (darkness) shall be the name of this place for ever', said the maiden. So hence are Dubad and Cnoc Dubada named.[3]

For a place that is named after darkness, the sun plays a big role at Dowth. It penetrates the southern chamber at midwinter. Until recent centuries, it probably also shone into the northern chamber around the time of Samhain and Imbolc sunsets (November/February). And there may be undiscovered passageways within its huge bulk. But as I said before, some of its secrets are in slumber. For now at least. And that's just the way I like it.

2.5

Buí and Englec:
The ancient goddesses of Cnogba

Many people look for meaning in the symbols carved in stone at the great monuments of the Boyne. Sometimes the most facile examination (and perhaps the most puerile too) is to indulge in pareidolia. When I took the photo of kerb stone 22 (shown on page 89) at Knowth/Cnogba, I was conscious of the image of the Cailleach, having been reading about her quite a lot:

> Rock is the hag's prime element, her stony spine.... Cailleach time moves form moon to moon, harvest to harvest. It is pagan time, rooted in the eternal return rather than the once-off redemption.[1]

Seeing this stone again – known under the archaeologists' counting system simply as kerb 22 – I was struck at how much it seemed to look like a large smiling face with two bulbous eyes and a big, broad grin.

These rocks were already eternally old when they were hauled into place – all 127 of them – to create a giant kerb or belt of stones around the gigantic mound that we know as Knowth. And now the carvings that were carefully etched into the surface of these slabs are eternally old, and the rocks that bear them speak of the beginning of time.

Once upon a time, so the story goes, this great mound of stone and earth was known as Cnoc Búa or Cnoc Buí, the hill of the daughter of 'red-haired Rúadrí', wife of Lug, son of Cian, of the ruddy spears.

A summer shower approaches Cnogba (Knowth).

It is there [Cnogba] her body was buried; over her was built
a great hill.[2]

What shall we say about Buí today, except that she is remembered
still, in these many aeons since her image was first conceived in stone, at
the mighty Brug na Bóinde where the hag never dies. The hag's breasts
are imagined as mounds in the Boyne landscape[3]; her passage-wombs,
creaking and groaning under the weight of the ages, live on to tell the
story of the undying sons who were born within them – Oengus the
young, who was conceived and born in the same day; and Sétanta,
whose crossing of the threshold of initiation brought him from innocent boy to murderous warrior. In there, Elcmar the magician of Brug
na Bóinde, divined souls with his fork of white hazel; Dagda Mór, the
Eochaidh All-Father, offered satiation to those who were crossing over;

Oengus protected the beautiful Etaín from the jealous Fuamnach in his sunny, crystal bower.

At ancient Cnogba, it is said that Englec the daughter of Elcmar was stolen away by Midir, much to the heartache of her lover, Oengus Óg.[4] At Newgrange, Oengus had protected Midir's lover Etáin, and yet at Knowth the two were love rivals for the woman Englec, whose disappearance was mourned greatly by the inconsolable Oengus. Lamenting the abduction of his beloved, Oengus engaged in a curious ritual … casting the 'blood-red nuts of the forest' on to the ground, and performed 'a lament around the little hill'.[5]

And so, in the confusion of tales so typical of the lore of the olden days, Knowth commemorates two distinct but perhaps not mutually exclusive events – both involving the passing (so to speak) of great women (goddesses even). As Cnoc Buí, Knowth remembers the great woman who was set to rest there beneath its heaving bulk, the undying hag of the ancient world who had many names and guises:

Kerb stone 22 at Knowth – the smiling face, perhaps, of the goddess Bua.

What we can say is that the notion of the caillech as chthonic goddess and goddess of death fits what have learnt of Buí from our various sources: the role of the earth-goddess in relation to sovereignty informs the imagery of 'The Lament'; in the Corc Duibne anecdote, Buí performs a rite of death and re-birth; and she is presented as the eponym Cnogba, which, being a mound in Bruig na Bóinne is at once an abode of the dead, and, as in Compert Con Culainn a telluric womb.[6]

As *Chnó-guba* (the 'nut-lament'), Knowth commemorates the passing of Englec into another realm, swept away by Midir to the Síd of Fer Femin, never to be seen by Oengus again.

On my visit to Knowth, I stopped in front of stone 22 during my round of the kerb (*deiseal*, sunwise, this time), and, having to stall a while under the modern concrete ledge to shelter from a summer shower, I imagined for a time that I was seeing the great women of

The setting sun casts a warm light on to kerb stone 65 at Cnogba (Knowth).

Cnogba, the abiding visage of the ancient hag that was known here as Buí, and the darling Englec, the beautiful daughter of Elcmar. And I wondered which would endure longer – the memory of these great mythic women, or the stone carvings bearing this image?

Cnogba (Knowth) and its satellite mounds viewed from the air.

3.

Sliabh na Calliagh

A marvellous vision of Tír na nÓg at Sliabh na Calliagh

When you climb Sliabh na Calliagh (the hill known today as Carnbane East, Loughcrew), it's difficult not to think of what motives and forces inspired a community of people in the far distant past to create great monuments of stone on the peaks of these hills.

How did they do it? Why did they do it? How did they stay warm up here, on autumnal days like today, when the wind is blowing and bringing water to the eyes? How many people laboured here, in honour of what gods, and at what cost to their physical and spiritual beings? You wonder about what could have driven them to such fabulous exploits, to create these permanent memorials of stone in honour of ideals and aims that we can only feign to understand.

It takes effort to get up the hill. Often, I trudge up the great prominence burdened heavily with camera equipment. I am usually out of breath half-way up. The effort required is all the greater on cold winter mornings, when the sharp bitter chill of the air stings the lungs. On these journeys, I wonder about whether all of the stone material that makes up the cairns was there, on the top of the hills, when those ancient master builders and astronomers of the New Stone Age began their gargantuan task of constructing these chambered cairns. Granted, none of these monuments is as big as Newgrange, Knowth or Dowth, but some of the larger cairns at Loughcrew (Cairn T, Cairn L and Cairn

The rays of the setting sun are cast beautifully over Carrigbrack and
Carnbane West viewed from Carnbane East.

D, for instance) are still quite substantial and contain a huge amount
of rock. Did they have to transport the stone to the hilltops from the
lower slopes or, even worse, from the lowlands beneath the hills? I can
manage the climb with a weighty camera bag on my back. How might
I manage with a large stone? And several such journeys each day for
weeks on end? It doesn't bear thinking about.

But, in the fading light of a late autumn day, I catch sight of a marvellous vision. The clouds and the sun create a powerful drama, a
play on the stage of the western horizon, causing sudden and thrilling
changes in colour and light that bring a sense of rapture. I am witness
to another dazzling moment in nature's constant dance.

The haze causes the landscape to fade into ever-dissipating layers
of mistiness, and the scattered beams of the sun create the impression
of a golden opening to something wondrous beyond the cairn-topped

hills. Perhaps this is as close as you can get to actually seeing Tír na nÓg, the Land of Eternal Youth. The eye beholds; the mind tinkers with possibilities, and the heart is greatly warmed by the glory of the scene.

Here, at this sanctified spot where the ancestors gathered in the ancient yesterday, I feel like I have made a connection with them, across time and space and landscape. I grasp with the notion of an otherworld in the here and now, one that transcends time and place, so that I can call out to them and they will answer.

And I wish and hope that the landscape will stay like this forever. Forever ancient.

The setting sun at the time of Lughnasa (early August) is seen to shine into the passage and illuminate a stone in the chamber of Cairn S, Loughcrew.

3.2

Sunrise at Cairn U

In 1983, Martin Brennan suggested that the passage of Cairn U, one of the smaller cairns on Slieve na Calliagh (known today as Carn-bane East) at Loughcrew, was aligned on the November/February cross-quarter sunrises.[1] One team of observers was situated in Cairn U on 3 November 1980, which was five days before the correct date for Samhain cross-quarter on 8 November. Brennan implies, although falls short of explicitly stating, that Cairn U is aligned to the cross-quarter sunrises. Regrettably, no further observations were possible, due to weather (not altogether unsurprising due to the Irish climate!) until November 12th.[2]

I was unaware of any photographic proof extant showing the sun aligning with the passage of Cairn U. Probably the best-known photographer of ancient megalithic sites and their alignments is Ken Williams.[3] Ken indicated to me that although he had been at Cairn U around the time of the cross-quarter sunrises, and although he had some photos, he hadn't been there on the exact day.[4]

At Imbolc in 2017, Ken, along with artist Lar Dooley and I, decided to try to witness and photograph the February cross-quarter sunrise at Cairn U. I set out from Drogheda at 6.25 am with the intention of getting to Loughcrew (which can take an hour or so by road) and climbing up the hill to be ready for sunrise, which occurs at around 8.08 am at Imbolc. It's always advisable to allow extra time, especially for the hike up the hill, the speed of which is often impeded by the weight of the

A beautiful red sky greeted the dawn viewed from the chamber of Cairn U at Imbolc.

camera equipment. I arrived safely and made the journey up the hill, where I was greeted by Lar. Ken arrived soon afterwards.

A red sky was forming because of some cloud towards the south-east. Positioned in the rear recess of the cairn, it was clear to me that the sun would come up in the approximate direction to which the passage was pointing.

The sun was obscured by cloud for the first few minutes after the actual moment of sunrise. So I was unable to make direct observation at the moment the sun appeared on the horizon. However, what was immediately clear was that the sun's position was still somewhat to the south of where it needed to be for a direct alignment. I observed the sun's azimuthal position from the light that it was projecting on to the clouds. Crouched in the rear recess, I couldn't see the sun or its light. However, on leaning slightly into the left-hand recess, I could see the sun coming out from behind the clouds in alignment with the passage.

We were delighted with the show nature was putting on. It was a great thrill to see the sun emerging. From my observations that day, I ascertained that it would be a week or maybe more before the sun would rise directly in alignment with the rear of the end recess. This was just a rough guess based on observation and there was no empirical method to my conjecture. The alignment was such that I had to lean towards the left-hand recess of Cairn U in order to see the sun through the passageway. It is obvious that the cairn (at least in its current condition) focuses on a range of sunrises, maybe lasting a couple of weeks. This is something that requires further observation. A return visit at either Imbolc or Samhain will be required.

One very, very interesting thing which I did not realise until that morning was the fact that the Imbolc sunrise, as viewed from Cairn U, was coming up over the Hill of Tara in the far distance. I imagine that is not a coincidence. Neighbouring Cairn T faces Slane (looking across Hill of Lloyd near Kells) for equinox sunrise, such that when an observer is crouched in the end recess of its chamber, looking out through the passage, the distant Hill of Slane is framed by the entrance.[5] Some of the cairns on Carnbane West point to cairns on Carnbane East.

I put the telephoto lens on the camera to zoom in for a picture of Tara from Cairn U. Tara is conspicuous from a distance not because it presents a particularly striking eminence against the sky, but because of the huge trees that grow in and around the churchyard there. These trees can be seen from a long distance away, making Tara easily visible from the great Brú na Bóinne monuments as well as Loughcrew, among other places.

It's such a great pleasure to be able to observe astronomical occurrences at prehistoric buildings. There are numinous qualities to such moments because they transcend temporal boundaries and take us back, in a way that is both spiritually and empirically connective, to a remote era when our early ancestors observed heavenly phenomena. We can only conjecture at a possible greater purpose behind such

Imbolc sunrise aligned with the passage of Cairn U, Loughcrew.

alignments, and inevitably such conjecture takes us into realms that are both scientific and spiritual. On the one hand, early people were marking out the distinct patterns of the sky, making the ancient chambered cairns of Ireland primordial sundials (and doubtlessly moondials too). But their construction was such that they were a statement, tacit or explicit, of permanence, of longevity, in a world where the cycles of nature spin all too fast, especially where human life spans are concerned.

In the Neolithic, a great many people would not live to see even one completion of what was known in later Irish as the *Naoidheachda*, meaning 'the nineteenth' – the 19-year cycle of the moon which is known today as the Metonic Cycle.[6] The best a Neolithic cairn builder could hope for was to see two complete Metonic Cycles. Because of the much lower life expectancy, there were no elders in the New Stone Age, certainly not in the sense that we have elders today; spiritual elders, perhaps, but not aged octogenarians or centenarians. At 40, you were a wise elder of the Neolithic community. If you lived to see 50, you might have been seen as a freak of nature.

Furthermore, the ancient passage-cairns weave a connective web suggestive of awareness or consciousness of a greater cosmos, in which the sun and astral bodies are not so much seen as things that are 'out there', totally beyond reach or influence, but rather things with which humans and the animate world have a distinct interaction. The light and heat of the sun can be seen to directly influence growth and seasonal patterns in nature, in addition to the many migratory patterns which would have been observable in the vicinity of the Boyne and Slieve na Calliagh tombs in the Neolithic. The moon's distinct and powerful effect on the tides led the megalithic people to make a detailed study of lunar movements.[7]

The labour involved in creating cairns on hilltops must not be underestimated. Even a fit young person finds the climb to the summit of Slieve na Calliagh an exertive and physically demanding activity. Imagine repeating this exertion, with the additional burden of carrying a boulder, or several boulders. When one factors weather and the lack of any significant capable engineering or construction technology into the equation, not to mention the smaller physical size of the builders, the creation of the cairns on the hills of Loughcrew seems a gargantuan task. These structures certainly deserve to be described as immense and monumental. As well as being prodigious feats of construction, they are monumental memorials to the humans who laboured hard to complete them. Their fastidious observations of discernible natural phenomena were ingeniously combined with an imaginative vista which opened towards realms that were supernatural, transcendental and otherworldly while retaining a physical connection to the telluric, sublunary sphere. At Loughcrew, this world and the next are seen to coalesce. Up there, on the hills of the hag, one gets a sense of detachment from the ordinary mortal dimension. Reaching out towards the sky above and the horizon beyond, the young humans who had just discovered agriculture and who were setting in place the foundations of civilisation, stepped out through the inter-dimensional threshold of the cairns into whatever realms of the spirit or imagination lay beyond.

There is yet at least one place on the earth where the ancient spirit dwells. When the fast-revolving clock of astronomical circuits ticks down on each of us at our own appointed time, we might aspire to those realms that were so anciently envisioned. Can we yet countenance the possibility that we will perhaps, some day, meet those who left their bones behind in the cairns of Loughcrew, out there, beyond that threshold?

A view of the passage and chamber of Cairn U just before sunrise at Imbolc in early February.

3.3

The Hag's Chair at Loughcrew: The throne of an ancient queen of the sky and the land

Although it is part of the kerb surrounding the cairn, the Hag's Chair at Cairn T, Sliabh na Calliagh, is unlike any other kerb stone on any Irish passage-tomb. We know very little about it, except what myth and folklore offer by way of mysterious and vague explanation.

The Cailleach (hag/witch/crone/goddess) of Loughcrew is ubiquitous on these hills. The story of the cairns is the story of this ancient figure of mythical intrigue. The creation myth of Loughcrew (for that is how it can be best described) suggests that she built the cairns, somewhat haphazardly, by dropping stones from an apron full of rocks as she jumped from hill to hill. She is said to have come from the north, which is interesting, because towards the northern aspect we find the rounded mountain of Slieve Gullion in Armagh – another place associated with the Cailleach (who goes by different names) and has a chambered cairn on its top which has a passage that points towards Loughcrew for winter solstice sunset.

> This is a very old lady whose shade still haunts the *lake* and carn of Slieve Guillion in the county of Armagh. Her name was *Evlin*, and it would appear from some legends about her that she was of De Danannite origin.... Does her name, *Eibhlín bheurtha inghin Thuilinn*, appear in the genealogies of the Tuatha De Dananns?[1]

The Hag's Chair at Cairn T (The Hag's Cairn) at Loughcrew with the rising moon.

Some sources suggest that the ancient Cailleach might have been the Queen Tailte,[2] in whose honour the Tailteann Games were held at nearby Teltown. As the Cailleach Bhéartha, she is the one who brought the cairns into existence. Not untypically of such creation myths, she is killed in the effort:

> There are three hills about a mile asunder in this parish, having three heaps (carns) of stones on their summits, with which the following wild legend is connected. A famous old Hag of antiquity called *Cailleach Bhéartha* (Calliagh Vera) came one time from the north to perform a magical feat in this neighbourhood by which she was to obtain great power if she succeeded. She took an Apron-full of stones and dropped a *carn* on *Carnbane;* from this she jumped to the summit of *Slieve Nacally* a mile distant and dropped a second carn there; from this hill she made a second jump and dropped a carn on another hill about a mile distant. If she could make another leap and drop the fourth carn it appears that the magical *feat* would be accomplished, but in giving the jump she slipped

and fell in the townland of Patrickstown in the parish of Diamor, where she broke her neck. Here she was buried and her grave was to be seen not many years ago in a field called *Cul a' Mhóta* about 200 perches to the East of the moat in that Townland, but it is now destroyed.[3]

I would speculate that the second part of her name, *Bhéartha*/Vera possibly derives from the Irish word *bert* or *beirt,* meaning 'burden, load, bundle'.[4]

It is interesting that the hag has several different names – *Cailleach Bhéartha* (Cally Vera), *Evlin* (Eibhlín), *Garvoge* and even *Tailte.* The hills also go by different names. Carnbane (*carn bán*) is the one we know to-day as Carnbane West. In one version, it is called Carnmore (from *carn mór,* the big cairn). Indeed, the largest cairn in the whole Loughcrew complex, Cairn D, is on Carnbane West. Carrigbrack, which does not feature in some versions of the creation myth, is from *carraig* (stone) and *breac* (speckled), thus 'speckled rock', but is also known as Sliabh Rua (Red Mountain), for which there is a very obvious and fascinating astronomical reason connected with local alignments (see chapter 3.6). Sliabh na Calliagh (also anglicised as Slieve Nacally) is apparently also known as Carnbeg (*carn beag,* the small carn). Although there is a middle hill called Loar, one wonders if Loar was Carrigbrack or Carnbane East, possibly making Patrickstown Hill the Carnbeg of the variant.

I have often wondered if the story of the old hag dropping stones as she leaped from hill to hill is not somehow related to the movements of the sun, moon and the stars. We know that several cairns point to other cairns (Cairn L points to the cairn on Carrigbrack, for instance; Cairn I points to Cairn T, etc). Is the Cailleach the moon? We know from research into the Boyne Valley monuments that Venus (the Morning Star) was known as *caillichín na mochóirighe,* meaning 'early-rising little hag'[5]. It is tempting indeed to view the moon, with its darker areas, as an apron or bag full of stones. As the Cailleach drops the stones, the moon becomes smaller, until it fades to a slender crescent into the

The Hag's Chair.

growing light of morning, before eventually disappearing (in the east) as the dawn comes. In Irish, the last-quarter moon is known as *goin-ré*, *goin* meaning 'act of wounding, slaying', and *ré* being 'moon'.[6]

It is possible also that the cairns might mark out various important lunar risings and settings which indicate the moon's course through the sky during the 18.6-year rotation of its nodes. Observation of this cycle leads to the observation of lunar standstills and the prediction of lunar eclipses. Martin Brennan and his team of researchers (including Jack Roberts) made several important discoveries at Loughcrew in the 1980s, revealing a number of probable astronomical alignments of the ancient chambered cairns. They made several observations of lunar events. It would be nice if this work was followed up. In the fullness of time, a greater story about the astronomical complexity of Loughcrew might emerge, and with it, perhaps, a 'solution' that cracks the meaning of the myth of the Cally Vera.

Until then, we can only suggest that some day this ancient queen might return, and claim her throne once more.

3.4

The story of the Cailleach of Loughcrew and its meaning

Many visitors to Loughcrew have probably heard the story of the Cailleach (hag or witch). The hills of Loughcrew are known to-day as Carnbane West, Carrigbrack, Carnbane East and Patrickstown Hill.[1] The hills (three of them at least) were collectively known in the nineteenth century as 'The Witches Hops',[2] and in the seventeenth as 'the Calliagh Steppes'.[3] In some versions, Carrigbrack is omitted, and in the fifteenth century the remaining three were referred to as *Trí Choiscéim na Caillighe,*[4] the three footsteps of the hag.

There is an old poem told about the Cailleach of Loughcrew, that goes like this:

> I am the Chailleach Beara
> Many wonders have I seen
> I have seen Carn Bawn a lake,
> though tis now a mountain green.[5]

The story about the Cailleach tells how she came from the north and she tried to jump from hill to hill, some say from the Carnbane (the westernmost hill) to Patrickstown (the easternmost), alighting on the other hills in between.[6] If she could succeed in this magical feat she would obtain great power. She was carrying an apron full of stones. As she jumped from hill to hill, she dropped some stones from her apron, forming the cairns on each of the peaks. When she

Rainbow over Cairn T, Sliabh na Calliagh.

reached Patrickstown (which is undoubtedly a Christian name, and perhaps we might some day learn what its original name was) she fell and broke her neck. According to Jean McMann, a pile of stones at the bottom of the eastern slope of Patrickstown Hill was known until recently as the Cailleach's grave.[7]

In earlier times, the hill we know today as Carnbane West was known just as the Carnbane (*Carn Bán*, the white cairn or the white heap of stones). The hill known today as Carnbane East was known as Sliabh na Cailliagh,[8] the mountain or hill of the hag/witch.

There is no doubt that the story of the Cailleach of Loughcrew contains essences of an ancient creation or origin myth. This great woman, whose status has been reduced to an old crone, was probably a goddess of the land who was greatly venerated in ancient times. McMann says of her:

> This cailleach is famous in Irish folklore. Other storytellers have described her as a superhuman woman who could

harvest a field faster than any man, a crone lamenting her youth, a banshee announcing a death, or a Christian nun. She is best known as Cailleach Bhéarra, but has been called by many other names, including not only Waura but Beri, Buí and Vera ... and may be a later version of the ancient pagan sovereignty queens whose consent was required for kings to rule. Some scholars think she represented wild nature, as a prehistoric earth goddess.[9]

Michael Dames suggests that 'the apron is the divine womb, translated into the language of dress'.[10]

In this context, we can see the apron as a womb of creation, and perhaps, in the tradition of Marija Gimbutas, we can think of the cairns not so much as tombs, but more like wombs.[11] As a creation or origin myth, the story of the Cailleach of Loughcrew shares some similarities with another origin myth, the one about how the River Boyne was formed. In that story, Bóinn approaches Nechtain's Well, something

The entrance of Cairn T (the Hag's Cairn) at twilight in winter.

which is forbidden for a woman. The well gushes forth into a fountain, carrying Bóinn along as it creates the River Boyne. Bóinn is mutilated by the waters – she loses an eye, and her arm and leg are broken. Eventually, she is washed out to sea, where she is drowned. Her lapdog, Dabilla, is transformed into the Rockabill islands.[12] In both cases, a female deity is credited with an act of creation, and in both cases at the completion of the act of creation the women are killed.

But there is more to the story of the Cailleach of Loughcrew than meets the eye. I'm inclined to think that the imagery of a woman jumping from hill to hill forming cairns is, perhaps, some memory of an ancient astronomical system in which the sun and moon were seen to rise up out of various hills and cairns when viewed from other parts of the complex, and possibly from other observing locations at a distance from the Loughcrew hills, and conversely they were seen to 'set into' hills and cairns from other vantage points. I'm inspired in this respect by the *Cailleach na Mointeach,* the 'Old Woman of the Moors' at the Callanish stones on the Isle of Lewis in Scotland. The local people there refer to her as the 'sleeping beauty' and once every 18.6 years, the moon at its major standstill southern extreme rises from some part of this sleeping beauty and sets again at the bottom of Mount Clisham.[13]

Until 1980, little was known about any astronomical aspect of the Loughcrew cairns. But in that year, Martin Brennan and Jack Roberts discovered the equinox alignment of Cairn T, during which the light of the rising sun on the equinoxes shines into the passage within the cairn and illuminates what Brennan described as 'solar emblems' on the stone at the rear of the chamber. They also discovered that the chamber of Cairn L appeared to be aligned towards the November and February cross-quarter sunrises, and several other small cairns appeared to have alignments towards solar events. In some cases, the passage of a cairn is pointing towards another cairn. For instance, from the chamber of Cairn I on Carnbane West, the sun appears to rise over Cairn T on Carnbane East at the beginning of September.

Megalithic art on a stone in the chamber of Cairn T at Sliabh na Calliagh.

The imagery of a woman, or goddess, jumping from hill to hill is possibly symbolic of a system of alignments from various parts of the megalithic complex, focusing on sunrises and moonrises, and also sunsets and moonsets. In the fullness of time, an even more comprehensive study of the alignments of Loughcrew might reveal an interest in the extreme lunar declinations – the minor and major standstills of the moon. At Dowth, for instance, my own studies of the alignments of its two known passageways indicate that the setting moon at both its major and minor southern setting positions might have been the primary, or even shared, targets of the southern and northern chambers, while the setting sun at winter solstice (southern chamber) and November/February cross-quarter days (northern chamber) were also targets.[14] Perhaps the death of the Cailleach is allegorical, referring to the lunar extreme, and maybe the 'death' of one 18.6-year cycle and the beginning of the next one? The fact that she was said to have 'come from the north' is also interesting, because of the fact that the maximum northern rising and setting extremes of the standstill moon are located in the far northeast and northwest.

Until a more comprehensive study of possible lunar alignments at Loughcrew can be undertaken (and I must admit I would be very happy to be involved!) we can only reflect on the possibilities. We know that there are certainly solar alignments. We can't be sure that these alignments were an intended principal function of the monuments, but they constitute a fascinating and indeed almost mystical aspect of these ancient structures. To be lucky enough to have been witness to some of these alignments makes me feel an extraordinary connection with the builders.

We cannot know how far back the story of the Cailleach of Loughcrew goes. Certainly, as Jean McMann acknowledges, 'People have probably been telling stories about the Loughcrew hills for more than five thousand years'.[15]

Is it too bold a step, too wild a conjecture, to suggest that the story of the Witches Hops or the Cailleach's Steps is in fact some remnant of a very ancient myth, one which goes right back to the time when these cairns were constructed?

Addendum: Watching the moon

Of interest to our discussion about lunar standstills at Loughcrew is the fact that a society carefully observing and recording the moon's cycles would become aware of several things. The number of sidereal months (the time it takes the moon to complete a circuit of the sky, ie from a particular place on the zodiac back to the same place again) and synodic months (a particular phase back to same phase, eg, full moon back to full moon) does not fit neatly into a solar year. Twelve synodic months is 11 days short of a 365-day solar year. In fact, the number of lunations only fits the solar year after 254 sideral months, or 235 sidereal months, which is equal to 19 years. This 19-year cycle is known today as the Metonic Cycle.

The moon rises over the ruins of Cairn V at Carnbane East, Sliabh na Calliagh.

Observers watching the Metonic Cycle would also naturally become aware of the rotation of the moon's nodes, an 18.6-year cycle during which the point where the moon's path crosses the sun's path (the moon's path is inclined to the ecliptic by 5.15 degrees, so its path intersects the sun's path at two points in the sky each month) appears to complete a full circuit of the sky. As this happens, the moon appears, at certain times during this 18.6-year cycle, to go through maximum and minimum extremes, which are observable by the moon's rising and setting places relative to the sun's solstice positions. When the

113

moon's node is located exactly on the sun's solstice positions, there is a likelihood of eclipses occurring at the time of the solstices. Conversely, when the moon's nodes are located exactly on the sun's equinox points, not only is there a likelihood of eclipses at the time of equinox, but the moon's path will be at its maximum separation from the ecliptic at the sun's solstice positions. If the moon's declination is at that time within the range of the sun's path, we get what is termed the 'minor standstill', while if its declination is outside of the sun's range, we get the 'major standstill'.[16]

It is possible the builders of Cairn T at Loughcrew were not exclusively focused on the equinox sunrises, but also on observing the moon, and in particular at those times when its node was crossing the ecliptic at the sun's equinox points. If this is the case, as we can merely speculate, then we can envisage observers within the rear recess of Cairn T watching for the rising moon at such times. The natural extension of this argument is that if the moon is visible through the aperture of Cairn T and is in the same position in the sky as the equinox sun, then seven days later (ie one-quarter of a circuit around the sky), the moon will be at its major standstill rising position (provided it is on its ascending node when visible within Cairn T) or at its minor standstill rising position if it is on a descending node. In other words, the Hag's Cairn might have been used to indicate the times of the extremes of the moon, when an 18.6-year cycle was ending (the death of the hag?) and a new one was beginning.

3.5

A glorious dawn announces the beginning of winter at Cairn L

Standing on the top of a great hill in County Meath in the pre-dawn cold, one is struck by the harshness of the environment in which the ancient megalith builders carried out their fervent work. At Samhain (early November) 2016, I was waiting with fellow megalithic explorers, artist Lar Dooley and photographer Ken Williams, to witness something that had been happening at Cairn L, Carnbane West, for thousands of years.

I hadn't been to Cairn L in a good few years, and to go there in the pre-dawn twilight, with Orion and Sirius looming above the ancient cairns, was really something very special. But what was to follow was one of the highlights of many years of being present at ancient and sacred sites. At 7.44 am, the sun appeared above the remains of a cairn on the summit of one of the Loughcrew Hills – known as Carrigbrack (from Irish *carraig breac,* meaning 'speckled rock'), and also known as Sliabh Ruadh (Red Hill).[1] One wonders just how ancient some of these place names really are.

In his volume three of his *Dolmens of Ireland* books, Borlase says the following of the word *breac*: 'Brack, or Breac, usually translated "speckled," is a term which, in one form and another … is so frequently associated with megalithic remains and venerated rocks…'[2]

As the sun appeared, its light immediately streamed into the passage and chamber of Cairn L, where it illuminated a limestone pillar in

*Samhain sunrise emerges from the ruined cairn on Carrigbrack
as viewed from the entrance of Cairn L.*

the chamber – a feature that is unique to Cairn L and not found in other ancient cairns with apparent astronomical alignments.

Martin Brennan and Jack Roberts and their team discovered this alignment in the early 1980s.[3] It is one of many suggested astronomical alignments at Loughcrew. The most famous is the equinox alignment of Cairn T (the Hag's Cairn). Although I had been to Cairn L a couple of times, I had never been there at sunrise, and certainly not at Samhain. It was an immense pleasure, and a moment of pure joy and rapture to see the beautiful warm sunlight illuminating the interior of the cairn.

The significance of this event is that Samhain was a very important pre-Christian festival, possibly having its origins in prehistory.[4] It was considered the beginning of winter, and as a so-called 'cross-quarter' day, it marks the halfway point, measured in days, between the autumn equinox and the winter solstice. But unlike Newgrange, where the sun shines into its chamber around winter solstice, Cairn L will be illuminated twice – once in early November and again in early Feb-ruary, for the ancient festival of Imbolc, or the February cross-quarter day.

Of particular interest here is the fact that, although the central axis of Cairn L's passage does not point to Carrigbrack, and nor does it align towards the cross-quarter sunrises of Samhain and Imbolc,[5] it is the curious limestone pillar at the edge of cell 6 of the chamber – the right-hand recess with its impressively decorated backstone (stone C16) – that receives the light of the sun at two very significant moments in the calendar. These moments are coincidental with the beginning of winter and the beginning of spring – Samhain and Imbolc.

In winter, the sun begins to shine into Cairn L around October 1. Direct sunlight reaches cell 4, the rear recess of the chamber, around mid-October, and as the sun moves southwards each morning, the fi-nal illumination of the chamber (specifically the aforementioned lime-stone pillar) occurs around November 7.[6] In other words, the last light entering the chamber occurs at the time of Samhain. In spring, the very first sunlight to enter the chamber strikes the pillar on February 4,[7] around Imbolc. Is this coincidental?

Archaeo-astronomers do not think that supposed cross-quarter alignments of passage-tombs had any calendrical significance. Frank Prendergast says:

> Although sunlight will penetrate to the edge of cell 6 … around these dates, any claim for the alignment of the passage axis being calendrically significant in an early prehistoric context has little basis in fact. Tomb L was built in the Neolithic, and, as such, predates (by almost three millennia) any late Iron Age/early Medieval evidence for calendrical subdivision of the solar year.[8]

However, the fact that the sun rises out of the ruins of the cairn on the peak of Carrigbrack hill at Samhain and Imbolc must be significant. The visual drama is quite profound. The sun rises out of Carrigbrack

*Samhain sunrise spectacularly illuminates cell 6 of Cairn L and its
beautifully decorated back stone (stone C16) in this fabulous image by
Martin Byrne (www.carrowkeel.com) taken on 5 November 1997.*

(also known, significantly, as Red Mountain[9]), emerging from the ruined tomb on its peak. As it does so, its golden light enters through the
entrance of the passage of Cairn L and shines into its interior, lighting
up the limestone pillar at the edge of cell 6. The light is then reflected onto stone C16, the largest of the chamber stones, and the most
lavishly decorated. The impressive visual dynamics of this alignment
would suggest an importance attached to those dates. At Cairn U, we
saw how the sun at Samhain and Imbolc would be rising above the
distant Hill of Tara when viewed from its chamber. Perhaps there is
some room for a reassessment of the significance of Samhain and Imbolc in the Neolithic? It is difficult to believe that these alignments are
accidental, and not part of some deliberate astronomical or calendrical
orientation, which is accompanied by impressive visual phenomena
and alignment towards other ancient sites.

Of further interest is the fact that the cross-quarter days have a
practical and observable function. They bracket the periods when the

sun's daily movement along the horizon is at its fastest and slowest. For instance, the fast-moving sunrises of spring equinox are bracketed on either side by Imbolc and Bealtaine. After Bealtaine, the sun's daily movement slows down again towards summer solstice, and it is only at Lughnasa that it picks up speed again. In winter, the slow movement of the sun's rising position is marked on either side of the midwinter period by Samhain and Imbolc.

In local folklore, it is said that a hag (Cailleach) carrying an apron full of stones created the cairns as she jumped from hill to hill, dropping piles of rocks as she did so. Another tale says the hills are sacred to the Garvoge, a 'monster woman', who formerly lived here.[10] The following is an old verse, sometimes attributed to Jonathan Swift, about Garvoge and Loughcrew:

> Determined now her tomb to build,
> Her ample skirt with stones she filled,
> And dropped a heap on Carnmore,
> Then stepped one thousand yards, to Loar,
> And dropped another goodly heap;
> And then with one prodigious leap
> Gained Carnbeg, and on its height,
> displayed the wonders of her might.
> And when she approached death's awful doom,
> Her chair was placed within the womb
> Of hills whose tops with heather bloom.[11]

One cannot help, while looking out from Cairn L towards the other hills (Carnbane East and Carrigbrack, both of which are topped with cairns), envisioning the Paps of Anu or the Paps of Morrigan, and to see in the landscape the earth goddess herself. Perhaps, if one allows a little imagination, one can think of the breasts and the belly of that great woman, so venerated in ancient Ireland, as the earth itself, topped with these cairns that are attributed to her as miraculous works.

In religious art, the human body symbolizes myriad functions beyond the sexual, especially the procreative, nurturing, and life enhancing. I believe that in earlier times, obscenity as a concept surrounding either the male or female body did not exist. Renditions of the body expressed other functions, specifically the nourishing and procreative aspects of the female body and the life-stimulating qualities of the male body. The female force, as the pregnant vegetation goddess, intimately embodied the earth's fertility. But the sophisticated, complex art surrounding the Neolithic goddess is a shifting kaleidoscope of meaning: she personified every phase of life, death, and regeneration. She was the Creator from whom all life – human, human, plant, and animal – arose, and to whom everything returned.[12]

Ancient though she may be, the Cailleach will never be forgotten at Loughcrew, because the Cailleach *is* Loughcrew.

The golden light of the rising Samhain sun strikes the limestone pillar in the chamber of Cairn L, viewed from the entrance. Within a couple of days, the light no longer enters the chamber and winter has begun. The light will re-enter the chamber, striking the pillar, at Imbolc, the beginning of spring.

3.6

Why Carrigbrack is also called Red Mountain

The hill at Loughcrew known as Carrigbrack might be the least famous of the four hills[1] upon which the Cailleach of ancient times was said to have built a scattering of cairns. Today, it has the remnants of just one passage-tomb on its top, and is somewhat forlorn. However, it has another name – Sliabh Rua – meaning 'red mountain'.[2] Following a weekend of observations on the hills of Loughcrew around Samhain 2016, it's now clear why it has that name.

At dawn on the ancient festival known as Samhain, in early November, the halfway point in days between autumn equinox and winter solstice, the sun rises out of the breast of Sliabh Rua and immediately its light shines into the chamber of Cairn L on Carnbane West. As we saw in the previous chapter, its light dramatically strikes a bright, slender limestone pillar in the chamber. Standing outside the cairn, looking at the dawn sky, one sees Carnbane East (topped by Cairn T) and Sliabh Rua (topped by the remains of an old cairn) as the image of the breasts of the hag.

On November 7, 2016, I went back to Loughcrew. This time, I went to Slieve na Calliagh (Carnbane East) to see if I could determine where the sun goes down on Samhain as viewed from the Hag's Cairn (Cairn T). To my delight, it was a beautiful evening and the sun and sky put on a dazzling show for my camera. And as it sank towards the horizon, I could see that the sun was setting over Sliabh Rua/Carrigbrack. It was easy to see from the resulting light show how that hill might have got its name – Red Mountain.

The higher elevation of Slieve na Calliagh means that one is looking 'down' at Sliabh Rua for the sunset, whereas because Carnbane West and Carrigbrack/Sliabh Rua have the same elevation, one is simply looking horizontally at the sunrise. (Cairn L is 236 metres above sea level; the cairn on Sliabh Rua is 237 metres and Cairn T on Slieve na Calliagh is 258 metres above sea level).

Just to reiterate – at dawn on Samhain, the sun rises out of Red Mountain when one is situated at Cairn L, which is one of the largest cairns in the whole complex, and which has a chamber that faces towards Carrigbrack. At dusk, the sun sinks into Red Mountain when one is situated at Cairn T, also one of the largest cairns, known as the Hag's Cairn.

One of the fascinating things about the Samhain alignments is that the hag in other parts of Ireland is sometimes characterised as the Hag of Winter. The November cross-quarter date appears to have been important in pre-Christian times, although there is some debate about its

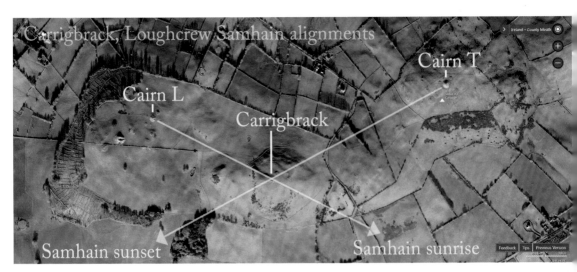

A map showing the Samhain alignments involving Carrigbrack.
Samhain sunrise emerges from Carrigbrack when viewed from Cairn L,
and in the evening of the same day the sun sets into Carrigbrack when viewed
from Cairn T. (Image: Bing Maps)

Samhain sunset goes down behind Carrigbrack, viewed from Carnbane East.

true antiquity, and whether it was considered important in the Neo-lithic. Samhain was said to have marked the beginning of winter, or the beginning of the 'dark half' of the year (the bright half beginning at Bealtaine in early May). Samhain was considered the principal festival in the ancient calendar.

Moreover, the visual aspect of the alignment system at Loughcrew leaves one in little doubt that the placement of cairns was set out with deliberate alignment in mind. With good weather for both the sunrise observation at Cairn L and the sunset at Cairn T, I can certainly say that both phenomena are very dramatic and awe-inspiring. The view from Cairn L towards Slieve na Calliagh and Carrigbrack presents the impression of recumbent female breasts. This is a feature noted in Sligo, where the Ballygawley Mountains present the form of a prostrate pregnant female.[3]

It is worth noting too that the hill over which the sun rises on winter solstice when it shines into Newgrange in the Brú na Bóinne complex is also called Red Mountain.[4]

4.

Megaliths and Monuments

4.1

Neolithic passage-tomb construction: Cooperation or enforced labour?

One of the major questions surrounding the construction of the giant chambered cairns of the Boyne Valley is whether the builders laboured hard at this immense monument-building project out of zeal and community cooperation, or as a result of enforced labour. The greatest of the cairns – Newgrange, Knowth and Dowth – appear to have been constructed by a large body of people, and the scale of the project was regional,[1] if not national.

Emeritus Professor of Prehistoric Archaeology at Queen's University Belfast, J.P. Mallory, says that in the Mesolithic, hunter-gatherers considered most material possessions 'as impediments to mobility'.[2] In the Neolithic, however, the emergence of agriculture led to many changes in the way we lived. Interestingly, fish was apparently 'off the menu' as there was a major shift from a marine diet to a terrestrial one.[3] We should not be altogether surprised by that, but it seems to have been a fairly dramatic change. The landscape changed too – there was significant cutting down of virgin forests for the purposes of agriculture and monument building. Interestingly, this is mentioned in mythology:

> Slaine, king of the Fir Bolg, and their judge, by him was its wood cleared from the Brugh.[4]

> Brega son of Breogan was the eldest of Breogan's children, and by him the plain was cleared (of trees), and from him it takes its name.[5]

*Newgrange and some of the monuments of the Bend of the Boyne,
viewed from the air.*

In the Neolithic, Mallory says there was an evolution of the concept of 'surplus, wealth and social ranking' or, as he puts it, 'if you prefer, waste, greed and discontent'.[6] Sounds familiar, doesn't it?

And so, as the seeds of agriculture were sown in the Boyne Valley and other parts of Ireland, introducing a new way of life to the island, the seeds of a modern civilisation were also sown, one that, despite all its benefits, has seen us painfully divorced from cosmos and the natural world, such that we're trying to kill our planet – by overpopulating it, by stripping it bare, by choking it and by many other means.

> It is with the Neolithic that we see the emergence of the 'ethic of fertility', encapsulated in the biblical injunction to 'increase and multiply', which is now being challenged by world overpopulation.[7]

The point (or rather the question), in terms of the whole idea of social ranking and wealth and 'discontent', is this: were the monuments built by a community of people that was unified in its beliefs, and content to contribute to this mammoth effort to enshrine its beliefs, and perhaps immortalise its 'moment in time' monumentally in stone?

Or, as the result of a hierarchy – a system of social ranking – was that community coerced, compelled or otherwise forced into these monumental labours against its wishes?

I would like to be able to tell you that there is a definitive answer to that question. There does not seem to be enough archaeological evidence to place ourselves on either side of the fence (let's call it a Neolithic palisade) that divides these two options. There might, of course, be a third option – it is possible that some people did it because they wanted to and some were coerced, compelled or otherwise forced.

However, Mallory does lean a little bit towards one side of the Neolithic palisade when he says this, offering a glimpse at the theory he might prefer:

> ... while mutual cooperation is always possible, large labour projects have often been seen to indicate the emergence of some form of social elite.[8]

Personally, I have always leaned towards the 'we're all in this together' idea, and see in the monuments of the Boyne a collective and cohesive effort representing the endeavours of a community that was largely working as one. What is my evidence for this supposition? I see monuments large and small, apparently built to a system based on alignments and on cosmology, representing an effort to record and understand the passing of time, and cycles, but also representing a spirituality whose complete depth and complexity we might never understand. There was an artistic zeal too, an expressive competence, perhaps indicating a community that was at the height of its creative output. It certainly doesn't seem like a project that was undertaken or completed under duress.

Climate change may well have played a significant role in the motivation of the community towards the construction of ever more

Modern agriculture at Brug na Bóinne. The mowing of grass silage takes place under the light of the full moon at Newgrange Farm.

gigantic passage-tombs. Archaeologist Robert Hensey says that while the first generations of farmers on this island might have been 'pleased with the rich soils and favourable climate they encountered', there was a significant change in the climate from 3600BC to 3000BC, bringing cooler conditions and more precipitation.[9]

> Farming communities must have been placed under significant pressure by these changes. A curious, and thus far unexplained, aspect of passage tomb construction is that the monuments increase in size and complexity even as the climate was degenerating and agriculture becoming more difficult. Particularly, there seems to be a greater investment in passage tomb construction in parallel with the deteriorating conditions.[10]

Kerb stone 52, dubbed the 'Calendar Stone' at Knowth, demonstrates a keen interest in the 19-year Metonic Cycle of the moon.

Yet again, this appears to have been hinted at in the mythology. In the section about Dowth, we saw how the Dindshenchas myth suggests there was a cattle 'murrain' and that the king, Bressal Bó-dibad, brought all the men of Erin to build him a tower to reach heaven. The Irish word for murrain in the Dindshenchas passage is *díth,* which can mean 'loss, absence, lack, need, desire'.[11] And so, not for the first time, the archaeology and the mythology agree. As Hensey suggests, the monuments were getting bigger as the climate deteriorated and agriculture became more problematic. It could be that the Dowth legend is more than just a fable, and perhaps incorporates some core of remembrance of actual events.

If you allow for this possibility, then the Dowth legend might also offer us an insight into the main question for discussion here, about whether the monuments were built by collaboration or enforced labour, or a mixture thereof. The cattle murrain – which might have been something like an infectious disease such as redwater – affected 'every place in Ireland', according to the Dindshenchas.[12] Hensey says the cooler, wetter climate from 3600BC onwards brought the additional challenge of disease and pests, which he says may have become an increasing problem during this time.[13]

On the 'big question' (forced labour versus community collaboration), neither of the Dinshenchas passages about Dowth can settle the matter for us conclusively:

> All the men of Erin were gathered from every quarter to Bressal, to build them a tower after the likeness of the Tower of Nimrod, that they might go by it to Heaven.[14]

> The men of all Erin came to make for him that hill…[15]

One version says they were gathered from every quarter to Bressal, perhaps suggesting that they were coerced. The other says that they (willingly, one presumes) came to make his mound for him. We might never know.

The early agricultural practices at Brug na Bóinne would have been very labour-intensive. Modern agricultural machinery makes it much easier to grow crops such as this field of barley near Newgrange.

What material evidence would there be, if there had been an elite, and they had compelled the population to haul the giant stones up the banks from the Boyne, and to sail to Cooley and Wicklow and perhaps other areas in search of materials? How would we know one way or the other? The paucity of human bone remains found in the chamber of Newgrange suggests it was possibly a burial chamber for a chosen few – the elite, perhaps. However, the fact that the chamber was open for more than two and a half centuries before the excavations means that we cannot know how much organic material might have been re-moved or disturbed during that time. And the remains of many individuals were found at Knowth and Fourknocks, for instance.

It may be that the downturn in the climate conditions over Ireland brought an increased urgency around the scale and nature of monument and ritual that were obviously closely tied to studies of the movements of the heavens. If the weather was worsening, perhaps the community considered the need to create grander edifices to the gods, in order that the warmer, drier weather might return.

We should not be surprised, therefore, to find that the chief god Dagda, who is associated strongly with Newgrange/*Síd in Broga* in *Tochmarc Étaíne* and other stories, was the one who:

> ...performed miracles and saw to the weather and the harvest...[16]

Dagda was the 'Red Man of all Knowledge',[17] whose radiance was renowned:

> Who was king over all Erin, sweet-sounding, radiant? Who but the skilful Dagda? You hear of none other so famous.[18]

One of his epithets was 'Deirgderc', meaning 'red eye', which is taken to mean the sun.[19] He is credited with being the actual builder of Newgrange,[20] and in one episode in the Dindshenchas, Dagda is said to have drained a magical sea which had covered the land known as

Mag Muirthemne, translated as the 'darkness of the sea' or 'it is under the sea's roof'.[21] This land, Muirthemne, is today County Louth, and anciently reached as far south as the River Boyne, so that the great monuments of Brú na Bóinne were within its borders.

> … there was a magic sea over it, and an octopus therein, having a property of suction. It would suck in a man in armour till he lay at the bottom of its treasure-bag. The Dagda came with his 'mace of wrath' in his band, and plunged it down upon the octopus, and chanted these words: 'Turn thy hollow head! Turn thy ravening body! Turn thy resorbent forehead! Avaunt! Begone!' Then the magic sea retired with the octopus; and hence, may be, the place was called Mag Muirthemne.[22]

I take this story to be a variation of the ancient creation myth about the monster known as Mata.[23] Indeed, Dagda is credited with having killed the Mata at the Lecc Benn, as we saw in an earlier chapter. The octopus which he encountered in the magical sea over Brú na Bóinne may have been a different type of creature. Lady Gregory described it as a 'Sea-Turtle that could suck down a man in armour'.[24] The word 'octopus' is a translation from the Irish *muir-selche*.[25] The word *seilche* means a turtle or tortoise, or a snail.[26] The form of the monster appears inconstant in the manuscripts, but there are aspects of the ancient creation tales that are reasonably consistent. The Mata licked up the Boyne, causing a deprivation of water. The *muir-selche* was expelled with the receding sea, causing another deprivation of water, 'thereby causing to surface the plain of Muirtheimhne'.[27] To my mind, they are both versions of a very early creation myth.[28] There are aspects of the Mata/*muir-selche* myths that may echo a very ancient deluge that is remembered in hundreds of similar myths from diverse parts of the world.[29]

His ability to make the sea recede marks Dagda out as a distinctly solar figure. Perhaps the megalithic builders of the late Neolithic constructed the greatest of their monuments – Newgrange, Knowth and Dowth – to try to appease or encourage the Dagda, in order that another environmental catastrophe be averted? In this milieu, with the memory of the warmer weather of the earlier Neolithic still extant, and a sense that conditions were gradually worsening – making farming more difficult – one can more easily imagine a certain level of active participation, zeal and urgency among the community.

If there was a sense that the midwinter sun was imagined to be weakening, and that by association the weather was deteriorating and agriculture (and therefore survival) was becoming more difficult, a monument aligned towards the sun (Dagda) at its lowest ebb on winter solstice seems more like the sort of project that would unify the community towards a goal that would help avert a climatological doomsday scenario.

It is interesting that Dagda was said to have kept two pigs in New-grange, one roasting on a spit, the other ready for slaughter, as a means, perhaps, of eternally satisfying hunger in the otherworld:

> There are three trees there perpetually bearing fruit and an everliving pig on the hoof and a cooked pig, and a vessel with excellent liquour, and all of this never grows less.[30]

There may be aspects of the declining climatological conditions that explain why, in the mythology, the older gods in the form of Dag-da, or (depending on the version) Elcmar, were deposed by the young son, Oengus Óg. It wasn't just a case that the old sun of the year had lost its strength and was being dethroned by a new, vigorous young sun. It might have been just as likely that the old sun that had been the friend of the Neolithic farmer since the earlier introduction of agrarian practices into Ireland was seen to be gradually waning over the centu-ries and that the arrival of Oengus Óg as the new owner of Síd in Bróga signified the wish of the community that the climate be turned back in their favour.

*Climate change might have made agriculture more difficult at the time
Newgrange and the great monuments were built.*

Notwithstanding the possible climatic implications for the construction of the Brú na Bóinne trio of passage-tombs, there is the un-
doubted cosmological aspect. It has been reasonably demonstrated that
all three had significant calendrical alignments, tied to the movements
of the sun, moon, and possibly some of the planets and stars.[31] Was the
symbolic information encoded upon some of the stones of these giant
mounds intended, even in part, to serve as a teaching guide for the
younger community, so that they could become adept at the seemingly
more complex lunar and planetary astronomy? Or were they, in fact,
the arcane etchings of an elite and aloof priestly caste, a minority of
learned druids or astronomers who kept their knowledge secret and
whose carvings were designed to remain mysterious to the mainstream
community? Certainly in the latter scenario one could imagine that
such a druidic stratum might indeed be seen to possess powerful abilities. A druid, for instance, who could predict that the next full moon

The 'new monuments' of the Boyne Valley ... housing developments and the M1 motorway bridge at Drogheda. Are we now painfully divorced from the cosmos?

would turn red might be a very powerful individual. Outwardly, it would appear that he had direct access to esoteric knowledge, and that his prognosticative abilities were indeed magical. Inwardly, however, he was accessing his own knowledge of the predictable pattern of lunar eclipses, something that he had learned through patient study and observation with his druid colleagues – knowledge which was likely passed down through the generations and which was perhaps remembered through story or mnemonic. This could be implied from Hicks' interpretation of *Tochmarc Étaíne.*[32] People told the stories, but maybe they didn't know the mysteries contained therein. Perhaps the early myths were transmitted from generation to generation by every member of the tribe or community, but the secrets behind the myth – the astronomical data among other things – were known to only a few.

It is not easy to answer the question about how willing the community was to become involved in the grandest construction projects of prehistoric Ireland. We can only suggest possibilities based on very limited evidence. A great deal of what has been written about the ancient monuments and their builders is based upon sometimes sparse or inconclusive material evidence, and a great deal of speculation or hypothesis based around same. We can suggest one thing – that a large community of people was involved in building Newgrange, Knowth and Dowth. What we cannot prove, or suggest with any level of certainty, is how willing they were to participate.

And so we will leave the final words in this matter to archaeologist Robert Hensey, who thus summarises what is probably the most acceptable consensus on the matter given the available evidence:

> A centralised authority would have been necessary for the gathering of materials and construction work to be accomplished, yet a certain amount of willing cooperation and community 'buy-in' must have been present for the project to be a success.[33]

4.2

Ceremonial dismemberment and excarnation in prehistoric Ireland

One of the most fascinating aspects of the Irish passage-tombs is the fragmented nature of the human remains that have been found inside these enigmatic monuments. In terms of the unburnt bone human fragments found during the O'Kelly excavations at Newgrange, 'apart from some complete hand and foot bones, all human specimens consisted of small fragments'.[1]

There were a total of 750 unidentifiable pieces. The fragmented remains of dozens of individuals were found in the chambers of nearby Knowth. Layers of disintegrated remains were found in the passage and chamber of Fourknocks.[2] So how do human bones – especially those that are not cremated – become so fragmented?

Eileen Murphy of Queen's University Belfast studied Irish Neolithic bones and found that our early ancestors had dismembered and defleshed their dead.[3] Murphy had worked on the excavation of graves in Aymyrlyg graves in Siberia, Russia.

> There she learnt to look for the tell-tale signs of what is thought to have been an ancient religious practice – short, fine scraping marks on the bone and cuts where tendons and ligaments were joined.[4]

> 'After studying the dismembered and defleshed Russian remains, I decided to have another look at Irish neolithic

bones. It is something that has been overlooked before and will now require a reassessment of our understanding of these ancient burial sites.'[5]

The researchers from Queen's made the findings when examining bones from the 4,000-year-old Millin Bay tomb in County Down, and the discoveries mirrored those found by Swedish archaeologists at Carrowmore in County Sligo. Body parts, notably skulls, are thought to have been kept on display for religious purposes.

Gabriel Cooney, professor of archaeology at University College Dublin, said:

> In these tombs you rarely find single skeletons, but rather groups of cremated remains. In this way these neolithic people would seem to have been creating a new identity from their treatment of the dead. You also find different parts of the body treated in different ways, such as unburnt parts of the skull in with cremated remains. This would point to dismembering of the corpses.[6]

The chamber of Newgrange looks like a man-made cave.

The western recess of Fourknocks. Burnt remains that were found in the tomb were believed to have been cremated at the Fourknocks II mound nearby before being brought here for interment.

Were the Brú na Bóinne bones dismembered or defleshed by humans (or defleshed by the process of natural outdoor excarnation)?[7]

A new study of bones uncovered during excavations of Carrowkeel in County Sligo by Professor R.A.S. Macalister in 1911 has revealed that the unburnt specimens 'displayed evidence of dismemberment',[8] indicating that 'the bodies of the dead were dismembered before they were placed in the tombs'.[9]

Dr Jonny Geber of the Department of Anatomy at University of Otago, New Zealand, said: 'We found indications of cut marks caused by stone tools at the site of tendon and ligament attachments around the major joints, such as the shoulder, elbow, hip and ankle.'[10] There was, he suggested, a particular focus on 'deconstructing' the bodies. 'Attempting to understand the reasons these ancient communities dismembered the bodies is one of the real fascinations with this research,' said Sam Moore, one of the authors of a paper about the discovery.[11]

Not all corpses were deconstructed by other humans. The process known as excarnation, or defleshing, is well documented. This involves leaving the human corpse out in the open (sometimes known as sky burial), or in a cave or even in a temporary grave, for the elements and wildlife to assist in the process of speedy decomposition. Some 'excarnation sites' were out in the open, while others were in caves. It is estimated that a human corpse left out in the open can be reduced to a pile of bones in a matter of weeks or months. However, there seems to have been a deliberate effort, in some cases, to slow down the process of excarnation by leaving a corpse in a cave.

A chance find of a bone fragment in a cave at Knocknarea in Sligo led to the discovery of more bone fragments belonging to an adult and a child which may have been evidence of cave excarnation. Radiocarbon dating put the age of the bones at over 5,000 years old. It is thought that the process of excarnation in a cave took much longer – perhaps up to two years – but eventually the deceased's relatives would come

A replica of the giant basin stone from Knowth's eastern chamber, with a recreation of what it might have looked like with bone material placed in it.

*Simulated solstice light in the passage of Newgrange. The 'cave' of Newgrange
might have been the place from which the journey to the spirit world commenced.*

back to collect the bones for burial elsewhere. In the case of Knocknarea, this burial might have taken place in one of several monuments on
the top of the mountain.

> We can imagine, therefore, that Stone Age people in Sligo
> between 5,000 and 5,500 years ago carried the corpses of their
> dead up the mountain. After an arduous climb, they then
> squeezed through the narrow cave entrance, and laid the
> dead person on the cave floor.[12]

What's also interesting in Ireland is that osteoarchaeological analysis has revealed an absence of animal scavenging marks, suggesting
that the entrance to the excarnation caves was sealed during the process of soft tissue decomposition.

> This reveals a conscious decision not to speed up
> decomposition . . . By creating a protective environment in
> which excarnation took place undisturbed, people controlled

the process, pace and space. The living may have sought to observe the slow and gradual disintegration that was taking place inside a cave. The underground was therefore a place of transformation, which in turn transformed caves as places. It may have been in caves that the journey into the spirit world commenced.[13]

There are no caves in the vicinity of the great passage-tombs of the Boyne Valley.[14] It would be interesting to postulate on how the fragmented unburnt remains there – and indeed at nearby Fourknocks – came to be in that condition. Of course another question that begs to be asked is how many of the flint scrapers and other flint tools found at Newgrange and other passage-tombs were used in the dismemberment of human remains.

It seems to the modern mind that the practice of cutting up a relative's body is something quite revolting and disturbing. However, the ancients were undoubtedly closer to their dead. In modern western civilisation, the tendency has been to move away from death and the dead:

> For the last two centuries, Western society has slowly striven and largely succeeded in removing the dead and the dying from public sight. We have pulled the curtains across, privatised our mortality and turned death into a whisper… The Western Death Machine has a collective way of both diminishing the physicality of death – the contact with the actual body itself – and professionalising it, from the medical profession to cemeteries and crematoriums.[15]

Closeness to the deceased, exemplified in the Irish wake, is reminiscent, perhaps, of ancient funerary rites of the Stone Age:

> The wake is the oldest rite of humanity, once practised in some form by every culture on earth, reaching back beyond the fall of Troy to our Neolithic ancestors and further still.[16]

4.3

Climbing Slieve Gullion to see the highest passage-tomb on the island of Ireland

I was up at Slieve Gullion around Easter and decided to go and visit one of the ancient archaeological gems of Ireland – one that I had never seen before – the Calliagh Berra's House. This is a passage-tomb with covering cairn located on the summit of Slieve Gullion in County Armagh. At 570 metres above sea level, it is the highest passage-tomb in Ireland.

Thankfully, there's a roadway that brings you to a small car park that is already 360 metres above sea level, so the walk/climb on foot is only a further 200 metres or so in elevation. Still, despite our brisk pace, it took my teenage sons and I about half an hour to make the climb. It was a dull day, although not cold, with only a light breeze. All the time it felt like it was going to rain but it mostly held off except for a very light drizzle for a few minutes at the top.

The pathway up the mountain offers some beautiful views over the surrounding countryside. This was an excursion that stirred some excitement for me. I have long been a visitor to Sliabh na Calliagh, Loughcrew, those magical hills in Meath scattered with ancient megalithic remnants. The two – Loughcrew and Slieve Gullion – are not only connected through their eponymous hag goddess, but also through an alignment involving winter solstice.

The name of the Calliagh Berra, in all its different forms,
is ubiquitous across Ireland.

The path twists and turns and has been nicely laid out with smooth rocks in places, gravel in others, and in other parts just turf pathways. However, about halfway up things become more steep and the climb is a wee bit more arduous. This was no deterrent for my 14-year-old twins, who looked as nimble as Legolas running along the mountain ridges of Middle Earth. We met a man who said he was waiting on a bus. I suggested perhaps he was waiting on a helicopter. Truth be told, it might even be possible that a fairy bus does pass this way every once in a while.

The top of the mountain is remarkable. It has a small lake on it, known as the Calliagh Berra's lake. There is a story about Fionn Mac Cumhaill and this lake:

> Fionn walked up the slopes of Slieve Gullion to the lake near the summit to find a beautiful young lady sobbing on the water's edge. Being a gentleman he enquired as to why she was crying; to which she replied that she had dropped her golden ring in the bottomless lake. Without a moment's

hesitation Fionn ripped off his shirt and dived in, swam down until he found the ring, grabbed it and returned to the top only to find an old hag laughing, the Calliagh Berra. The witch had tricked Fionn and he fell out on the lake's shore as an old withered man. When Fionn came down the mountain, no-one recognised him, not even the Fianna! However, when his trustworthy Irish Hounds smelled the old man they knew that he was their Master. Fionn, the Fianna, and the hounds forced the Calliagh Berra to restore Fionn to his youth, but it is said that his hair remained white like an old man's for the rest of his life, and that his fate is said to befall anyone who bathes in the lake to this very day. Are you brave enough to dip your feet in the Calliagh Berra's lake?[1]

The chamber of the Calliagh Berra's House on Slieve Gullion. In midwinter, the rays of the setting sun enter through the doorway and flood the interior.

The cairn itself is known as Calliagh Berra's House and is just one of many ancient megalithic remnants that is named in her honour.[2] At last we got the opportunity to enter its ancient passageway. It seemed like I had been waiting to do this for a long time. I've only ever imagined what it would be like because I had never seen it before. You have to hunker down at the entrance which takes a bit of nimble movement, but once inside the main thing to concern yourself with is the rocks on the floor. It would be very easy to sprain an ankle in there because the stone-strewn floor is so uneven.

You certainly get the sense of a devoted, determined and stoic people. They built this cairn out of rocks – large and small – on top of a mountain in a far-distant age (around 5,000 years ago, maybe more) at a time when there was no proper footwear, and no construction site health and safety. Building passage-tombs must have been a dangerous occupation in those times. It takes effort just to climb the mountain. But then to start hauling stones around the place in the cutting wind and inevitable rain must have been an undertaking requiring serious devotion to the task. Calliagh Berra obviously commanded a pious respect among the ancient megalithic builders.

Another thing that strikes you is the lack of megalithic art. And indeed the lack of enormous structural stones such as those you find at Newgrange, Knowth and Dowth – the large corridor orthostats, the bulky ceiling cap stones, the three-tonne kerb stones. This is a different type of structure to the Brugh na Bóinne complex. Similar in some respects, but different in others.

They say first impressions last though. And Calliagh Berra's House made a deep impression on me. Such that I can say I would love to go back; ideally in better weather, which makes for better photos. A trip up there for winter solstice sunset would be a distinct possibility. I'd love to see the sun shining in there as it sets beyond the distant hills of Loughcrew.

Upon turning to leave, it's not difficult to see how landscape made such a deep impression upon the imaginative and creative sensitivities of ancient people. Ireland is a beautiful country. I am reminded of this constantly. The journey back down the mountain created a greater awareness of that fact than the journey up. When you climb a hill or mountain, you are ever looking ahead, upwards, towards the summit, the goal. You have a determination, and must concentrate your energies on getting there. On the way down, it's as if you have lightened your load, and the landscape unfurls beneath you. Even with the approaching rain, it looked heavenly. And that's a stark reminder of the real power that elevated megalithic sites must have had – engendering a sense of detachment from the sublunary world, providing an encroachment into the upper, divine levels, away from humdrum civilisation and altogether closer to something austere, numinous and regenerative.

The Calliagh Berra's Lake on top of Slieve Gullion.

4.4

The huge monoliths of Ireland's Stonehenge were buried

For years I have been drawing attention to a monument, sadly now destroyed, which has been dubbed 'Ireland's Stonehenge'. This was a remarkable and unique monument, consisting of several concentric circles of stone surrounded by a large earthen embankment, all of which was encompassed by ten enormous monoliths.

Ireland's Stonehenge was documented by antiquarian and astronomer Thomas Wright in 1746.[1] His drawing is the only known representation of this once great monument, which was located in a townland known today as Carn Beg, not far from the town of Dundalk, in the north of County Louth. I first wrote about Ireland's Stonehenge in *Island of the Setting Sun*. The story of Ireland's Stonehenge is tinged with sadness. It is a tale of something magnificent, something unique and very ancient, which disappeared into the mists of time. Is there yet some possibility, I wonder, of a resurrection?

This huge monument vanished from existence sometime between the time Wright's 1746 drawing and brief description of it in appeared in *Louthiana*[2] and the construction of the Drogheda to Portadown section of the Dublin-Belfast railway line in 1855. Historian Henry Morris, writing for the *County Louth Archaeological Journal* in 1907[3], gave us a tantalising insight into what the monument's purpose might have been when he wrote:

I have read or heard it stated somewhere that this place was the site of a school of astronomy. Its position on the plain, with a semicircle of mountains around would enable an ancient astronomer to observe and mark the places where the various heavenly bodies appeared on the horizon at different times of the year.[4]

Regrettably, Morris was unable to recall the source of this valuable detail. However, he might have read about this in James Bonwick's 1894 book *Irish Druids and Old Irish Religions.* There, Bonwick referred to a place called 'Carrick Brauda of Dundalk', which, he said, 'was renowned for astronomical observations'.[5] Adam Hodgson, in his Letters from North America, elaborated somewhat:

> Tradition sometimes conveys along the stream of time, a name attached to these stone monuments, which informs us of their use. In Erin's bright green isle, which was a famous resort of the Druids, these stone circles, placed upon an eminence, are called in the Irish language, Carrick Brauda; and in Wales, similar structures have retained the name, Cerrig Brudyn, to the present time; the appellation is the same in both countries, and means Astronomers' Circles.[6]

The now destroyed Ireland's Stonehenge might have looked something like this in ancient times. The monument has been recreated in this 3D computer model by artist Kerem Gogus.

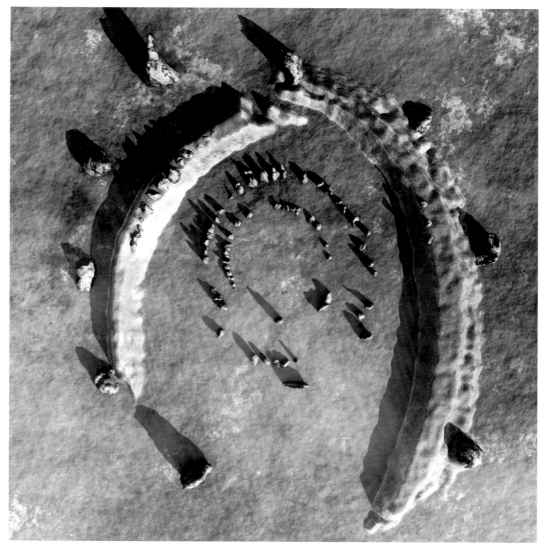

Kerem Gogus' rendition of the stone henge based on
Thomas Wright's 1746 drawing.

Neither Bonwick nor Hodgson elucidate the etymology of the word *brauda*. However, a number of sources repeat this supposed etymological link between Carrick Brauda and Cerrig Brudyn. Carrick is from the Irish *carraig*, rock, but the derivation of *brauda* is a little bit obscure to say the least. In volume one of *Munimenta Antiqua* published in 1799, Edward King similarly asserts that 'there is also an *Astronomers' Circle of Stones*, not far from Dundalk, called *Carrick Brauda.*'[7] King cites

Wright's *Louthiana* as his source. However, there seems some confusion here. The 'Fort of Carick-Braud' described by Wright in Louthiana is a different monument to the one at Carn Beg we have come to know as Ireland's Stonehenge, and is (or rather was, as it too has since been destroyed) in fact located in the townland of Raskeagh,[8] two and a half kilometres to the north of Carn Beg. Wright does not propose a name for the stonehenge, other than to say it is located 'on the Planes of *Ballynahatne*, near *Dundalk*'.[9] Clearly, the stonehenge at Carn Beg and the fort at Raskeagh/Carick-Braud are two different monuments. Is it possible that one 'scholar' mistakenly identified a linguistic link between Carick-Braud and Cerrig Brudyn, and that all the others subsequently copied this mistake? Did the same scholar perhaps confuse the monuments described in Louthiana and somehow come to believe that the great stonehenge of Ballynahatne was in fact called Carick-Broad?

Whatever the answer to that question is, the fact remains that both of these now-destroyed monuments were located relatively close to each other. Perhaps there was a stronger local tradition, or some indigenous source, referred to by Henry Morris, that was more explicit in describing the stonehenge as a school of astronomy. We may never know. What we can say with certainty is that there is a hill just to the north of these monuments, now located just across the border in County Armagh in Northern Ireland, in a townland called Carrickbroad. This hill has a prehistoric cairn near its summit.[10] The name Carrickbroad is derived from *Carraig-brághad*, 'rock of the neck or gorge'.[11] In place names, the word is applied to a gorge or deeply-cut glen.[12] It is suggested locally that the gorge might be *an Gleann Dubh*, 'on the edge of Carrickbroad and neighbouring Tiffcrum townland where a narrow road sweeps through under steep rocky inclines on both sides'.[13]

In recent years, it has been suggested that the lost monument we now know as Ireland's Stonehenge might have been part of Oenach Airbi Rofir,[14] the place where Cúchulainn is said to have buried his son, Connla, and 'the site of an assembly he planned to host at the

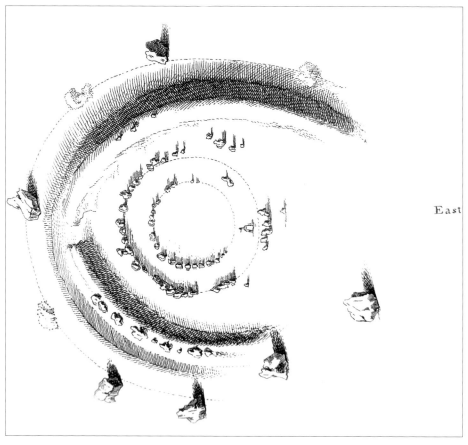

East

Thomas Wright's drawing of the giant monument at Carn Beg (the 'planes of Ballynahatne') was completed in 1746 and published in Louthiana *in 1748.*

end of the harvest, at Samhain, which he was prevented from convening because of a spell cast upon him by two women of the *sídhe*.'[15] An *oenach* is a traditional assembly site. Ronald Hicks of Ball State University in Indiana has attempted to identify some of the *oenach* sites, demonstrating that they occur in conjunction with monuments known as henge enclosures. Hicks has devoted four decades of his career to identifying henges from 'among the 40,000 or so circular prehistoric earthworks known'.[16]

The place-name tales in the Dindshenchas assert that, at least in the case of the more illustrious oenach sites (*oenaige*), they 'resembled historical fairs, but with political and ritual overtones'.[17] Many of them had links with the celebration of Lughnasa, but the Oenach Airbi Rofir is an obvious exception, with its Samhain assembly. One of the greatest difficulties of Hicks' task in identifying the *oenaige* is that 'there is no clear description' of them.

> '...such sites are usually thought of as open areas. But there is evidence ... that at least in some cases the term may refer to an enclosed area or structure.'[18]

Furthermore, the *oenaige* are 'not isolated monuments but, rather, part of complexes that include other monuments of various sorts'.[19] Ronald Hicks says that these complexes were likely to have covered a lot of ground.

> 'One other bit of supporting evidence is that two of three possible stone circles in County Louth listed by the Archaeological Survey are within three kilometres. Also, the townland names of Carn Mor and Carn Beg suggest that at least two other prehistoric monuments existed nearby.'[20]

Not long after Wright's drawing of Ireland's Stonehenge was published, the Armagh Road was built, probably in the early 1750s,[21] and there can be no doubt that this was a significant factor in the destruction of the stonehenge. I overlaid Wright's drawing of the monument on to satellite imagery of the site and this makes it obvious that at least some of the monument was flattened to make way for the new road. This very straight section of road intersected the monument and its construction would have wrought much damage. But the road was not the only destructive factor at work. Some of the stones from the Carn Beg henge were taken for other uses too. Writing in 1880, James Bonwick said:

> ... many of the best circles have been destroyed to furnish road-metal, gate-posts, &c.[22]

Ireland's Stonehenge at sunset. 3D image by Kerem Gogus.

Henry Morris could find no remains of the monument in 1907, say-ing that it was 'Gone! Cleared away, its very site not exactly known'.[23]

It was not until 1988 that the exact location of Wright's druidic tem-ple was finally rediscovered. Archaeologist Victor Buckley was able to discern the monument's 'footprint' in an aerial photograph which had been taken in 1970 for the Cambridge University Collection of Aerial Photographs.[24]

There was some archaeological geophysics carried out at the site in 2006, in advance of a proposed housing development which didn't materialise because the Irish economy subsequently collapsed. Stand-ing at the site of the stonehenge, which is now part of a disused golf course attached to a hotel, it is very difficult to get any sense that it was anything other than a field. There are simply no stones remaining.

However, I've recently discovered something significant about what might have happened to the large stones – or at least some of them – in the most unlikely of sources.

Reading George Henry Bassett's *Louth County Guide and Directory* (1886), we find that early on, he makes reference to the area's antiquities:

> The remains of antiquity are very numerous, and extend through every part of the county. They continue in very much the same condition that they were found more than one hundred and twenty-five years ago by Thomas Wright, author of *Louthiana*. His work was instrumental in stimulating the curiosity of many of the residents of the county in regard to the precise nature of the contents of the Danish and Irish forts and Druidical camps.[25]

And here we find the most valuable information pertaining to what happened to this once marvellous monument:

> It had not the effect, however, of preventing a tenant, near Dundalk, from effacing the Druidical circle at Ballynahatna. Of the ten stones which were said to represent the generations from Adam to Noah, only one now stands in the original position. Most of the rest were dropped into holes sunk behind them, and covered at a sufficient depth to escape the plough.[26]

This is most interesting. Bassett says that instead of being broken up, like the smaller stones, the large ones were dropped into huge holes to bury them. This is quite exciting as it leads to the possibility that at least some of these large megaliths are still there – buried where they once stood. Perhaps this is information which might lead archaeologists towards further investigation of the site at Carn Beg?

Certainly Ronald Hicks thinks so:

Another henge, this one a lot smaller than the Carn Beg monument. It's a recreated 'wood henge' near the eastern entrance of the great Knowth passage-mound.

> The 2006 resistivity survey makes it clear that significant traces of the monument remain. If indeed the stones were buried, a survey of the whole site using other modern geophysical prospecting methods, such as magnetometry or ground penetrating radar, should have no difficulty in locating them.[27]

One of the greatest tragedies connected with the disappearance of Ireland's Stonehenge is how and why it was vandalised during the time the Coulter family were resident at Carn Beg. Records show that the Coulters, who lived at Carn Beg during the time of Wright's visit and the probable subsequent destruction of the stonehenge, had an interest in antiquarian matters and the preservation of monuments. Beginning around 1731, Samuel Coulter rented lands at Carn Beg and the adjoining townland, Carn More, from James Hamilton, Viscount (or Lord) Limerick.[28] It was Lord Limerick who was likely to have been the one who invited Thomas Wright to Ireland.[29] *Louthiana* was actually dedicated to Lord Limerick, and during his time in Ireland

Wright even taught mathematics to some of the well-to-do families of the day.[30] In his journal, Wright wrote that, in October of 1746, he:

> Collected and drew all the plans of Louthiana & taught Mr. Hamilton & Miss Fortesque & Mr. Read &c. mathematicks &drawing.[31]

Samuel Coulter died in 1760. The farm probably passed at that stage to his younger brother, Thomas, and after his death in 1769 Carn Beg 'would have been administered by his executors until 1776' when Thomas's son Samuel came of age. This Samuel, a nephew of the Samuel who was at Carn Beg during Wright's era, was described as a 'scholarly man' who kept a small library at Carn Beg.[32] Among his books was a copy of Wright's *Louthiana*. This is hardly surprising, given that Wright had probably spent a lot of time at Carn Beg years previously. His other books included a copy of *The Táin*, a copy of Edward Lhuyd's *Archaeologia Britannica* and a copy of Charles Vallancey's *Irish Grammar*. Samuel evidently passed on his love of antiquities to his son, Dr. Thomas Coulter, who became a botanist. According to his biography, Thomas was upset about how locals treated a monument on his lands at a townland called The Stump. The monument, known as the 'Ship Temple', had an Irish name, *Fás na haon-Oíche*, 'the work of one night'. He prosecuted individuals who were carting away stone from that monument,[33] probably to use for field boundaries and gate posts.

Was Thomas Wright's action in prosecuting these vandals borne out of some sense of guilt for what had happened to the stonehenge back in his uncle's stewardship of the Carn Beg lands when the Armagh road was built? Or was the building of the road, and the vandalism of the stonehenge that likely resulted, out of Coulter's hands? Did Lord Limerick, perhaps, allow the road to cross his land?[34] If so, did he allow for the destruction of the monument, and, more importantly, did he benefit financially from the construction of the road? We might never know.

One of the authors of the biography of Dr. Thomas Coulter was E. Charles Nelson. In correspondence a number of years ago, he said that he was unable to add anything to the information he had included in the book, and that 'there was nothing in the Coulter papers that I saw that is likely to shed any light on the destruction of the monument'.[35] He added:

> It is an interesting problem, certainly, but as Murphy must know, there was no respect for archaeological sites in the past – even in the present the government does not protect archaeological sites in the appropriate manner.[36]

Did the builders of Ireland's Stonehenge watch the rising and setting of the sun, moon and stars from their circles of stone?

Whether archaeology or the Irish Government can do anything in the near future to rescue this lost monument from the mists of time remains to be seen. In the meantime, however, the monument we know as Ireland's Stonehenge has come back from the dead, so to speak, thanks the magic of 3D computer modelling. A Turkish 3D design artist, Kerem Gogus, has recreated a vision of Ireland's Stonehenge based upon Wright's eighteenth century drawing. Gogus's work presents to us the first really exciting visual insight into this fascinating monument – in a way that Wright's two-dimensional drawing could never do.

The computer modelling allows the monument to be shown in different lighting and weather environments, and because of this we are afforded a dramatic and somewhat poignant look at something unique in terms of monumental architecture and scale that was foolishly and tragically torn apart.

We may never see the monument restored to its former glory. But I hold firm to the hope that it might, in time, be at least partially restored. And, with enough will and a little bit of imagination, perhaps someone in the locality of Carn Beg/Ballynahattin will eventually build a full-scale replica of Ireland's Stonehenge in the vicinity of the original site. Wouldn't that be an exciting prospect?

4.5

Only the guardian of Fourknocks knows its true name

Inside the ancient stone chamber of Fourknocks, a seemingly small yet very impressive monument of the late Neolithic, there are a number of intricately carved stones, some pristinely preserved.

The modern visitor is able to see, at close quarters, the careful work of Neolithic artists, people who lived and died in a remote age, when only the most basic technologies were afforded use by human hands. At Fourknocks, the lozenge (diamond) and the zigzag predominate. The angular manifestation of the glyphs is curious. There is one stone, above the passage, bearing concentric circles, and another – the original entrance lintel – bearing a rough spiral, among other peculiar designs. Most of the other decorated stones are devoid of curvature, containing the distinct angles of diagonal and serrated patterns.

The stones of Fourknocks demand from us an answer, an answer to an unanswerable riddle – why is the spiral, so predominant at Brugh na Bóinne, almost absent from this wondrous little passage-tomb, and why do the angles predominate? We can only answer the question with a question:

Who can know?

I have a theory. But that's all it is – a theory. Unfortunately, we cannot travel back in time to speak with the artists of the New Stone Age, whoever they were – farmers, astronomers, poets, priests or magicians. (Likely a combination of these). We have to make do with our own

Fourknocks is deceptive. It looks tiny from the outside, but its chamber can hold many more people than that at the much larger monument of Newgrange.

speculations, and our own vivid imaginations. My theory is that the absence of the spiral is directly connected with the absence of the sun. No sun can shine into Fourknocks. Its passageway points to a place in the far north, some 14 degrees (approximately) east of north. No sunlight can enter into its cold interior. Fourknocks, whatever its other purposes might have been, was definitely not a solar observatory; not in its own right at least. There are other mounds in the district, and who knows what secretly oriented chambers they might contain?

The spiral is a convenient and potent symbol representing solar movement. Over the course of the year, the sun appears to wind a series of contracting and expanding spirals in the sky.[1] At Newgrange, the great entrance stone, facing the sunrises on winter solstice, is adorned impressively with huge spirals, one of which appears to end in a line that seems to point in towards the entrance to the cave, perhaps beckoning the sun to 'enter in here'.

There is no such theatrical meandering spiral at Fourknocks. Here, we see zigzag lines and diamonds, almost exclusively. Almost. There is one stone that stands out above all others. It is one of the chamber orthostats, positioned just to the right of the passageway as one looks out from the chamber. It is said, by some, to be a crude representation of the human face. Not having access to the artist, or the instruction manual from which he or she was working when they carved it, I can neither agree nor disagree with this contention. There are more angles, and diamonds, and curves. If it's a face, it's a strange one. And yet I find myself drawn to the idea that it is a type of 'guardian' stone, if such a concept even existed when these structures were built 5,000 years ago. There is a stone in the western passage of Knowth that has been said, by some, to represent some type of guardian. It has an almost owl-like presence – the owl being the Cailleach of the night, its call often attributed to the *Bean Sídhe,* the woman from the otherworld mound who sometimes cries out before a death. As a place of burial,

An owl-like face with huge eyes looks down from a carved stone
above the passage of Fourknocks.

(top) The passage of Fourknocks, looking in towards the interior.
(bottom) The southern and western recesses inside Fourknocks.

Fourknocks might have needed just such a presence – a woman of the *sídhe* to watch over as the souls of the deceased crossed over from this world to the next.

Fourknocks is indeed a sad place. When it was excavated in the 1950s by P.J. Hartnett, the remains of at least 21 children were found, along with burnt and unburnt remains of adults.[2] By the time its period of use was coming to an end, the entrance passage had been filled almost to the top with material, with three separate layers or deposits of human remains.[3] The passage was deliberately blocked up. It was intended that Fourknocks be sealed off. And so it was ... until the 1950s.

It is a sad fact that all of the burials/deposits were removed during the excavation. There is a sense that the monument has lost an aspect of its sacredness, that the final resting place of so many people would later be stripped out so that nothing of the burials remains. In this sense, we see how archaeological excavation of prehistoric monuments is a destructive and invasive process,[4] and in many cases the chambered cairns that have been excavated, which represent some of Ireland's oldest manmade structures, have been stripped clean to the extent that they can be considered to have been sterilised.

In being sealed up, Fourknocks shares a history similar to that of Newgrange (which points towards it, incidentally). Archaeologists maintain that Newgrange was sealed for the best part of 4,000 years, until Charles Campbell and his labourers rediscovered the passage entrance in 1699. Fourknocks lay concealed in the landscape for a long time. Because it probably did not have a stone vaulted roof and thus it didn't have a large cairn covering it, it was likely to have had only a gentle profile in the landscape. As the soil deposits gradually built up in the vicinity of the mounds, the surrounding landscape progressively rose to the extent that it might have been almost level with the remains of the Fourknocks complex. Like the 16 satellite mounds at Knowth, the remnants of Fourknocks might have been largely invisible in the landscape before excavation. They were not large, imposing,

The 'face' stone inside Fourknocks, said by some to be a guardian stone.

mound-like hillocks like the reconstructed ones at Knowth. However, they had not altogether disappeared from view. It is reported that a local man, Paddy Maguire, brought Fourknocks to the attention of archaeologist P.J. Hartnett.[5] The name Fourknocks is said to be derived from the Irish *na fuarchnoic,* meaning 'the cold hills'. But I don't buy it. It doesn't 'feel' like an authentic name for a complex of ancient monuments. And thus I think its real name has been lost to time. Local historian Brendan Matthews once proposed to me the possibility that Fourknocks was derived from the 'four cnocs', meaning the four *cnocs* or artificial mounds. That seems more plausible to me than the cold hills.

The proximity of Fourknocks to Clonalvy tempts one to look for a link there. Clonalvy is from *Cluain Ailbhe,* the meadow of Ailbhe, whoever she might have been. It might also be connected with the Delvin River (An Ailbhine). I am curious about the mention of a possibility that Clonalvy was the location of a monument called *Lia Ailbhe,* a huge standing stone described as the 'chief monument of Brega', until it fell in 999 and was broken into four millstones by Máelaschlainn, the high king.[6] That seems like an avenue worthy of research, for there is something that has been nagging away at me for years and that is to find out the ancient name of Fourknocks, and its associated mythology.

I wonder if, in time, some astute and dedicated scholar will find, buried somewhere in the manuscripts, perhaps, indications of the ancient name of Fourknocks. They might find that it is connected with Síd in Broga, especially in light of the fact that Newgrange points towards it. Maybe it might also have mythological associations involving swans.[7]

In the meantime, perhaps only the guardian of Fourknocks knows its real name.

4.6

An investigation of the alignment of the passage of Fourknocks

Several years ago, I wrote about the apparent orientation of New-grange towards Fourknocks and the orientation of Fourknocks towards a place on the horizon where the brightest star of the swan constellation (Cygnus) would have been rising after its brief glance with the horizon towards the north.[1] In recent times, a more detailed examination of this alignment system has been carried out, and that study has yielded further interesting results and fascinating possibilities.

A summary of the 'Cygnus Enigma' is first required. In a nutshell, Newgrange points towards Fourknocks, although neither site is visible from the other. Fourknocks lies about 15 kilometres (approximately nine miles) to the southeast of Newgrange. There are two intervening hills that prevent intervisibility of the sites – Red Mountain and Bellewstown. Fourknocks lies at approximately 137.95 degrees of azimuth from Newgrange.[2] This would place it on the edge of the range of azimuths covered by the Newgrange solstice alignment.[3] The best way to try to visualise this is to think that as the sunlight is retreating from the chamber of Newgrange at winter solstice, the sun is directly above Fourknocks.

Fourknocks, in turn, has a passage that is aligned to approximately 14° azimuth, in the far northeast. Richard Moore and I had suggested that Fourknocks is aligned in the direction of the Baltray standing

*A view from the interior of Fourknocks looking out through
the passage towards Mullaghteelin.*

stones on the northern side of the Boyne[4] and that the two stones lined
up to point back towards Fourknocks, even though neither site was
visible from the other.

It is this alignment – the axis of the Fourknocks passage (that is,
where it points to) – that has yielded fascinating new information.

Sitting on the sill stone of the rear recess of the Fourknocks chamber,
looking out through the passageway to the far horizon, one is looking
at a hill towards the north-northeast called Mullaghteelin. Near the
summit of Mullaghteelin, directly on the alignment as viewed from
Fourknocks, is a barrow,[5] probably dating to the Bronze Age.

Using a map, or better still Google Earth, the alignment can be seen
to continue through Donacarney village before crossing the Boyne river
and pointing towards the Baltray standing stones. This is where Google Earth has real value in the investigation of long ley lines or straight
track alignments. Zooming in on Baltray, we see that both stones are
situated precisely on the axis of this alignment from Fourknocks.

The axis of the Fourknocks passage points towards Clogherhead, where the large greywacke slabs used in the construction of Newgrange were sourced over 5,000 years ago.

Whether this alignment was created intentionally is an entirely different matter, but one wonders, given the existence of several long-distance alignments of ancient monuments, if indeed the ancients had skills beyond which we give them credit for.

If you continue the line[6] from Fourknocks beyond Baltray standing stones, you will find that it eventually hits the shoreline on the Irish Sea coast at Clogherhead. It then travels across Dundalk Bay and eventually meets a stony beach on the southern shore of the Cooley peninsula at Rathcor/Templetown. Both of these shores – Clogherhead and Rathcor/Templetown – were locations where stone for Newgrange was sourced.

Clogherhead was the source of the greywacke slabs that were used as kerb stones, passage orthostats and large structural stones in the chamber of Newgrange.[7] An estimated 200 of these rocks, weighing on average three tonnes apiece, were brought from the shoreline at Clogherhead by boat down along the Irish Sea and up the river Boyne to Brú na Bóinne.[8]

Rathcor and Templetown beaches are littered with rocks of all different types and sizes. Most interesting of these are the granite cobbles which, it is said, were brought from this area to Newgrange to be placed among the white quartz stones that decorate the front of the monument.[9] Again, these would have been transported by sea, across Dundalk Bay, around Clogherhead and then up the Boyne.

So, whether by accident or design, the Fourknocks passage points towards two of the three locations from which it is said that stone was sourced for the construction of Newgrange.

Just for the sake of it, I looked at the alignment in the opposite direction, as if one could imagine following the axis of the passage south-southwest from Fourknocks. Interestingly, it points towards the Blessington Lakes in County Wicklow, some 30 miles or 50 kilometres distant approximately. Now this really is a stretch of the imagination, I'll readily admit, but we've all been told that Wicklow is the likely source of the milky quartz at Newgrange,[10] although the

The wide chamber of Fourknocks, looking towards its passage with the door closed over.

*The larger of two standing stones at Baltray. The axis of this stone points
towards Rockabill, where the winter solstice sun rises.*

exact location or quarry from which it was extracted has never been found. I've heard it suggested that Blessington is a possible source. It could have been transported from that area by barge or currach down the Liffey River into the Irish Sea and from there up to the Boyne.

If the Blessington area turns out to be the source of the Newgrange quartz (and that is by no means anything other than a possibility at this point in time), then the Fourknocks alignment would 'point to' all of the major sources of stone for the construction of Newgrange – the greywacke from Clogherhead, the granite cobbles from Cooley and the quartz stones from Wicklow. As it stands, we can say that Fourknocks definitely does point to two areas from which stone was sourced. The third remains an unknown, but Blessington is a possibility.

More recently, the Rockabill islands off the coast of Dublin have been suggested as a possible source of the milky quartz at Newgrange.[11]

This is equally interesting, because the larger of the two standing stones at Baltray points towards Rockabill for winter solstice sunrise.[12]

The Fourknocks passage also points to a peak called Eagle Mountain in the Mourne Mountains in the far distance towards the north, mountains which are easily visible from Fourknocks on a clear day. Geologists have told us that the cobble stones from Rathcor/Templetown have their origin in the Mournes.

It seems rather unlikely that a chambered cairn such as Fourknocks would be constructed with the intention of pointing to sites where the stones for another monument were sourced. However, that it accidentally does so is still fascinating. This author has previously suggested the passage of Fourknocks was aligned on a stellar event – the rising of the bright star of the constellation we know today as Cygnus, the swan, after its brief setting in the north.[13] There seems little doubt that the passages of stone age chambered cairns were often aligned so that they pointed towards other monuments or landscape features. In this case, whether by design or accident, Fourknocks points to Mullateelin[14] and beyond that to the Baltray standing stones.

Putting aside speculation and postulation, we can state a fact with certainty. Fourknocks points towards at least two of the known sources of the Newgrange stones. Whether this is intentional is highly debatable, but it is interesting nonetheless, especially in light of the circumstance that Newgrange points to Fourknocks.

5.

The Boyne Valley

5.1

Cleitech, Rosnaree and the ancient ford of the Boyne

In ancient times, long before stone bridges, the places where you crossed rivers were called *áth* (fords). These were generally shallow parts of the river, sometimes stony, where one could expect to be able to walk or wade across in general safety, except when the river was in full torrent.

Ironically, there is no modern bridge across the River Boyne between Slane and Oldbridge – around the whole Bend of the Boyne – except for the pedestrian footbridge that is used by visitors to Knowth and Newgrange to access their buses from the visitor centre.[1] However, in the olden days there were fording points along the Boyne, and one in particular that may have been where an ancient road from Tara crossed the river as it headed north.

This road was the Slighe Midhluachra, and it crossed the Boyne very near to the old mill house which still stands at Rosnaree. The ford was a paved ford, and was in regular use until the early years of the 20th century[2]. Elizabeth Hickey, writing a half century ago, says this of the ford:

> This was the *Áth na Bóinne* of the ancients. Near here Mananan, son of Lir, tied up his magic boat, the Ocean-Sweeper, the craft which knew his thoughts; here came the Sons of Turenn to borrow it in order to pursue their quest. Across this ford the builders of the great tombs, which tourists see today, passed

to and from their work. Milesian fleets rowed past these tombs to battle with De Danaan magic. Warriors from the North descended to the ford, King Conchubar with Cuchulainn and his army, to fight at Rosnaree. St. Patrick and his followers passed to Slane.[3]

In ancient times, rivers and watercourses formed the only effective transport network. The builders of Newgrange, Knowth and Dowth relied on the Boyne as a means of bringing huge stones, many weighing three tonnes and more, to the Bend of the Boyne using barges. However, they did not haul these stones beyond the shallow waters of the Boyne at Áth na Bóinne. It is likely that they landed much further east, somewhere in the vicinity of the lands that now form part of Dowth Hall, and hauled their stones from there.[4]

The ford of Rosnaree was paved, that is, it was artificially augmented with stones placed by people so as to raise the river bed and provide a solid causeway over which the crossing could be made. The owners

A view of the Boyne looking from the old salmon weir at Roughgrange westwards towards Rosnaree and Cleitech.

*An aerial view of the mill house at Rosnaree and the location
of Áth na Bóinne, the ancient ford of the Boyne.*

of the mill house in the middle of the twentieth century were the John-sons. Mr. Johnson told Elizabeth Hickey 'of travellers on horseback, travellers on foot, and hay-carts passing over, and men at work to keep it paved, not so very long ago'.[5]

The precise location of the ford is still known, of course, not only because it is pinpointed on the older Ordnance Survey maps, but because a crossing is still possible in modern times, as pointed out locally, and indeed the rocks that undoubtedly form the augmented crossing cause the surface water of the river to rise and ripple over them.[6]

Close to the ford of the Boyne at Rosnaree is a place anciently called the House of Cletty (spelt variously as Cletigh, Cleiteach, Cleitech and Cletech, among others). Cleitech is said to have been the place where King Cormac Mac Art died after choking on a salmon bone,[7] something that is very interesting because of Cleitech's proximity to Rosnaree and the Boyne, and the locality of Fiacc's Pool, where Fionn Mac Cumhaill and Finnegas were said to have caught the Salmon of Knowledge.

For a long time there was some mystery as to where Cleitech was located. The antiquarian William Wilde (father of Oscar Wilde) suggested it might have been at Clady, near Bective, south of Navan.[8] O'Donovan, in his notes on the *Annals of the Four Masters*, placed it 'near Stackallen Bridge, on the south side of the Boyne.'[9] Both were wrong. O'Donovan was closer, but Stackallen is several miles upstream from Rosnaree, west of Slane. It was Elizabeth Hickey who finally pinpointed its location through 'considerable research'[10] and a healthy dose of doggedness. Here is her own account of the matter, based on her reading of the various myths and manuscripts. It is an excellent piece of detective work:

> The *Táin* tells us that Cuchulain, when he went to woo Emer, descended to the Boyne on its lower reaches, between the Brugh of Oengus [Newgrange] and the Sidhe of Bresal to the west, and crossed the river between the houses of Cleitech and Fessi. From the story of the death of King Cormac we know that Cleitech was on the southern bank and was likely to have been near to Rosnaree, certainly not too far below the ford, for Cormac's bier was carried from the House of Cleitech to the river and borne by the river down to Rosnaree. Another story tells us of autumn games held between Newgrange and the House of Cleitech, and from these games and young folk ran to Knowth. The story of the death of Muirchertach gives us more detailed topography – the House of Cleitech was above the Boyne and above the green-topped Brugh; a glen lay to the south of the house; the grave of Muirchertach was to the north-east, according to another poem... There is only one spot on the map which fulfills all the conditions and this is the plateau-like elevation where Rosnaree House stands today.[11]

Whatever the House of Cletty might have been, it is gone now. Its earliest mention as a house above the Boyne is in the Táin. One can imagine it might have been an Iron Age ringfort, something the Irish would have called a *ráth* or a *lios*. But because it was the abode

*Rosnaree House, believed to be the site of the ancient sídhe of Cleitech
by Elizabeth Hickey, viewed from Newgrange.*

of kings (Muirchertach was the last king to live there), it might have
been something more special, like a multivallate fort or even a passage-tomb.[12] The Edwardian mansion of Rosnaree House is the most
likely location of Cleitech, according to Hickey. The house is situated
high above the river and from the terrace upon which it sits a great
deal of the area can be seen, and there are views across to Knowth and
Newgrange. According to archaeologist Geraldine Stout, a fourteenth
or fifteenth century reference 'indicates that Cleitech lay near the *Síd in
Broga* (Newgrange) and opposite Knowth'.[13]

What might be the meaning of this name, Cleitech?

In a dialogue between Cúchulainn and his lover Emer, in the Táin
Bó Cuailnge, Cúchulainn refers to a journey and masks the locations
with obscure references, including: 'over the Marrow of the woman
Fedelm, between the Boar and His Dam', 'That is, between Cleitech
and Fessi. For Cleitech is the name for a boar, but it is also the name for

a king, the leader of great hosts, and Fessi is the name for a great sow of a farmer's house.'[14]

Pigs and boars are prominent in Irish mythology. Long before the arrival of the builders of Newgrange and the Neolithic farming revolution that saw the introduction of cows, wild boar was part of the staple mesolithic diet.[15] Pigs are plentiful in myth too. Lugh Lamhfada's father, Cian, took the shape of a wild pig to try to avoid the attention of the sons of Tuirenn. Diarmuid, one of the greatest warriors of the Fianna, was gored by a wild boar and consequently died. He was later brought to Newgrange by Oengus an Broga, 'to put aerial life in him so that he will talk to me every day'.[16]

But there is, perhaps, another meaning for Cleitech that makes sense in the context of a paved ford across the Boyne. In Shaw's dictionary, there is a word *cleitach* which means 'full of rocks', and a similar word, *cleitadh*, meaning 'a ridge of rocks in the sea'.[17]

Whatever its meaning, Cleitech was an important place, although its house is long gone. However, the area around the ford at Rosnaree and the eminence upon which the House of Cletty once sat retain an ancient feel, and it's not difficult to see how the *file* (poet) or the *draoi* (druid), who must have drawn great inspiration from being close to the flowing waters of the Boyne, might have felt himself in heaven in these places.

> ... from just such ancestral visions the stuff of ancient history was made. This gentleman knew the river as the men of old, the number of the cygnets with the swans, the way the salmon ran, where lay the deep pool which must have been Linn Feic, the fox's way, the badgers' earth, the sunny sheltered place, a likely spot for hermitage. If Cleitech has disappeared, its environs remain unchanged – Cuchulain could cross the river today, and thinking of Emer, see nothing of the twentieth century but a slight untidiness of overgrowth.[18]

5.2

Up close with the
Rosnaree Sheela-na-gig

I was very fortunate not too long ago to have been given an opportunity to see and photograph an enigmatic and fascinating relic of Ireland's past. I had long known that once upon a time there was a Sheela-na-gig built into the wall of the old mill house at Rosnaree on southern bank of the River Boyne.

About quarter of a century ago the ancient stone-carved figure was removed from its place in the wall of the mill for safekeeping. Before that, it had been whitewashed over so many times that its features were becoming difficult to see.

The owners of the old mill, Georg and Barbara Heise, beautifully and lovingly converted the old structure into a modern habitable home. I was delighted to be given an opportunity by the Heise family to examine and indeed take photos of the Sheela-na-gig.

Sheela-na-gigs are:

> ... female exhibitionist carvings found on walls, abbeys, convents, churches, pillars and other structures in Ireland, England, Scotland and Wales, as well as in other parts of Europe. They come in many different shapes and sizes, but all share the same characteristic of a prominent and often enlarged genitals, often held open by the figure's hands. Most date from the middle ages.[1]

The Rosnaree Sheela-na-gig.

Sheela-na-Gigs are figurative stone carvings of naked females, typically depicted as standing or squatting in a position generally described as an 'act of display'. Sometimes they are shown with thighs widely splayed and often one or both hands are shown pointing to, or touching, the genitalia – deliberately accentuating the focus upon this part of the anatomy.[2]

The old mill house at Rosnaree in winter floods.

There are various theories as to what their intended meaning or purpose was, but we simply don't know for sure. Some suggest they were fertility figures,[3] and that touching them was considered a blessing for assured pregnancy. Others say the fact they were often positioned on the walls of churches meant they served as a grotesque warning against the 'sins of the flesh'. Is the Sheela-na-gig supposed to represent a goddess? Or a crone or hag, like the cailleach?

Regardless of the theories, these ancient carved figures are fascinating. I was fortunate to be allowed to take some photos of the Rosnaree Sheela. In order to capture as much of the detail as possible, I used a remote flash and illuminated the figure from left, right, above and below.

A description of the Sheela-na-Gig is given in the Sites and Monuments Record (SMR) taken from the Archaeological Inventory of County Meath:

Sheela-na-gig now in private possession. Figure formerly built into wall beside door of mill that was not its original location. Removed from wall of mill and kept safe in store. Described by Freitag as a figure, 'crudely carved on irregular stone slab; widest at bottom part which is cut straight, allowing figure to sit firmly on ground. Elongated, deeply hollowed out groove in crown of head (presumably for libations) further indication of figure originally free-standing. Left side defaced, and some damage also to chin, right forearm, right foot and lower part of leg. Large head, no ears, big owl-like eyes with eyebrows, clearly marked nostrils, jagged incision indicating mouth and possibly teeth. Four striations on right cheek running down to side of slab. No neck or breasts, but clearly marked navel. Right arm reaches under leg which is widely splayed, but no hands or fingers traceable. Genitals indicated by deep semi-circular depression' (Freitag 2004, 140).[4]

There is another, more well known, Sheela-na-Gig on one of the standing stones in the churchyard on the Hill of Tara. It is often passed by and not noticed by visitors. The stone is covered with lichen, making the figure difficult to see under certain lighting conditions.

Recently, a link has been suggested between these grotesque Sheela-na-gig figures and the wife of Saint Patrick, who was called Sheela. The scholar who suggested that link, UCC folklorist Shane Lehane, says the following of the Sheela-na-gigs:

Sheela-na-Gig is a basic medieval carving of a woman exposing her genitalia. These images are often considered to be quite grotesque. They are quite shocking when you see them first. Now we look at them very much as examples of old women showing young women how to give birth. They are vernacular folk deities associated with pregnancy and birth.[5]

We should, perhaps, leave the last words about the Sheelas to Patricia Monaghan:

> Call it a stance of power or a posture of sexual invitation; call it yoni yoga or vulva vaudeville. We may not know what the original sculptors intended her to mean, but we can certainly say this: Sheela-na-gig is one old woman who does more than just wear purple.[6]

A Sheela-na-gig on a standing stone in the churchyard on the Hill of Tara.

5.3

The remarkable geological secret
of the Newgrange kerb stones

The giant kerb stones of Newgrange, and many of those at Knowth, weighing up to five tonnes apiece, were sourced along the coastline at Clogherhead, and brought by sea and river to the Bend of the Boyne, where the great megalithic monuments at Brú na Bóinne were built more than 5,000 years ago.

What is not widely known is that Clogherhead holds a fascinating geological secret, one that is extremely unlikely to have been known by the ancient megalithic builders of the Boyne Valley. At this promontory of land that projects out into the Irish Sea from the coast of what is now County Louth, there are rock formations which are vertical.[1] The stones jut up out of the land in jagged layers. It was here that, over five millennia ago, the builders of Newgrange, Knowth and Dowth sourced many of the large stones that were used for kerbs, and for orthostats and structural stones.

What the builders did not know was that these jagged rock formations are the result of a significant seismic event around 400 million years ago, in which two continents smashed together.[2] It's hard to imagine today, but there is a 'border' of sorts running from Clogherhead down to the Shannon Estuary. Everything north of this border was once on a continent that has been given the name Laurentia, while everything south of there was on a continent called Avalonia. The types

Spiral-shaped fossil on a rock at the Big Strand beach, Clogherhead.
My thanks to my daughter, Amy Murphy, who discovered this.

of fossils found either side of this so-called border, which is now called the Iapetus Suture, are very different.

> Rocks older than 400 million years north of this line have similarities to rocks of the same age in Norway, Scotland, Greenland and North America, while rocks older than 400 million years south of this line have similarities to rocks of the same age in England, Wales, Africa and Australia.[3]

In geological terms, Clogherhead is exciting because it is 'one of the few places where Lower Palaeozoic rocks are exposed adjacent to the supposed surface trace of the Iapetus Suture'.[4] One author says:

> The seam that joins North America and Europe runs approximately from Limerick to Louth. Clogher Head is the only place in Ireland where it can be seen in the surface rocks.[5]

It's hard to believe that Laurentia and Avalonia, and by extension the northern and southern parts of Ireland, were once separated by

3,000 kilometres of ocean. This ocean has (in modern times of course) been given the name the Iapetus Ocean – hence the Iapetus Suture.

The collision of these continents results in the discovery of very different types of fossils on the northern and southern side of Ireland's ancient border:

> The half of Ireland that lies north of the seam was originally joined with Scotland, Greenland and North America in the ancient continent of Laurentia. The south-eastern half of Ireland, along with Wales, England and Brittany, formed the smaller continent of Avalonia. Some 500 million years ago Laurentia lay at the Equator, Avalonia lay further south, and between them was the Iapetus Ocean (Iapetus was the father of Atlantis, after whom the Atlantic Ocean is named).

> Fossils from this time found in the northern Laurentian, or 'American', half of Ireland are very different from those found in the Avalonian, or 'European', half. This reflects the fact that they came from distant parts of the world once separated by 3,000 kilometres of ocean.[6]

Almost-vertical rock formations at Clogherhead, one of the few places in Ireland where the Iapetus Suture is observable.

The builders of Newgrange used the vertical formations of layered greywacke at Clogherhead to their advantage. They were, it seems, able to prise specimens out using something like wooden poles and, we are told by archaeologists, strap them to the underside of a boat or barge.[7] At high tide, the sea would lift the raft, with stone underneath, and the 'pilot' of this barge would steer it down the coast and up the River Boyne.

One wonders how intrigued they might have been by fossils which they undoubtedly discovered during their many journeys to and from Clogherhead. Is it possible they saw spiral-shaped fossils which can be seen on some rocks in the area, and that these fossils provided some of the inspiration for the spiral carvings upon the stones?

Sunrise at Clogherhead, where the greywacke kerb stones for Newgrange were broken free from vertical rock formations.

5.4

On the quest for the Cailleach of Clogherhead

When you stand at the giant amphitheatre-like henge monument near Dowth – the one archaeologists ingloriously named 'Site Q' – on the morning of summer solstice, the longest day of the year, you will see the sun rising out of the landscape towards the northeast near Castlecoo Hill, at Clogherhead. Site Q has two large openings, one at its south western end, and one at the north east, which both appear to line up towards the solstice sunrise position.

The name Castlecoo comes from *Caisleáin Có,* meaning the 'stone fort of the hound'.[1] But another townland name on the hill of Castlecoo has long piqued my interest.

That townland is Callystown, which has generally been translated as *Baile na gCailleach,* the 'town of the nuns'. Tradition says that there was once a nunnery at Callystown, hence the name.[2] But the issue is not as straightforward as that. As we have seen in previous chapters, the Cailleach was an ancient goddess, revered in prehistoric Ireland in places far and wide. She was known in some localities as the Cailleach Bheara/Cally Vera, and although we might consider her hag imagery to be somewhat grotesque, it seems that at one time she was a female deity held in very high esteem. Indeed there are distinct comparisons between the great Cailleach and some of the Boyne Valley goddesses such as Bóinn and Buí.[3]

*The summer solstice sun rises over Clogherhead in line with the openings
of the Dowth Henge (Site Q), viewed from the air.*

We know that the Cailleach was revered in this region in ancient
times. The hills of Loughcrew, upon which sit ancient passage-cairns
that are older than Newgrange, Knowth and Dowth, are called Sliabh
na Caillighe – the hills of the witch/hag/crone/old woman. She is said
to have formed the cairns upon Carnbane East and Carnbane West as
she jumped from peak to peak, carrying an apron full of stones, some of
which she dropped as she jumped. Curiously, the same story describes
the construction of the round tower at Monasterboice in County Louth.
According to folk tradition, gathered in the Schools Folklore Collection, the round tower was formed by the Cailleach dropping stones
from her apron.[4] In one version of the tale, the Cailleach becomes the
Virgin Mary. In another version, she slips from the top of the tower
and is killed in the fall to the ground. Not too far away is a stone age
wedge tomb called the 'Cailleach Bhirra's House'.[5] Monasterboice is
only six or seven miles west of Clogherhead and Callystown.

I've long wondered if the Callystown area of Clogherhead was perhaps named more anciently than the arrival of the nuns. A case has
been made suggesting a link between the goddess Bóann/Bóinn and

the moon and Milky Way.[6] Similar connections could be made with the Cailleach, who was venerated all over Ireland and whose name survives in many townlands and even on the Beara Peninsula in Cork, along Ireland's southern extremity, where she has a long-standing association.[7]

A trawl through some of the sources pertaining to place names and other locally available historical information has cast considerable doubt about the supposed connection between Callystown and the nuns, or at the very least the origin of the name Callystown. While there is a strong tradition of nuns in the area, the link between those nuns and the name Baile na gCailleach is tenuous to say the least. According to local history, the nuns arrived in Callystown at the turn of the sixteenth century.[8]

Writing in 2003, Liam Mac Raghnaill said of Callystown:

> In 1508, a small community of nuns, known as the Black Nuns, arrived at Callystown, where they held 128-acres, a cottage and possibly a small church. They are believed to have moved from Termonfeckin to Callystown as a result of a dispute with the Lord Primate of the time. The convent buildings were thought to have been situated near to the site where Callystown House was later built, but no trace remains.[9]

The case would appear to be closed. Clogherhead's Callystown is so called because the Black Nuns lived there from the sixteenth century. However, I decided to reference the Online Placename Database of Ireland[10] to see what further information, if any was available, could be gleaned about this place name.

Imagine my surprise, upon browsing the archival records about Callystown, to see that it appears to have been called Callystown before the nuns ever arrived there. The earliest record, going back all the way to 1301, suggests it had that name a whole two centuries before the nuns came along. As with most place names, the spelling varied throughout history, but it seems that it was known in some form as

*Local folklore says the round tower at Monasterboice was built
by the Cailleach when she dropped stones from her apron.*

Callystown in the years and centuries before the nunnery existed there.
Here are the various spellings of the name through history:

1301 Balykellath

1416 Calyaghtoun

1426 Kylkloghir

1431 Kaillaghton

1431 Cayllaghton

1440 Caalaghton

1471 Kallyaghtown

This last spelling, the one immediately preceding the arrival of the
nuns, is almost definitely a rendition *Cailleach* or *Cailliagh* and 'town'.

So there was a nun in Callystown before the nuns. Or a hag/crone/ancient goddess.

Because of the prominent position of Callystown/Castlecoo Hill as a horizon foresight for summer sunrise from the great Boyne Valley monuments, and because of the very strong association of those monuments and their river valley with the goddess Bóinn, it should be possible to at least re-consider the origin of Callystown, and to acknowledge the possibility of another inception for its name.

It is, of course, still possible that there was some sort of nunnery or convent at Callystown before the arrival of the Black Nuns. Interestingly, there is a place at nearby Termonfeckin called Nunneryland, and we were told the old Irish name for that place was 'Cailleach Dubh', meaning 'black nun' or usually just 'nun', but also just 'a hag'.[11] Cailleach also means 'veiled woman',[12] and there is a general tendency to associate the word with nuns. However, as previously stated, the Cailleach is one of Ireland's most ancient divinities. Cailleach Dhubh can also refer to the cormorant (a bird)[13], while cailleach oidhche (Cailleach of the night) is an owl,[14] and indeed the cry of the bean sídhe (banshee) is said to resemble that of an owl.

Local tradition in Termonkfecin suggested that there was once an old laneway that ran all the way from Nunneryland to Callystown. Declan Quaile, writing about the old townlands and placenames of the area, said that:

> Callystown was always pronounced 'Calliaghstown' by the old people, harking back to the original Irish word.[15]

5.5

The Tara Brooch: Ireland's finest piece of jewellery

The Tara Brooch has rightly been described as Ireland's finest piece of jewellery. It dates from the seventh century AD and represents the zenith of craftsmanship by the early medieval Irish metalworkers.

However, the brooch has no known connection with either the Hill of Tara, after which it is named, or the High Kings who ruled there. It was, supposedly, found on Bettystown beach in County Meath, a mere nine and a half miles (15km) from the great mound of Newgrange and some 18 miles (29 kilometres) from the Hill of Tara.

The story goes that it was found at Bettystown in 1850 by a peasant woman's children. They allegedly found it in a box which had been buried in the sand. However, there is a suggestion that the brooch was really discovered somewhere else and that the peasant woman's family had changed details of the story to avoid any dispute with the owner of the land where it was really found. On 24 August 1850 (and remember this was just after the Great Famine, when times were tough), the woman offered the brooch for sale to the owner of an old iron shop in Drogheda. Can you imagine receiving such a fabulous and priceless artefact into your hands and then deeming it to be of little worth? That's what happened:

> [He] refused to purchase to light and insignificant (sic) an article; it was subsequently bought by a watchmaker in the town, who, after cleaning and examining it, proceeded to

Dublin and disposed of it to us (Messrs. Waterhouse & Co.,
Jewellers, Dame Street), for nearly as many pounds sterling
as he had given pence for it.[1]

A different story about the discovery of the Tara Brooch later
emerged. Sir William Wilde (father of Oscar Wilde) had compiled a
*Catalogue of the Silver and Ecclesiastical Antiquities in the Collection of the
Royal Irish Academy* in 1862. This was not published until 1915. In it,
Wilde refers to certain silver objects found 'in the excavation for the
harbour wall at the mouth of the river Boyne, near Drogheda, in an oak
box, and along with them the brooch called that of Tara'.[2]

The only thing in common with the two stories is that the brooch
was found in a box and that it was found somewhere along the coast
near the Boyne estuary.

Whatever the truth about the location of its discovery, the Dublin
jeweller George Waterhouse was the one who named this most precious item the Tara Brooch, linking the find to the Irish High Kings,
'fully aware that this would feed the Irish middle-class fantasy of being descended from them.'[3]

An aerial view of the Boyne Estuary, with its harbour walls.
The Tara Brooch was said to have been found here.

The Tara Brooch. (image Wikipedia)

And it worked. The Tara Brooch was displayed as a standout showpiece at The Great Exhibition in London in 1851 and the Paris Exposition Universelle, as well as the Dublin exhibition visited by the Queen in 1853. Prior to this, it had even been specially sent to Windsor Castle for her inspection.[4]

Around 1867, the brooch came into the collection of the Royal Irish Academy. It was sold to the RIA for the sum of £200, quite a lot of money in those days, and sold 'on the express condition that it should never be allowed to leave Ireland'.

The Tara Brooch is currently on display at the Treasury room of the National Museum (Archaeology) in Kildare Street, Dublin, where the public can see it for free. Here is the museum's description of the Tara Brooch:

> It is made of cast and gilt silver and is elaborately decorated on both faces. The front is ornamented with a series of exceptionally fine gold filigree panels depicting animal and abstract motifs that are separated by studs of glass, enamel and amber. The back is flatter than the front, and the decoration is cast. The motifs consist of scrolls and triple spirals and recall La Tène decoration of the Iron Age.
>
> A silver chain made of plaited wire is attached to the brooch by means of a swivel attachment. This feature is formed of animal heads framing two tiny cast glass human heads.
>
> Along with such treasures as the Ardagh Chalice and the Derrynaflan Paten, the Tara Brooch can be considered to represent the pinnacle of early medieval Irish metalworkers' achievement. Each individual element of decoration is executed perfectly and the range of technique represented on such a small object is astounding.[5]

There is much historic and mythical significance attached to the Boyne Estuary, if that is indeed where the brooch was found. This is where the builders of Newgrange brought the stones for the monument in from the sea. This is, according to myth, the place where the Milesians entered Ireland when they came to take the country from the Tuatha Dé Danann. It is also reputedly the place where Saint Patrick landed when he arrived to bring Christianity here.

One wonders if the brooch was not part of a haul that was either being brought into the country, or, more likely, being secreted away to be sold abroad; and, if the latter was the case, what misfortune came upon its then owner at the mouth of the Boyne. Whatever happened, we are exceedingly fortunate to be able to marvel at its splendour today.

The Tara Brooch has no known connection to the Hill of Tara.

5.6

Tracing the goddess of the Boyne river

When one studies the mythology of ancient Ireland and Europe, it is likely that, before too long, one will encounter the name of Carl Jung. One of the things that has struck me since I recently began to earnestly probe the life and work of this hugely influential individual – only within the past couple of years – is how I have managed to live this long without encountering his writing, and the tremendous influence he has had, not least upon our understanding of mythology, but of the idea of the collective unconscious and the archetypes that emerge from some sincere yet imponderable depth within us.

Marie-Louise Franz's biography of Jung was one of the most exciting things I've ever read.[1] Then I followed up with Laurens van der Post's biography,[2] which I found equally enthralling. I have read a limited amount of Jung's own writing, but in not untypical fashion I sometimes find that an account of a person of such greatness by a third party – in both these cases people who were lucky enough to know Jung while he was alive – provides a fuller insight into not just their work, but their whole being.

In a similar vein, my prejudice towards the biographer, if it hadn't been immediately obvious, was manifested in the case of Nietzsche when I found myself underlining and highlighting many more passages in a Janko Lavrin biography of him[3] than I did in Nietzsche's own work, *Beyond Good and Evil.*

*The Boyne river at Oldbridge. The river is named after
the bright bovine goddess Bóinn.*

In many respects, I had already met Carl Gustav Jung, through the
work of someone who has often been described as a Jungian disci-
ple, Joseph Campbell. Campbell's work crossed into fields of common
interest with my own researches into the myths of the Boyne Valley
and Ireland, and indeed he became firmly focused in my crosshairs
when his discussion of a myth about Venus shining into Newgrange
once in eight years set the hairs on the back of my neck all tingling in
one of many great and exciting revelations that occurred while I was
researching for *Island of the Setting Sun*.

Campbell was, I now realise, a stepping stone on the crossing
of a great river, towards an even more fertile land, inhabited by the
thoughts and works of a person (Jung) of such great standing in the
human story that it can be suggested, even though subjectively, that he
deserved to stand alone from the human race, deified perhaps by those
of us who can only tread softly in his shadow, so great and yet gentle

is his presence in the great work of understanding the sacred, and the symbol, and the myths of mankind, and indeed his participation in the great mystery of his own existence.

And so I followed by bliss, and my bliss led me to Newgrange, and thereafter to the works of C.G. Jung.

In his biography, Laurens van der Post discusses Jung's association with the Rhine, and how Jung believed that no-one could truly live without being in the presence of water, whether lake or river. The biographer believes it was a portentous event that Jung, born on the shore of Lake Constance, should four years later move close to Basle, where he spent 21 years in the presence of the great Rhine, 'so that ... the presence of this great river ... was in and around his senses'. But here, van der Post makes a stark observation:

> The Rhine is one of the great mythological rivers of the world, not yielding place to the other immense mythological rivers representing the searching and inquiring spirits of men and their cultures, such as the Ganges, the Nile, the Yellow River of China and so on. But unlike those rivers which appear as rivers of light, resolution and are full of a natural, maternal solitude for life, the Rhine is a dark, angry and outraged masculine stream ... It was as if the Rhine had its source in the heart of the darkness of European history.[4]

How can one say that a river, a restless body of water flowing ceaselessly from source to sea, has gender? I thought immediately of the Boyne, which has never been too far from me, either physically or consciously, and her very feminine name, Bóinn, she who is the illuminated bovine goddess of some considerable antiquity. The following words from van der Post made me somewhat enamoured that my local river, the river of my youth and that is ever-present in my story upon this earth, should have such a stark feminine association:

Like Heine, I could not understand why it should make me feel sad when the tops of the hills above the Rhine sparkled in a long evening sunlight of summer. I wondered why the story of Lorelei should trouble me? ... Perhaps it was because the imagery evoked by Heine of the feminine being of irresistible beauty and siren song, combing out her hair of gold with a comb of gold, represented all the feminine values which European man, particularly German man, had rejected. German culture, embedded as it was in a civilisation almost entirely man-made, was deliberately and wilfully masculine.[5]

In fact, van der Post wrote, 'the infinitely renewing and renewable moon that swings the sea of change and symbolises all that is eternally feminine in the spirit of man, by some ominous perversity ... was rendered into a fixed and immutable masculinity.[6]

And I thought, upon reading all the above, that no-one who had lived by the shores of the Boyne river, having heard her gentle lappings or the incessant babbling of her salmon weirs, could ever go to war against another man, or tribe, or nation. Naively, perhaps, I thought that a feminine name and a feminine myth were enough to ensure that those of us who lived within hearing distance of the bright cow river had within our grasp some sense of the feminine aspect of ourselves, allowing it an amount of balance with the masculine in order that some good human decency would prevail that would impel us not towards conflict with our brethren in the greater world, but towards some greater accord. The moon, I felt, was itself a bright wandering cow, and in my own work I had been satisfied that Bóinn (also sometimes spelt Bóann) represented more than just the river which has her name – she was river, but also moon and Milky Way. The philosopher John Moriarty described it thus:

Boann, the moon-white cow.
Boann, the gleaming river.
In dreams I know it as cow.
Awake I know it as river.[7]

I thought that no-one who lived by the shores of the Boyne, shown here at Ardmulchan, could ever go to war against other humans.

Ireland did not have a 'father' identity (like Germany or Japan), rather being named Éire, after one of a triune of goddesses. We did not make war, but rather we suffered it, and often were the unnecessary victims or players in someone else's conflict, or someone else's incursions upon Éire's sovereignty. This is written indelibly into our mytho-historical story, exemplified in the *Lebor Gabála*, the Book of Invasions, which has been imprinted upon the very essence of our spirit as a people.

I thought of the poet Francis Ledwidge, who was born near Slane, high above the Boyne on its northern bank, and who died in the Great War at the age of 29. He wrote:

> ...Since the poets perished
> And all they cherished in the way,
> Their thoughts unsung, like petal showers
> Inflame the hours of blue and grey.[8]

A bust of the poet John Boyle O'Reilly at Dowth cemetery.

Another poet of the Boyne Valley, John Boyle O'Reilly, wrote of his longing to return to the river of his youth:

> And I long for the dear old river,
> Where I dreamed my youth away;
> For a dreamer lives forever,
> And a toiler dies in a day.[9]

And when I stood by Bóinn's shore, beneath looming Rosnaree, the wood of the king, I watched in flame the grafted embers of Ledwidge's twilight vision, of cherished things that were no more than barely formed thoughts, flowing down in a stream from hills beyond sight. And there, glistening in a pool of Bóinn's tender making, the relinquished dreams of that Éire passed into song would be gloriously resuscitated by the ancient poet, a Ledwidge in the guise of Finegas the Wise, singing merrily by the shore in an Ireland that is more famous for song than sword.

The Boyne at dawn on a misty spring morning.

And we could not make kings of Jung nor Ledwidge nor Finegas, for even as a king at Rosnaree, I was, in the words of Shirley, sceptered and crowned, yet I tumbled down, and in the dust I was equal made with the poor crooked scythe and spade.

Often have I stood by Bóinn's brooding waters in the blue hour of evening, after the sun's departure, and listened there for the sounds of those stories of ancient glory, sweetly told. I never realised how that unfathomable something within my deeper self could be so brilliantly exemplified in the symbolism and sound of water until I had spent many a lonely hour in her presence.

And maybe from now on, lingering at Bóinn's border as I ponder incessantly at the edge of the unfathomable, I will tip my hat to the great C.G. Jung, whose whole work, in the words of van der Post, 'was the rediscovery of the great feminine objective within the objective psyche of man, as to make possible as never before a reconciliation of the masculine and feminine elements in life.'[10]

Some old names for the town of Drogheda

My home town is today called Drogheda. The commonly accept-
ed nomenclature of Drogheda says that it is derived from the
Irish *Droichead Átha,* meaning 'Bridge at the Ford'. I've always been curious about that, mainly because a ford or crossing point is something
that obviously pre-dates a bridge, so that the name seems to refer to
two distinct and different methods of crossing the river. Before bridges
were built, rivers were crossed at shallow places called fords, or indeed
at shallow places where the crossing was augmented by some sort of
stone causeway built along the river bed.[1]

An ancient ford of the Boyne at Rosnaree, several miles upstream
of Drogheda, is marked on early Ordnance Survey maps. It might have
been one of the principal crossing places of the Boyne in prehistory,
and was possibly the place where the great northern road from Tara,
the Slíghe Midluachra, passed through the Boyne Valley adjacent to
the great monuments of Brúg na Bóinne.[2]

In *Island of the Setting Sun: In Search of Ireland's Ancient Astronomers,*
Richard Moore and I presented evidence that the name of the Boyne
river might have been inspired by the Milky Way, the great 'river of
the sky' and that the Boyne might have been considered its earthly
counterpart.[3]

So I have this pet theory, and it's only a theory, without much foundation, that perhaps the old name of Drogheda does not mean 'Bridge

Drogheda has grown over the centuries on either side of the River Boyne.
On its eastern flank, the Dublin-Belfast railway line crosses the river
on the Boyne Viaduct, completed in 1855.

on the Ford', but maybe something like 'Ford of the Wheel' – *droichead* being related to the word *droch,* which means wheel'.[4] I've also seen it written somewhere (although I cannot recall the source) that suggested the word *droichead* stems from *droch* representing the wheel-shaped arches of a bridge. My theory is that the 'ford of the wheel' is the crossing point of the earthly Milky Way, the river Boyne. Indeed, another great wheel of the sky – the zodiac, through which the sun, moon and planets journey through the sky – was recognised in earlier times by the Irish phrase *rael-draoch,* the 'circle or wheel of the stars'.[5]

In prehistoric times, the area where Drogheda is situated today was likely known as Inber Colpa (spelt different ways, including Inbher Colptha). There are a couple of different stories accounting for the origin of this name. One of these says that it is named after the shin-bone (*colptha*) of the great monster the Mata, which was said to have been slain by the men of Erin at a mysterious stone on Newgrange. Another story says the name is accounted for by the death of the Milesian brother Colpa during their battle with the Tuatha Dé Danann, who caused a fierce tempest to blow up as the Milesians attempted to land at the Boyne.[6] *Inber* is an Irish word that means 'the meeting of the waters', or a harbour or estuary.

Of particular interest to my little investigation here, though, are a couple of names for Drogheda which I had not previously encountered. Droichead Átha and Inber Colpa are well attested, but much less well known but equally interesting are some other names which were apparently given to the town, or features in its vicinity, in times long ago.

In their recounting of a famous story called 'The Colloquy of the Old Men', Cross and Slover refer to the separate journeys of Oisín (son of the celebrated Finn McCool) and Cailte, son of Crunnchu mac Ronain. After visiting Finn's old nurse, Oisín and Cailte split up, one going north to seek Oisín's mother, who is one of the Tuatha De Danann, the other moving south toward Tara:

> ... Oisin went to the fairy-mound of Uch Cletigh, where was his mother, Blai daughter of Derc Dianscothach; while Cailte took his way to Inber Bic Loingsigh which at present is called Mainister Droichid Atha (the monastery of Drogheda) from Beg Loigsech son of Arist that was drowned in it, that is, the king of the Romans' son, who came to invade Ireland; but a tidal wave drowned him there in his *inber* (river-mouth). He went on to Linn Feic (Fiacc's Pool), on the bright-streaming Boyne; southwards over the Old Mag Breg, and to the rath (stronghold) of Drum Derg, where Patrick mac Calpuirn was.[7]

There are a few things that are interesting in this passage. We know that Fiacc's Pool is likely situated on the Bend of the Boyne beneath Ros na Rí (Rosnaree) and was the celebrated place where Finneces caught the Salmon of Knowledge, from which Finn gained all his wisdom. The 'Inber Bic Loingsigh' which was better known as the Monastery of Drogheda, is a curious one indeed. Bic or Beg is probably the Irish word *beag,* meaning small or little. Loingsigh could be a variant of *loingeasach,* meaning 'abounding in ships or in fleets'.[8] Joseph Falaky Nagy

Drogheda on the Boyne from the air. The fording point of the river was located close to St. Mary's Bridge, the second bridge from the bottom of the image.

asserts that the Mainistir Droichit Átha referred to in the text is Melli-font,[9] the first Cistercian monastery founded in Ireland (in 1142). Not being a scholar in medieval Ireland, I cannot argue with him. Howev-er, the location of Mellifont a number of miles northwest of Drogheda, on a smaller tributary of the Boyne called the river Mattock, means it is some distance removed from the river mouth where Beg Loingsech was apparently drowned.

The story of the mysterious drowning of Beg Loigsech is interesting indeed. There are obvious parallels here between Inber Bic Loingsigh and Inber Colpa. Beg Loigsech was the son of the king of the Romans, who 'came to invade Ireland', but a tidal wave drowned him at the river mouth. Colpa was a son of Mil, the king of Spain, and he was drowned somewhere near the mouth of the Boyne by a storm whipped up by the Dé Dananns while trying to land for the purpose of taking Ireland from them.[10] The Milesians could also have said to be 'abound-ing in ships'; many of them were destroyed in the Dé Danann tempest. The parallels between these stories are so striking that one cannot but

*Millmount, now the site of a British military fort built in the early
nineteenth century, is believed locally to have been an ancient burial mound.*

draw the tentative impression that they are two versions of a single old
mythic narrative involving the naming of the Boyne estuary.

Another obscure ancient name from Drogheda is mentioned all too
briefly in O'Donovan's Ordnance Survey letters, and it would be interesting to see if further research into this name – and its variants – yields
information of interest. Here is what O'Donovan says, after writing
briefly about the name Droichet Atha:

> There are other ancient names of it still retained by some
> persons. Sarsfield, whom we have mentioned on our former
> letters, says the ancient name of it was Ath Dhunruaidhe,
> and Jones says the ancient name of it was Dun Dubhruaidhe
> . . . Others say it was called *Treda* prior to it having got the
> denomination of Drogheda – if it was so-called, *Treda* seems
> to have been the first Anglicized name of it. Droichet atha
> (Droichet Atha) occurs in several places in the Annals of the
> Four Masters ...[11]

The Boyne at twilight. The old ford was located adjacent to
St. Mary's Bridge, in the centre of the photo.

Literally translated, *Ath Dhun Ruaidhe* would mean 'the ford of the red fort' or something similar and *Dun Dubhruaidhe* would mean 'the fort of black-red/dark-red' or something to that effect.[12] O'Donovan puts a footnote in for the Sarsfield and Jones references which asks the question 'Are these names preserved in any document?' Regrettably, the answer would appear to be no.

In fact, the names are so obscure that it's doubtful that most residents of Drogheda today would ever have heard of them.

5.8

The Hill of Slane:
Where Christianity met prehistory

To me, the Hill of Slane represents the place where Christianity met prehistory. Saint Patrick is said to have lit the Paschal Fire here in 433AD, bringing the flame of Christianity to a very pagan Ireland.

Some of the headstones in the cemetery on the Hill of Slane are based on a Celtic Christian Cross design. This cross, to me, represents the conjunction of Christianity and whatever spirituality existed when it arrived. I see in the Celtic cross the cruciform shape that is inherent in the major megalithic monuments of the Boyne Valley, which probably predate Christ by more than three millennia. The inclusion of the circle of the sun in the centre of the cross is just another representation of the chamber of Newgrange – where sunlight intersected the centre of the cross in spectacular fashion on winter solstice over 5,000 years ago.

One thing that seems obvious when you walk up the eastern side of the Hill of Slane (which is the only way to walk up it) is that the monuments and remains relating to Christianity dominate, and that the 'pagan' remains – which lie further up the hill on the summit – are shrouded by trees and are largely obscured from view.

The dominant feature from prehistory is a mound or motte, said in place name lore to be Dumhach Sláine, the burial place of Sláine, a king of the Fir Bolg.[1] The Irish word *dumhach* usually refers to a burial mound.[2] In the summer time, it is virtually impossible to see the

214

The Hill of Slane at twilight.

mound, but in winter when the foliage is gone from the trees its large bulk becomes visible.

I have previously suggested that the mound on the hill of Slane might possibly be a passage-tomb monument dating from the Neolithic. In recent years, ground-probing archaeological techniques have been employed at the mound to try to determine if there is a possible structure within.

> The 2010 geophysical survey on the motte suggests a buried stone structure, and the circular enclosure surrounding it has similarities to a prehistoric barrow and enclosure at Mountfortescue, 5km to the north.[3]

The motte of King Sláine is very interesting for another reason. It marks the point of intersection of two ancient alignments of sites. We call these the Brigid alignment, or the Brigid's Way, and the Patrick alignment, which I prefer to call 'Patrick's Equinox Journey'.

The Brigid alignment connects Saint Brigid's birthplace at Faughart with her monastery in Kildare through a 65-mile (104 kilometres) straight alignment of sacred sites, which include Saint Brigid's Well at Faughart, the barrow cluster on Mount Oriel, the motte of King Sláine on the Hill of Slane, the Hill of Tara and the Curragh, the plain upon which Brigid was said to have grazed her cattle, which is located beside Kildare town where she founded her monastery.[4]

One thing that should be obvious about the Brigid alignment is that it must predate Christianity because it involves many prehistoric sites. Indeed, we find that Brigid was venerated as one of the Tuatha Dé Danann long before Christianity came to Ireland.

When Saint Patrick landed at the Boyne Estuary (ironically in the same place as the Milesian spiritual leader Amergin had reportedly done over two millennia previously) he made his way towards Slane. Another apparent alignment involving the motte of Slane connects it around the time of the equinoxes with Millmount in Drogheda (another motte, said in local myth to be the burial place of Amergin). If you trace the line of this alignment on a map, from Millmount through Dumhach Sláine, it continues through the town of Kells and on past the hills of Loughcrew, through the Cruachan Aí complex towards Mayo. In Mayo, the alignment follows the route of the Tóchar Phadraig, the pilgrim path from Ballintubber Abbey, through Aughagower, and eventually it lands exactly on the peak of Croagh Patrick.[5] Is this apparent arrangement of sites from the east of the country,

A statue of Saint Patrick looks out across the Boyne Valley from the Hill of Slane.

An aerial view of Slane.

where Patrick landed and lit the Paschal Fire, to the west, where he battled with the demons, a coincidence? Patrick's fire was said to have been ignited just after spring equinox, on March 26. Fascinatingly, viewing the equinox sunsets from the top of the mound of Millmount in Drogheda reveals that the sun does not set over the peak of the Hill of Slane (and thus Dumhach Sláine) on the day of spring equinox, but rather a couple of days afterwards.[6]

It may be that Slane's importance in the wider landscape is not yet fully understood. The Hill of Slane is the dominant feature in the landscape viewed from the east. From Slane (although the view is obscured today by trees), the dominant features to the west would be Loughcrew and Hill of Mael. The latter, which has a very impressive monument of unknown date on its peak, is situated exactly on the equinox alignment that stretches all the way from Amergin's burial mound in Drogheda (Millmount) to the summit of Croagh Patrick in Mayo, on the west coast of Ireland.

From the top of Mael, one can imagine the possibility that the pyramidal peak of Croagh Patrick might just be visible on a very clear day …

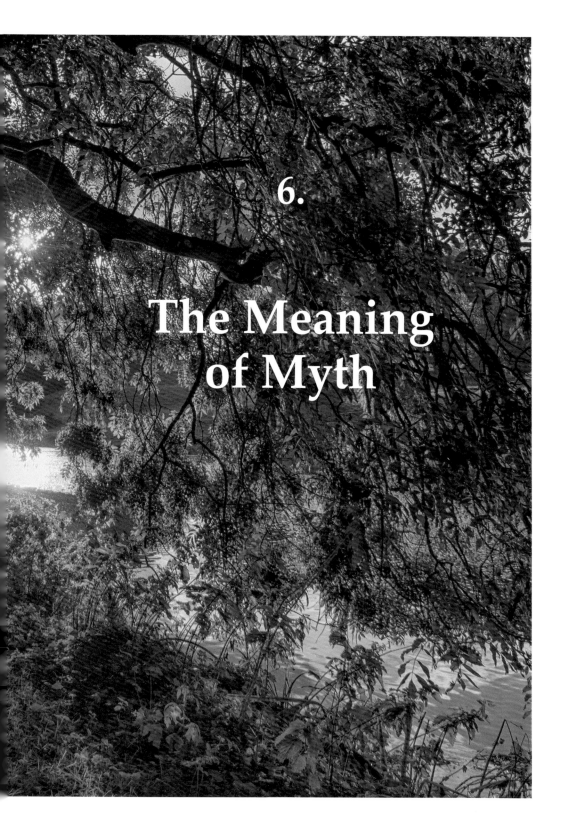

6.

The Meaning of Myth

6.1

All the dead kings came to me

There's a poem by Francis Ledwidge that I really love. Ledwidge was born at Slane and died in the Great War in 1917 at the age of 29. He loved the Boyne Valley, and shortly before he died he wrote of his great longing for home in a letter to fellow poet Katherine Tynan:

> I want to see again my wonderful mother, and to walk by the Boyne to Crewbawn and up through the brown and grey rocks of Crocknaharna. You have no idea of how I suffer with this longing for the swish of the reeds at Slane and the voices I used to hear coming over the low hills of Currabwee. Say a prayer that I may get this leave, and give us a condition my punctual return and sojourn till the war is over.[1]

Unfortunately, he never came home. He and five others were killed when a shell exploded beside them at the Battle of Ypres.

One of his poems, 'The Dead Kings', interests me greatly.

> All the dead kings came to me
> At Rosnaree, where I was dreaming,
> A few stars glimmered through the morn,
> And down the thorn the dews were streaming.
>
> And every dead king had a story
> Of ancient glory, sweetly told.
> It was too early for the lark,
> But the starry dark had tints of gold.

I listened to the sorrows three
Of that Eire passed into song.
A cock crowed near a hazel croft,
And up aloft dim larks winged strong.

And I, too, told the kings a story
Of later glory, her fourth sorrow:
There was a sound like moving shields
In high green fields and the lowland furrow.

And one said: 'We who yet are kings
Have heard these things lamenting inly.'
Sweet music flowed from many a bill
And on the hill the morn stood queenly.

And one said: 'Over is the singing,
And bell bough ringing, whence we come;
With heavy hearts we'll tread the shadows,
In honey meadows birds are dumb.'

And one said: 'Since the poets perished
And all they cherished in the way,
Their thoughts unsung, like petal showers
Inflame the hours of blue and grey.'

And one said: 'A loud tramp of men
We'll hear again at Rosnaree.'
A bomb burst near me where I lay.
I woke, 'twas day in Picardy.[2]

Rosnaree (more often spelt Rossnaree these days) is on the southern bank of the Bend of the Boyne, overlooking Fiacc's Pool, where Fionn Mac Cumhaill is said to have caught the Salmon of Knowledge. It is close to the river ford (*áth*) which would have been the main crossing point over the Boyne in ancient times. It is the place where the Boyne river swelled up so that Cormac Mac Art's body could not be brought to be buried at Brú na Bóinne.

The mural of Francis Ledwidge in Slane, commissioned by the Francis Ledwidge Museum Committee and executed by artist Ciaran Dunlevy.

I wonder, when reading some of the lines of Ledwidge's poem, whether it is perhaps infused with elements of a familiar legend from Rosnaree, one that might involve dead kings and the spectre of a loud tramp of men returning to haunt its woods. Being a native of the area, Ledwidge was very familiar with some of its stories. His collection of legends and stories of the Boyne, serialised in the *Drogheda Independent* newspaper beginning in 1913, has only just been finally published in book format in 2017.[3]

There is a legend about Rosnaree which tells of sleeping soldiers. It is a familiar story, being similar to that told about Garrett's Fort[4] at Hacklim, outside Ardee in County Louth.

The Rosnaree version of the story talks about a man who encountered a light at a fort near Rosnaree, close to the Boyne. He entered into the fort to find a lot of bags hanging on the walls and one of the bags had a sword stuck in it. This story was recounted to a collector from the National Folklore Collection in 1938 by Navan resident James Neill (aged 74), who in turn had heard the tale from an elderly gentleman called Johnny Murray:

He went over and he was lifting up the sword and according
as he was lifting it there was a man's head lifted up from this
big bag and a horse along with him, and he was riding the
horse, and as according as he drew out the sword there were
horsemen rising all around the wall. They were nearly clear
out of where they were and he got afeerd and he let the sword
drop back in, and as soon as he did he was told, 'Go home,
you coward.' I disremember the regiment he'd have lifted out
of prison if he lifted up the sword altogether.[5]

Legends of a sleeping army waiting for a hero to come and rouse
them for some great battle are present in other parts of Ireland too
(such as at The Curragh, County Kildare, and Lough Gur in Limerick).
Gearóid Iarla (Earl Garrett, Gerald) is sometimes said to be the one
who is the chief of the chthonic army. At Hacklim, some versions say
it is Fionn Mac Cumhaill.[6] The messianic theme of the legend in its
various forms is overtly political, the clear premise being that a great
leader from the past will return, from a supernatural subterranean domain, leading a great army to restore glory and freedom to Ireland. In
the context of a country under the sway of foreign rule and oppression,
it is no wonder that such tales might have found sympathetic ears in
Ireland.

According to the legend, the rousing of the army will occur when
a prophesied hero (those who have tried and failed are invariably referred to in less than favourable terms, such as 'coward') will pull a
sword out of a wall or a stone or a bag. If the sword in the stone sounds
familiar, think of King Arthur and Excalibur. The notion of a hero or
king sleeping in a cave can be found all over Europe and even further
afield. It is so familiar in folklore that it is referred to as the 'king in
the mountain' motif and has been classified in the Aarne-Thompson
system of folktale motifs.[7]

Ledwidge's opening lines, 'All the dead kings came to me / At
Rosnaree, where I was dreaming' are suggestive that he is familiar

with that location's mythic and even historic significance. Perhaps the dead High King Cormac Mac Airt, who is said to be buried at Rosnaree, was one of those of whom he writes.

'There was a sound like moving shields In high green fields and the lowland furrow.' Was Ledwidge, perhaps, describing the sound of the enchanted army of Rosnaree being awakened?

'A loud tramp of men We'll hear again at Rosnaree.' Granted, Ledwidge was in the battlefields of the Great War, and although he says he is dreaming at Rosnaree, the bomb wakes him to the reality that he is, in fact, in Picardy. Nevertheless, it's an interesting speculation that he was perhaps reflecting upon cultural aspects of his homeland. Rosnaree would have been visible just across the Boyne Valley from his home at Janeville, east of Slane. Interestingly, Rosnaree is a name that comes from the Irish *Ros na Ríogh,* meaning 'wood of the kings'.[8]

Had Francis Ledwidge heard the story of the sleeping army of Rosnaree, and did he incorporate it into The Dead Kings? Unfortunately, his book of legends and stories of the Boyne was never finished. He intended to complete the series of articles in the *Drogheda Independent,* but ceased when he was called into military action. The book remained incomplete, ending at Slane, so we sadly don't find out what Ledwidge might have written about Rosnaree.

The final lines of his poem are tragically prescient. 'A bomb burst near me where I lay.' He was killed when a shell exploded nearby on July 31, 1917.[9]

6.2

Kissing the Cailleach:
The sovereignty dream of Ireland

Not long after the beginning of 2017, I had a significant dream. I dream all the time, but often I wake up in the morning and, despite knowing that I had been dreaming the previous night, I can't remember the details. Sometimes I remember snatches of dreams, but forget others. And then occasionally, I have a dream that shouts out at me, as if saying, 'this is one you will not forget'.

I dreamt that I was descending through a spiralling tunnel, which was winding down into the darkness of the earth counter-clockwise. There were people running towards me, fleeing from something around the bend. They were shouting and looked terrified. I was momentarily afraid. Before I got a chance to ask 'what is it?', one of them shouted 'it's the Cailleach' and fled in terror. They all ran away, behind me, back up the tunnel, still screaming, as if running from some terrifying spectre or monster.

Instead of turning and running with them, I pressed on. Curiosity got the better of me and the fear gave way.

Out of the shadows, an old woman appeared. She was slight, and haggard, and was dressed all in black. The image wasn't terribly vivid, but I got the impression of grey or white hair under a shawl or head scarf. She was almost skeletal.

However, I did not feel fear not revulsion. We approached each other. She came towards me and I moved towards her. As we did this,

The Lia Fáil (Stone of Destiny) on the Hill of Tara.

the strangest thing happened. She began to lift her hand towards me, and as she did so, I reached my hand out towards hers. I instinctively took her hand, just as we were within reach of each other, and then I drew it towards my mouth and kissed it.

As soon as I did so, she changed into a younger woman. She was not a really young woman, but rather more like a woman in her forties, a more mature and yet healthy and youthful, voluptuous woman. She had a friendly, familiar face and was smiling warmly.

When I had kissed her hand, she smiled at me and said: 'You are ready to die now.'

And that's where the dream ended. It was fascinating and fascinatingly brief. I woke knowing that I had dreamt something very significant. And I could remember every detail, which is unusual. Knowing that I should write it down, because it was important, I sent a summary of the dream to several friends by email that day.

As I recalled the details, and dwelt on them during that day, several things occurred to me. The first and perhaps most significant aspect was the fact that this mysterious transforming lady told me I was ready to die. What did she mean?

I was not afraid of this apparent portent. I did not see it as a threat. The Cailleach was communicating a symbolic death. But what of?

My friends had some interesting insights.

> 'You are ready to die... perhaps meaning the old version of yourself, of who you thought you were, is ready to be let go... Time to shine my friend.'

> 'We all must die to the old and only we know what that is within each of us – perhaps old habits, ways of being in the world, jobs, whatever. It comes in many forms, this wake-up call.'

> 'It could be a death of your old self, any old parts of ego that may have held you back.'

> 'Death? Yes. Not physical. The dying of old constructs as you are ready for ever deeper connection with the ancestors ... and they with you. You are ready to die now. Into something altogether glorious.'

I could not but concur with these interpretations, especially in light of the dramatic transformation of the Cailleach from a hideous and frightening old crone into a friendly, more physically attractive and benign presence. Was this, I wondered, symbolic of a transformation that must occur within myself, in order that something of the old me must die so that something new should be born, as my friends were suggesting?

The darkness of the cave and the hideous nature of the old Cailleach were aspects, perhaps, of a tendency towards symbolising fear with blackness and ugliness. Considered symbolically, the fact that many people were running away in fear suggests, in my view, that they were not necessarily running from the fearful nature of the scene, but rather that they were refusing to engage with a fulsome introspective process – a peering inwards, so to speak – for fear of what they might have to confront within their own shadows. Joseph Campbell was famously said to have either uttered or written: 'The cave you fear to enter holds the treasure you seek.'[1]

It seems Campbell certainly did say the following:

> It is by going down into the abyss that we recover the treasures of life.

> The very cave you are afraid to enter turns out to be the source of what you are looking for. The damned thing in the cave that was so dreaded has become the center.[2]

In the dream, I ventured forwards where others fled in fear. My own cave, in the Campbellesque analysis, provided quite the transformative experience. But the initial descent, reminiscent in some respects of Dante, signified the crossing of a threshold, and the ingression into darker realms and deeper strata of the unconscious self.

In the story of Nechtain's Well, which is approached in provocation and curiosity by the goddess Bóinn (a woman who dares to enter a male-only domain), there is a similar theme relating to the breaking through of a fearful threshold in order to look down into the waters of the well, symbolising the unconscious:

> There was none that would look to its bottom
> But his two bright eyes would burst[3]

Why should anyone fear to look to the bottom of the well? The fear is that, peering too far, too soon into the depths of one's own unconscious, the initiate will become overwhelmed, and that the process will be a destructive one rather than a restorative one. The water is a 'living symbol of the dark psyche',[4] and the real danger is that the removal of the mask of ego will reveal an unfamiliar self, our own shadow:

Looking down the Lia Fáil on Tara.

> … whoever looks into the mirror of the water will see first
> of all his own face. The mirror does not flatter, it faithfully
> shows whatever looks into it; namely, the face we never show
> to the world … the mask of the actor.[5] … nothing is more
> disillusioning than the discovery of our own inadequacy.[6]

In Bóinn's case, she walks 'heedlessly' around the well three times,
and three waves burst from it, deforming her – she loses a foot, a hand
and an eye, and is washed down from the well towards the sea, where
she drowns.[7] The barriers and dams, represented by rite and dogma in
religious systems, were designed, says Jung, to 'keep back the dangers
of the unconscious'.[8] When these barriers collapse, 'the waters rise and
boundless catastrophes break over mankind'.[9]

The concept of *sídhe* as threshold, the doorway between the conscious and unconscious self, is a fascinating and invigorating possibility.

> The shadow is a tight passage, a narrow door, whose painful
> constriction no one is spared who goes down to the deep
> well.[10]

229

Can we be altogether sure that, among its other purposes, which no doubt included death and rebirth rites for the ancestors along with astronomical observations, Newgrange did not also serve as a place of initiation? Standing at the doorway of the great *sídhe* in the far-gone ages of the past, the initiate would be facing a journey into complete darkness – literally and perhaps metaphorically.

> And so it happens that if anyone – in whatever society – undertakes for himself the perilous journey into the darkness by descending, either intentionally or unintentionally, into the crooked lanes of his own spiritual labyrinth, he soon finds himself in a landscape of symbolical figures (any one of which may swallow him) which is no less marvellous than the wild Siberian world of the *pudak* and sacred mountains. In the vocabulary of the mystics this is the second stage of the Way, that of the 'purification of the self,' when the senses are 'cleansed and humbled,' and the energies and interests 'concentrated upon transcendental things'.[11]

The other most significant aspect of my 'kissing the Cailleach' dream was that it was, in many ways, similar to a story that comes to us right out of Irish mythology. That is the story of Niall of the Nine Hostages, one of the most famous of the early kings of Tara.[12]

Niall and his four half-brothers are all sons of the king of Ireland, Eochaid Mugmedón. Mongfhind is the mother of Brian, Ailill, Fergus and Fiachra, while Niall's mother is Cairenn. Apparently polygamy was acceptable in medieval Ireland. Mongfhind becomes jealous of Cairenn when she is pregnant with Niall, and forces her to perform manual tasks such as drawing water, hoping that she will miscarry the child. This fails and Niall is born. It later emerges that he is favoured to succeed his father as king, in place of one of Mongfhind's sons. Mongfhind is enraged. She tries to devise a trap by encouraging her four sons to quarrel with Niall and then kill him.

The five go hunting together. At night, they wish to cook their quarry but they need water. Fergus is sent to fetch some.

> He finds instead, next to a well, a horrible hag, black as coal, with hair like the tail of a wild horse, smokey eyes, a crooked nose, green teeth that can cut oak, and green nails; she is covered in pustules and is in every way loathsome.[13]

The hag asks Fergus for a kiss. If he refuses to comply, he will get no water from the well. He declines, saying that he would rather die of thirst. He returns to the camp empty-handed, and one by one the other brothers go seeking water. Ailill and Brian both refuse to kiss the hag and return with no water. Fiachra does, however, give the hag a peck on the cheek, but still returns empty-handed.

It falls to Niall to get water. When he encounters the loathsome old hag, he embraces her fully, throwing himself upon the old woman and giving her the most passionate kiss. When he does this, the hag transforms into a beautiful woman, dressed in royal purple and wearing bronze slippers on her feet.

Standing at the entrance of the sídhe (in this case the artificially lit eastern passage of Knowth), the initiate would be facing a journey into darkness.

She reveals herself as Flaithius, the sovereignty of Ireland, and tells Niall that he will reign as king and that his children will reign after him.[14]

What was the Cailleach of my own dream offering me? Sovereignty over myself? Over my ego? The woman of the *sídhe* came forward to me, and I met her as one girded against malevolent and destructive possibility and yet prepared for a significant initiation event. She gave her hand. I kissed it. She told me I was ready to die.

Did she portend the death of the ego, the crumbling of the old ways? Was she foretelling the birth of something new? What was I to reign over, if anything – my own self actuation and realisation? The empowerment of my better nature, my *sídhe* nature, perhaps? My Danann nature?

In terms of initiation, Jung said that the central element of the ceremony was always the same: 'death and symbolic resurrection'.[15]

> During the journey to the beyond the initiate receives instruction from the highest divinity of heaven or the underworld, from a dead ancestor or a great shaman of the past, from a female figure with magic powers or from a magic anima.[16]

I never got the chance to reply to the Cailleach. The dream ended when she uttered those powerful words. Apparently she needed no reply. She did not require an affirmation from me that, perhaps, I was indeed 'ready to die'.

Having crossed the threshold of fear, and entered the apparently dark underworld of the *sídhe*, I have returned to the world of mortals knowing one thing more than anything – that I am, indeed, ready to really live.

6.3

Killing the Evil Eye

Tory is a small island off the northwest coast of Ireland, nine miles out into the Atlantic Ocean near Donegal. Being acutely aware that the island is known in myth as the stronghold of the Fomorians – those dark, brooding forces of malevolence who sought to suppress and vanquish the Tuatha Dé Danann – I somehow felt that I should gird myself for my first visit to the island, in June 2016. Shortly before I went to Tory, I visited Síd in Broga, where I hoped that, in some way, the Dé Dananns would make their presence felt – that, somehow, I would be imbued with a supernatural psychological strength to repel any of that dark energy that might perhaps lurk on this mysterious island out in the ocean.

The rationalist in me balked at the whole idea. Supernatural forces indeed. What a load of nonsense.

However, at Newgrange I had a strangely unique experience. The place seemed bereft of presence. It felt bizarrely devoid of any energy or power. It had become, for the first time in my experience, just a heap of stones. Under the stars in the summer twilight, I felt very alone.

Upon reflection, it now seems clear that the perceived absence of energy at Newgrange was the unconscious realisation within myself of a distinct lack of presupposed personal energy of any form – good or bad, Dé Danann or Fomorian – that I might have used in my own imagined battle with the Fomorians out on Tory. In other words, while I went to Newgrange to mentally prepare for the trip to Tory, where

Midsummer sunset on Tory Island, viewed from Dún Bhalóir.

I feared I might encounter a darkness in my own nature, when I got to Newgrange and found it bereft of vitality, I should have realised that this was a blunt message from within, which might have said something like 'there is no need to gird yourself, because the only energy you will encounter on Tory is whatever energy you bring there yourself'.

Through such experiences, we realise one of the great truths about sacred sites like Newgrange. And that is the idea that they are expressions of our own numen-seeking nature. They reflect back to us the energy that we bring to them. Newgrange is a place of peace and power because we make it so. Does this mean we only imagine that it has power, and that in fact, as many archaeologists have perhaps concluded, it is merely a man-made cairn of stones and nothing more? Does this mean it has no power at all?

The answer to that question depends entirely on your own perception of it, and indeed your own general approach to such issues. For many of us, Brug Maic Ind Óc has an intense power. The monument functions as a mandala of sorts. It activates for us great sources of awe and wonderment, of some deep awareness within us, or perhaps even a sense of our greater connection to the cosmos, and to forces of spiritual vitality and oneness that lie beyond rational explanation. It has this power because we allow ourselves to be open to the possibilities.

How can we know whether any of this power with which we imbue it was an intention of the builders? We can't. Therefore, we must allow it to be whatever it will be for each and every individual. And therein lies the great power of Newgrange.

Arriving on Tory Island in June, coming towards midsummer and the longest days of the year, I can truly say that I was enchanted. It did not hold any sort of dark energy perceptible by me, except for whatever feelings such a remote and windswept and barren piece of rock might instil in the human spirit. While I enjoyed my time there and really warmed to Tory, I can imagine that the place must be much bleaker in winter time, when the island often becomes cut off from the mainland, sometimes for several weeks or even months.

On most days, you can see the mainland, and the mountains of Donegal. But despite their relative proximity, there are times when they seem a lifetime's journey away. Tory is one of those unique places

*Dún Bhalóir (Balor's Fort) on Tory Island, pictured
at midnight around midsummer.*

where it is possible to experience a sense of loneliness and detachment, in a way that visits to Síd in Broga cannot possibly do. At Newgrange, you are just minutes away from civilisation – towns and cities, motorways and airports. At Tory, you are much more isolated.

Staying in the easternmost property on the island gave me the opportunity to visit what is perhaps the single most powerful part of the island from the point of view of both mythology and dramatic landscape – Dún Bhalóir (Balor's Fort). This very striking promontory is the highest part of the 5km-long island, with dramatic precipitous cliffs that present almost-vertical drops to the surging Atlantic below.

Over the course of five days on the island, I made many visits to Dún Bhalóir. The first was undertaken with some trepidation, as I am not blessed with a good head for heights. Despite my fear, I was captivated and enthralled by Balor's Fort, which is a fantastic example of an Iron Age promontory fort. There are dramatic views of the whole island from up there, and indeed the Atlantic Ocean. It was here that Balor had his stronghold, and in a cleft on its eastern side, surrounded by high sea cliffs, was Príosún Bhaloir (Balor's Prison), in which he was said to have kept his prisoners. It was here that Balor kept his daughter, Eithne, who would eventually become the mother of Lugh, the one who would kill Balor.

I made repeated visits to Balor's Fort. It kept calling me back. This isolated spot, high on a rocky isthmus on this remote outpost of civilisation, had a power for me similar to Newgrange. It awakened within me some deep-seated sense of awe, and of rugged and raw isolation, such that it was possible, momentarily at least, to lose all sense of oneself. Of course the camera was always on hand, and the nature of the sunsets and long drawn-out, everlasting twilight of June meant that the constantly-changing scene presented dramatic pictures that transformed from one moment to the next.

Eithne's son Lugh built himself a fort called Dún Lúiche, at the base of mount Errigal on the mainland. It was here that Balor was said to

Port Challa, Tory Island.

have been killed by Lugh with the help of Gaibhdín Gabha, a Tuatha Dé Danann smith. They killed him by thrusting a red hot spear through the back of his head and out through his evil eye. Gleann Nimhe (Poison Glen) is named from the liquid which poured from Balor's eye.

On one of my last visits to Dún Bhalóir, while climbing up its steep slopes, I reflected on this story of the killing of Balor by Lugh, and the version from the Second Battle of Moytura with which I was more familiar. In some variations of this story, his eye was said to have burned the landscape. While pondering the symbolism of the evil eye, a thought suddenly came into my head, very clearly: 'We must kill the evil eye within ourselves.'

Reflecting on the metaphor of the story of Balor's evil eye, and how he was killed by a spear or slingshot from Lugh, it became clear to me that what the evil eye represents is our own shadow, the dark aspects of ourselves which we might perhaps project on to others – in this case, these others are represented by Balor and the Fomorians. They are not some dark or evil race, some shadowy mythical beings. The Fomorians are our shadow. In the human lifetime, there is an everlasting conflict between the Tuatha Dé Danann and the Fomorians. This battle, or counter-positioning of the forces of light and darkness, is present to some extent in all of us.

But furthermore is the notion that the evil eye of Balor represents the human weakness of projecting our own shortcomings and failings, and prejudices, onto others, as exemplified by Matthew 7:3:

> And why beholdest thou the mote that is in thy brother's eye,
> but considerest not the beam that is in thine own eye?

This problem of the evil eye – the eye that sees malevolence and misdeeds in others and perhaps wants to act upon this prejudice – is present in very destructive and threatening forms in the world today. This current manifestation of the evil eye in Europe and America in particular threatens to bring the world to a new conflict – a clash of civilisations akin to the great battles between the Tuatha Dé Danann and the Fomorians.

We must not seek to kill the Fomorians. For one cannot kill one's own shadow. One must merely acknowledge its presence and, to an extent, 'make friends with the devil'. Jung might have referred to this as assimilation of the shadow. We can retain an awareness of our own shadow, but not identify with it.

It is more important that we kill the evil eye, that prejudice within us that wants to blame others for the ills of the world. Let us pierce that evil eye with a great spear, or break it with a slingshot, so that the world of mankind does not bring itself towards a Third Battle of Moytura.

'We must kill the evil eye within ourselves.'

6.4

The Dawning of the Day

There are many strange tales in the myths and folklore of Ireland. One, several variants of which can be found in different localities, concerns the idea of a city or village beneath a lake or the sea. Sometimes, as in the legend of the mysterious island of Hy Brazil, the underwater realm becomes visible once every seven years. An extraordinary deluge tale was once recounted in the folklore of a fishing village called Blackrock (Na Creagacha Dubha), on the County Louth coastline near Dundalk.

This village, which mostly fronts on to Dundalk Bay, faces out across the restless waters, offering its residents enchanting views of the Cooley Mountains, whose undulating peaks roll out eastwards into the Irish Sea.

Blackrock's flood lore relates to a local version of a well-known song called Déalradh án Lae, 'The Dawning of the Day', written by James Clarence Mangan. A note appended to the song in a manuscript by transcriber Nicholas O'Kearney says:

> This song is founded on a tradition prevalent among the people in the vicinity, that an ancient city, with fine land adjoining it, are seen every seventh year by the fishermen off Blackrock shore near Dundalk. The bard, remembering the legends of Gerald Iarla in Mullach-Elim, and O'Neill in Aileach, considers the appearance a favourable sign for Ireland's liberation.[1]

Legends of cities lost beneath the waves are encountered in different parts of Ireland.

It may have happened, time out of mind, that a city and land in this part of the Island were encroached on by the sea. A great causeway, built with huge mountain stones, has been traced from Dunany to Cooley Point, a distance of more than seven miles across the Bay of Dundalk ... The old people used to tell many stories of the inhabitants of the enchanted city, and assert that some of their offspring still live at Blackrock.[2]

Here is Mangan's translation of the song:

'Twas a balmy summer morning
Warm and early,
Such as only June bestows;
Everywhere the earth adorning,
Dews lay pearly
In the lily-bell and rose.
Up from each green leafy bosk and hollow

Rose the blackbird's pleasant lay,
And the soft cuckoo was sure to follow.
'Twas the Dawning of the Day!

Through the perfumed air the golden
Bees flew round me:
Bright fish dazzled from the sea,
'Till medreamt some fairy olden
World-spell bound me
In a trance of witcherie.
Steeds pranced round anon with stateliest housings,
Bearing riders prankt in rich array,
Like flushed revellers after wine-carousings—
'Twas the Dawning of the Day!

Then a strain of song was chanted,
And the lightly
Floating sea-nymphs drew anear.
Then again the shore seemed haunted
By hosts brightly
Clad, and wielding shield and spear!
Then came battle-shouts—and onward rushing—
Swords and chariots, and a phantom fray.
Then all vanished; the warm skies were blushing
In the Dawning of the Day!

Cities girt with glorious gardens
Whose immortal
Habitants in robes of light
Stood, methought, as angel-wardens
Nigh each portal,
Now arose to daze my sight.
Eden spread around, revived and blooming;
When . . . lo! as I gazed, all passed away—
. . . I saw but black rocks looming
In the dim chill Dawn of Day!

Reflecting upon the meaning of the drowned cities, one is tempted into a number of avenues of exploration. Because of the apparent proliferation in Ireland of myths pertaining to towns and cities lost beneath some sea or lake, one is drawn to wonder whether the myths are, at least in part, ancient memories of antediluvian civilisation, and perhaps of a deluge that caused this old civilisation to suffer a watery calamity.

> The legends of the lost cities, related in all cases to lands lost under the waters of the seas and oceans, even lakes, prevail in all countries in the East and in the West, and they all have the same central core of similarity suggesting the same factual origin, though separate and independent. In all these cases the peoples of these legendary accounts claim descent from the former inhabitants of sea lost lands. This is most true, of course, amongst people who live on lands abutting seas and oceans, both in Europe and the Americas.[3]

Another possibility presents itself in the reading of the words of Mangan's song. The immortal habitants of light could well be the Tuatha Dé Danann, waiting in that invisible realm beneath the green hills (or, in this case, the waves of the sea) for their long-awaited return to this world.

The political background of the nineteenth century, when the song was written, might well have been an influence in the belief that the appearance of the submarine city was a favourable sign for Ireland's liberation.

> Of course such tales might also have been the product of the imagination of the downtrodden, stories that stem from imperial oppression and the desire to be free once more. It is in this light that we can certainly view some of these narratives, which were no doubt woven during the long period of occupation by Britain.[4]

The Boyne river and the Obelisk Bridge on a misty spring morning.

Metaphorically, the song of Blackrock and similar traditions are fascinating. Should we also consider these things from a psychological standpoint? It was while reflecting upon the themes of water and otherworlds that the possibility of such an interpretation came to light, and I wrote the following:

Some day, I would like to try to sail down the Boyne, all the way from Carbury well to Inver Colpa. I know it's likely not possible, but I'd like to do it anyway. And I think that, in the doing of it, in the navigating of the puny Boyne, the restless Boyne, the mighty Boyne, I might have relived a drama encompassing the journey of life; not a linear life, flowing from beginning to end, but rather a cyclical life, one with no beginning and no end, just a constant flow from one form to the next.

And I wonder, merely by contemplating the journey of the eternal river, if perhaps I might enter eternity myself, on the strength of a thought. Before you were born, I knew you. Before you were the Well of Segais, you were a million raindrops. Before your ejaculation on the slopes of Sídhe Nechtain, you had been glorified on the slopes of Mount Fuji, and on Kilimanjaro you had been a spring of nimiety; on the Matterhorn you had been a darkling brook, and at Elbrus a frozen fountainhead.

Segais, the beginning and the end.

Segais, the Alpha and the Omega.

Bless me with your sanctifying waters, so that I might spring forth a river, a mighty body of water whose end cannot be known. Cry me a river – not a river of sighs, or of broody reflection. Become Boyne, and give birth to a multitude of almighties, so that not one god, but a thousand, can become deified in your pools of crystal absolution. And there, on your shores, John the Baptist and Finneces the Wise will immerse the poor in spirit so that they may have their eyes washed clean, and that they may see with perfect vision the *cloigtheach* beneath the waves.

The obscure belfry below, the one that chimes mysteriously from the bottom of the lake, or from the brooding sea in the evening, is not a stony bell-tower left standing from the time of Atlantis's destruction. Rather, it is that mystical something that must be awakened within you, that peeling of the bells that calls you to your ancient self – the you that was alive before the first of the ancient palaces were built, the you that is potent in the very matter of the universe.

Come down and ring the bells with the monks of the submarine domain, that realm that lies beneath the darkness of your unconscious, and there make music that will echo in the very caverns of the *sídhe*. Go down, and be a bell-ringer for the awakening of a multitude. Call the world to enlightenment with a chorus of sound and voice from the deep, and bring the unrestrained joy of that chthonic music to every ear and heart and soul.

6.5

Awaiting my salvation in Fiacc's Pool beneath Rosnaree

A good few years ago, I had a dream.

I was down at the River Boyne, at Rosnaree. That's a small but significant part of the world whose name, as we saw earlier, means the Wood of the King. I was surrounded by trees and water. The Boyne had burst its banks and the wood was flooded. I felt I was in danger. I don't know what from. I had a fear of water dreams. There was a belief in my family that certain water dreams are portents – warnings of a looming death. Dreams in which you are in peril on the water, or near water, were possible indicators of a coming passing. Having experienced such water dreams in advance of bereavement, I had come to believe in these portents.

In my dream at Rosnaree, I felt as if I was in some unquantifiable danger. Maybe it's just that I was in the water, and I could not see an immediate path to safety. Trees loomed up from the water, their lower parts invisible. There was no grass or dry land to be seen; no easy way out.

And that was it. There was no spectacular ending to the dream. No frightening occurrence, no uplifting finale. Rosnaree was flooded, and I was down there, in the river, in a familiar place that somehow seemed dark and foreboding.

I've never forgotten that brief dream. When I pass the scene, at the bottom of the steep hill that runs down from Rosnaree village into the dark woods on the southern bank of the Boyne, I think about that dream and what it might mean.

Years later, I'm still wondering if there was something about that short dream that is trying to address my mystical senses, to entice me to dissolve its arcane façade and to resolve its lucid deeper meaning.

And I wonder if, walking upon the road to Rosnaree, on the southern bank of the mighty Boyne, I might chance upon Finegas, pointing the way to Fiacc's pool, there in the Bend of the Boyne beneath lofty Cleitech.

With raised arm and outstretched finger, he might beckon me to the mystery pool, and tell me to become a fisherman.

'But I can't fish,' I protest.

'Everyone can fish,' he says.

'I don't have a fishing rod. And even if I did, I would not know how to use it.'

'If you say so,' he says impassively.

'If I say so? I do say so. I am no angler.'

'One day you couldn't ride a bike, and next day you could. So it will be with fishing.'

'I have no interest in fishing,' I retort.

'Then you have no interest in knowledge,' he replies, tersely.

'What knowledge?'

'All the knowledge that you will ever need,' he says.

Intrigued, I ask what this might have to do with fishing.

'I know about your dream,' he says.

'You do?'

'Yes. In the shadow of the trees, wading in the deep water, you are afraid. You fear that you will drown, and you see no obvious way out. You wonder if the flood is a portent. You fear that it means the death of someone, or something. So you ignore it, hoping it will go away. But it never does.'

'Maybe it has no meaning,' I say, wistfully.

The River Boyne in flood.

'Perhaps not. And if you really think that, you are welcome to leave my company immediately and carry on down the road.'

Before I learned to ride a bike, I thought that those who could were magicians. They could do something miraculous. I wanted to know how to do that. I wanted the knowledge.

I turn to Finegas.

'Show me how to fish.'

Finegas smiles.

'I don't need to show you,' he says. 'You already know.'

'Maybe I do,' I say, not knowing why I say it, because clearly I don't know how to fish.

'To get knowledge, you must wade out into the water, until you are chest-high in the waters of the Boyne. Can you swim?'

'Not very well.'

'All going well, you won't need to.'

'All going well?'

'Yes,' he replies. 'It's not possible to know what perils the future will bring. All you can do is make sure you are focused on the present. You can learn to swim now, just in case you need to swim later.'

I turn away again and look along the road into the distance.

'That's just fear,' Finegas says.

'What is?'

'You are still thinking about leaving – about returning to familiar roads and journeys. You worry that the water will overwhelm you.'

I don't answer. He might be right.

'There is a great salmon,' he says. 'It swims in the waters of the Well of Segais. It eats the nuts from the nine hazel trees that grow above the well. The salmon will come to Fiacc's pool, here beneath Rosnaree. The salmon will come to you. All you need to do is to brave the waters, to face your fears, and wait for the knowledge to come.'

'So I don't need to learn how to fish?'

'You must still catch the fish. And when you've caught it, you must eat it.'

'Should I cook it first?'

'Oh yes, you must cook it first. That's an important step.'

'Why?'

'You will see . . .'

᠀᠀᠀

There's nothing about fish or wise old druids in my dream. It's just a dream about water – a lot of water – in a location highly familiar yet gloomily distorted. And trees. Water and trees. The Boyne and the hazel, perhaps?

The great salmon, the one that brings knowledge, eats the nuts from the hazel trees at Segais.

How does a salmon gain knowledge from a hazelnut?

How does a salmon come to live in a well?

How does the salmon get from the well to the river, and from there to Fiacc's pool at Rosnaree?

These are all mechanical questions.

We should, perhaps, deal with mystical ones.

When and where did I burn my thumb on the *Bradán Feasa?*

When and where was I overwhelmed by the waters of Segais?

When and where did the *imbas* – the great knowledge – come to me, if at all?

Imbas – the great knowledge. Gnosis. Enlightenment. I wish that you would nourish me.

Perhaps I bought it in a bottle, sold by a street peddler on the road to Rosnaree?

'Enlightenment – one euro a bottle!' the peddler shouted.

Beware the peddler by the road, selling *imbas*. I would much rather have Finegas teach me to fish, than to quickly imbibe a bottle of false promises.

The Boyne at Oldbridge, looking south towards Glenmore.

And I wonder – who would I rather be, at Rosnaree? Would I rather be Fionn Mac Cumhaill or Cormac Mac Airt – both of whom are strongly associated with this ancient place known as the Wood of the King?

Finn burned his thumb while cooking the *Bradán Feasa*, and through fate and fortune he gained the *imbas* of the nine hazels of Segais.

Cormac did not wish to be buried with the 'pagan' kings at Brug na Bóinne. He died after choking on a salmon bone, or so it is said. Had Cormac denied himself the *imbas* – the sacred knowledge that so many would yearn for? Instead of eating the Salmon of Knowledge, did he choke upon it? Was he overwhelmed by it?

In my dream at Rosnaree, I felt I was in danger from the rising water of the Boyne. There seemed to be no way out. Was I afraid that I could become Cormac, cut off from the *imbas,* and denied, through my own obstinacy, a place with my ancestors?

Cormac's friends tried to take him to Newgrange, to be buried with the kings of old. So the story goes. But the Boyne rose up, and they could not cross. His bier was carried by the waters down to Rosnaree, where he was buried, on the southern bank of the river, on the opposite side of the Boyne to the great monuments of *Brug na Bóinne.* Cormac converted to Christianity in the years before his death. Had he forsaken the sacred *imbas* so that he could placate his new faith in a miracle worker from a far-distant land?

And I wonder now, all these years later, if the rising waters in my dream might have been related to my own misgivings – misgivings about the *imbas* that I sought and the faith that I longed to hold on to.

In my dream, was I trying to cross the Boyne, from the Christian side to the pagan? Was I afraid? Afraid to wade out from the southern bank, for fear that, in leaving my old faith behind, I might drown?

It seems to me now, in hindsight, that I might have feared choking on the salmon bone, instead of eating its flesh and gaining the great knowledge.

Who among us, setting out on a long journey, would choose dangerous and unfamiliar paths? Who would wade out into the Boyne at Rosnaree, instead of crossing the river by bridge at Drogheda or Slane? Which of us would stand in Fiacc's Pool beneath lofty Rosnaree, in peril, awaiting the arrival of a speckled fish that might never come?

❧   ❧   ❧

Bless me father, for I have sinned.

What is your sin?

I have forgotten the old ways, the ways of my ancestors.

The old ways are dead, my son. You must learn the new ways.

The old ways are not dead. They are merely sleeping, in the belly of a fish that swims beneath the nine hazels of Segais. I will wade out into the water now, towards Fiacc's Pool, and there await the coming of my salvation.

No one can come to the Father, except through me.

I do not wish to come to the Father. I wish to come to myself. I wish to come to myself through *imbas*, and to know myself in a way that I have never known myself. I will wait for the salmon, at Fiacc's Pool. And in the dim Wood of the King beneath Rosnaree, I will become Finn, wanting to be with my ancestors at *Brug na Bóinne*. And Finegas the wise will teach me poetry beneath Knowth, while we wait for the *Bradán Feasa*.

I cannot help you any more.

Thank you for trying.

Alone in my wanderings, I wonder if the waters will overwhelm me at Fiacc's Pool.

The waters rose at Segais, when faultless Bóinn approached it, against the wishes of the men who controlled it. Like the biblical Eve, Bóinn was castigated for desiring the knowledge of good and evil. Eve was forbidden from eating the fruit of the tree of the knowledge

An ancient salmon weir marks the likely location of Fiacc's Pool at Rosnaree.

of good and evil. Bóinn perhaps wanted to taste the salmon that ate from the sacred nuts of the hazel trees – the equivalent of the tree in Eden. They were *imbas* trees. They were knowledge. And knowledge is power.

And when I get to Fiacc's Pool, in the swirling waters of the Boyne, I hear Bóinn crying out to me.

'Go not widdershins around the well, as I have done,' she says. 'For it has not gone well for me.'

'What happened?' I ask.

'I went against the order of things. I ventured against the sun's course. I yearned to happen upon all the knowledge of deep Segais. But the *imbas* of Segais is very deep, and in a moment there I was overwhelmed.'

There is a sadness in her voice, a tone of regret. I meet that sadness, from time to time, at Brug na Bóinne. Alone in the evening, I hear the voice of Bóinn on the air:

'Go not wishershins around the well. For that is what I have done. And I have come undone.'

This section of the Boyne, between Knowth and Rosnaree, is the likely location of Fiacc's Pool where the Salmon of Knowledge was caught, according to tradition.

I tell her that they have named the river after her, and that her name lives on in the valley, spoken often by those from far and near.

'Yes,' she says. 'They named the river after me. But what for – fame or infamy?'

'I do not know.'

'Be careful how you approach the well,' she warns. 'There are none who can look to its bottom, although many have tried.'

And in my dream at Rosnaree, I fear being overwhelmed by the waters of Bóinn.

Sometimes, when the wind is right, I catch the sound of the Tara Mines train out at Brug na Bóinne. It runs from Drogheda to Navan, to collect the zinc ore mined there, and brings it back, through Drogheda, and on to Dublin Port. The train travels an old line beyond the hills on the southern side of the Boyne Valley.

Train signals are like traffic lights. Red means stop. Green means go. Amber means 'proceed with caution'.

Perhaps there should be an amber light at Segais, to warn the approacher to proceed with caution.

A salmon jumps the weir at the flood gate on the Boyne in Slane.

And I wonder sometimes, as we look out upon all the things we've done to the world and how we've tried to mould it to our liking, if we haven't dug too deeply at Tara Mines? Have we, perhaps, looked too deep into the well of Segais? Not knowing how to proceed with caution, are we overwhelmed by it?

Bóinn, bright Bóinn, a prehistoric mother archetype, a mother of our hopes, a river of our dreams – is the great river that flows from the spring that emerges from deep within the earth. Her clear waters emanate from the unfathomable depths of human thought and mind, and spirit – that pool of unconsciousness that we know exists within us, but which we seldom venture towards, for fear of peering into dark places.

'Water is the commonest symbol for the unconscious,' wrote C.G. Jung.[1] 'We must surely go the way of the waters, which always tend downward, if we would raise up the treasure, the precious heritage of the father.'[2]

'How deep is the well?' someone asks.

'There is none who can look to its bottom,' comes the reply.

But who can even stand there, and try? And why should we wish to look into the waters of the sacred well? Do we want *imbas*? Do we expect to drink the waters of Segais, and to taste honey? Or should we first expect to have to drink the soiled and spoilt water, before we reach the better parts? And what if we should walk to the well, and go sun-wise around it, on a proper course? Would we then avoid the fate of Bóinn, bright Bóinn, whose beauty was shattered by the gushing waters of a well that ran so deep it could form a huge river?

We would have a honey well, a fountain of delight, but we know, somehow, that in order to see to its bottom, we must go widdershins around it.

Finegas spent years by the Boyne.

There was a belief in former days that poetry was revealed to the poet on the verge of the water.[3] In the minds of the ancients, wisdom and water were connected. A spring or well was not just sacred because it was a source of water, a key ingredient of life, but because it was seen as a source of wisdom.

There is wisdom aplenty to be found at the well of Segais, if one cares to look deep enough. However, it is the nature of one's approach to the well that will determine what one finds in its depths.

We cannot venture to the well with the expectation of instant wisdom. One does not become endowed with wisdom simply by taking one look into the depths of themselves. A visit to Segais must be an immersive experience – metaphorically. And it must be a lasting experience. The wisdom initiate needs to come back repeatedly. Having learned how to correctly approach the well, one must continue to return there often.

In the pre-Newgrange days of the Mesolithic, when the inhabitants of the Boyne Valley were hunter gatherers, the food sources were rather interesting. Among the most popular foods in those pre-farming times were wild boar, salmon, trout, eels and hazelnuts.[4] There were said to have been two pigs in Newgrange – one nicely fattened, ready to be slaughtered for a feast, and one already on a roasting spit, ready to be eaten.[5] The legends of Newgrange might well recall the culinary preferences of ancient times.

The salmon magically finds its way to the one who prophecy says will eat it.

The initiate consumes the fish – through accident and fate and not through mere desire – and gains all the knowledge of Segais.

This is no apple from the Garden of Eden.

This is the salmon of the magic hazels, consumed at Brug na Bóinne, Ireland's early Eden.

The Bend of the Boyne: Ireland's early Eden.

6.6

The synchronicity of the swans

In recent years, I have found that my senses have come into sharp focus around certain mythical imagery associated closely with the Boyne Valley area. My study and research has taken me towards examining the metaphor and symbolism of myth. This has yielded interesting results. I told a friend how I seemed to be engaged in an interesting process of following 'hunches' and 'leads' and that this process almost always bears fruit.

When dealing with the area of science versus mysticism, I can, by and large, only deal with my own experiences and how they have forged my thoughts and beliefs around the whole question of the rational versus the esoteric. Currently, I am agnostic. The best and simplest definition of agnosticism I can offer is this – I neither have proof in the existence of a god or an afterlife, or of other worlds and other realms of spirit or consciousness; nor do I have proof that they don't exist. I remain very open-minded. I am grateful for this open-mindedness. It prevents me from blindly following a path of enquiry without considering the alternatives. Recently, my work has focused on the alternatives.

I have been experiencing synchronicities – strange and wonderful coincidences and happenings – since the very beginning of my researches into myths and monuments years ago. I initially thought them to be what Richard Moore and I called 'spooky coincidences'[1] but over the years I've come to see them less as something to be wary of and more something to be enthralled and inspired by. My own

Whooper swans at a pond in a field near Knowth,
where they regularly congregate in winter time.

experience has been that when a synchronicity occurs, it's like an affirmation that I'm on the right track with something.

But is all this just some sort of mystical woo? Is this just indulgence in some new age wishy-washy nonsense? Philip Freund, a novelist, poet, short-story writer, documentary film writer, television dramatist and playwright as well as essayist, literary critic and anthropologist, wrote about hunches leading to discoveries. Freund was a man described in his obituary as a 'true polymath'.[2] If ever there was somebody who embodied the persona of the *Samildánach* – the 'many-gifted' – it was Freund. Here's what Freund has to say about science and intuition:

> The history of science is filled with instances of noted workers in all fields who testify in their memoirs that a 'hunch', a perhaps inexplicable ray of light, suddenly led them to a major discovery. Is it Newton under the apple tree, or Galvani watching his wife cook frogs' legs? Some of these invaluable 'finds' seem to have been pure accidents... But what inspires

Whooper swans wintering near Newgrange.

the author of a scientific hypothesis to choose one route, one direction of approach, rather than another, when many offer themselves with equal persuasiveness to him or confront him with an equal opacity? Whence comes the 'hunch', what directs the 'ray of light', the seemingly lucky chance that without warning illuminates the right dark path to be followed?[3]

I was walking the dog on a Friday night, going to collect my sons from football. As I walked along on a very cold, icy night (the first of that winter), I thought about all the research I had been doing and how it all seems to have produced fascinating insights. A great deal of this research work involved stories about animals and mythic creatures. A great deal of it involved following hunches and intuition. And a great deal of it yielded interesting results. A thought came into my head, along these lines:

'You've really hit on something here, Anthony. This is the sweet spot.'

Just as I thought that, I heard what might have been children's voices in the distance. I looked along the road, half expecting to see my sons and their friends coming towards me. But the road was deserted. There were no cars and no people at all, which is unusual because it's normally a very busy road.

Again I thought I heard a voice or two, but this time they were above me, so I looked up instinctively, and caught sight of a formation of eight whooper swans flying southwards, directly over my head.

The significance of this beautiful creature (for those of you unfamiliar with the myths of Newgrange) is that the whooper swan has been wintering at Newgrange for a long time – quite probably since before the monuments were built there 5,000 years ago. Some of the predominant myths about Newgrange, and the supernatural characters associated with it, involve swans. The most famous of these is the Aislinge Óenguso, the Dream of Angus Óg.

An ancient Bronze Age enclosure, possibly the site of Caiseal Oenguso, where the whooper swans regularly converge when they arrive in the Bend of the Boyne in October.

Were these eight swans among the first to arrive into the Boyne Valley for the winter of 2015? Every winter, thousands of whooper swans come to Ireland from Iceland, landing *en masse* in Donegal and then diverging into smaller groups to winter at various sites on the island. The area around Newgrange is an important wintering ground. It regularly sees more than 50 swans in winter, making it one of the predominant sites for the whoopers.[4]

Less than two days after seeing the whooper swans fly overhead in Drogheda, I received an SMS text message from a friend of mine, Ollie Fitzpatrick, who keeps a close eye on things out in the valley. Over the past few winters, he has been keeping me informed about the arrival and departure of the whooper swans. This is what I received from him:

Whoopers at Knowth Anthony. About 8. Just arrived.

I smiled when I received it. The first thing to come into my mind was the thought that perhaps these were the same eight that had flown over my head on Friday night.

So I feel inclined to continue following these lines of mythic research that are opening up before me. There is something in the mythology of the Boyne monuments that begs to be explored, deeply and extensively, and open-mindedly, because they are more than just stories. I believe they contain an essence of what the monuments were all about, and an insight into the mind of distant ancestors. Are these stories at all relevant today? Absolutely. They are a revelation – a vista into the soul itself, and I don't believe it's at all coincidental that this mythology has survived from time immemorial to tell a story to the people of today.

The process of mythic investigation has been an epiphany for me, a process of recondite introspection that has been at times both intimidating and riveting. It's brought me right into the centre of my own story on this planet – the reason I am here.

6.7

Rekindling the powerful image of the druid Elcmar

Some of the oldest tales about Newgrange were written down in the Old Irish period. There is, of course, no easy way to tell when these stories first originated, but there are scholars who believe that it is possible that some of them have their origins in the Neolithic, when the great monuments of the Bend of the Boyne were built.

> In the case of Newgrange, we must therefore suppose not only that there was some cultural link between its builders and the first speakers of Goidelic in Ireland, but that this link exercised a formative influence on the belief system of the latter. Again, the survival of some versions of these ancient doctrines in the medieval literature indicates that the world-view of the Irish remained, at least in certain respects, astonishingly stable throughout the intervening centuries: the Boyne legends were still relevant, and important, in the Christian period.[1]

The ancient stories of Newgrange include *De Gabáil int Síde* ('The Taking of the Otherworld Mound'), *Tochmarc Étaíne* ('The Wooing of Étaín') and *Altram Tighe Dá Mheadar* ('The Fosterage of the House of Two Vessels'). In *De Gabáil int Síde*, it is Dagda, the chief of the gods, who owns Newgrange, and is tricked out of it by his son Oengus (known as the Mac Óc). In the latter two texts, it is Elcmar, the husband of Oengus's mother Bóinn, who owns the síd.

The crescent moon and Venus in winter over Síd in Broga (Newgrange).

In *Tochmarc Étaíne*, there is an incredibly powerful image of Elcmar, standing on Newgrange[2] at Samhain in druidic garb and carrying in his hand a mysterious but potent symbol – a fork of white hazel. It is Samhain, that very special time of the year at the threshold of winter, a time when 'when the dead might reach out to the living'.[3]

Elcmar has evidently arrived into the ownership of Síd in Broga through his power as a druid, and a poet, and a diviner. The vision is an extraordinary one, filled with druidic symbolism and divine energy. Here is the magician of Brugh na Bóinne, the one who occupies a privileged position as the wise elder of his community. In this guise we see Elcmar as the prehistoric cult leader, the chief priest of the tribe; the commander, perhaps, of the community that built the great monument. And, we might even venture to suggest, its chief astronomer?

As the supposed original owner of Síd in Broga, it is clear that Elcmar held a privileged position in our ancient stories. Some accounts hold that the original inhabitants of Newgrange were Bóinn and her spouse, Nuadu Nechtain (yes, the two names are sometimes combined), otherwise known as Elcmar. This name – Elcmar – translates as the 'envious one', quite possibly because of the extramarital wanderings of his wife, Bóann, with the Dagda; and yet, spellbound under the considerable magical abilities of this interlocutor, the spellbound Elcmar was said to have known nothing of their union – even though they produced the child Aengus Óg in his absence.

Perhaps the envy was wrought by Aengus Óg, who managed to trick Elcmar out of the ownership of Newgrange using little more than wit and ancient Ireland's version of a clever legal argument.

The most striking symbol of Elcmar's presence at Síd in Broga is undoubtedly the fork of white hazel. The hazel tree was revered in ancient Ireland for a number of reasons. It was said to have grown near water, and indeed the wood of the hazel was the primary tool of the diviner. But it was also said to have had mystical powers of protection, and could ward off snakes among other evils.[4] Hazel trees were said to have grown over sacred wells which were the source of Ireland's great rivers, the Boyne and the Shannon. The hazel nut is associated with wisdom – not necessarily wisdom of sciences, but perhaps a more esoteric perception, which included 'inspiration and the knowledge of poetry'.[5]

It was the sacred hazel nuts of wisdom that eventually gave Fionn his great insights, gained from the Salmon of Knowledge. In our tradition, it is said that the salmon gains its knowledge from the nuts of the hazel that drop into the sacred well. Every spot on the salmon's back represents each nut that the fish has consumed.[6]

Elcmar didn't need a weapon. He had a fork of hazel, and hazel was noted for its power of protection against malevolence. It gave protection against evil spirits and even snakes.[7]

We come to a question about Elcmar, a quandary that must be explored to better ascertain his influence – if there should be any – upon

The archaeologist's measuring poles.

the modern interpretation of Síd in Broga, the place the Cistercians first called the New Grange.

The question is this: was Elcmar a scientist or a mystic?

Was his rod of hazel a scientific instrument or a holy implement?

Was it, perhaps, both?

The modern-day rod-bearers are the archaeologists who come, by and large, to the Brugh by the Boyne with little care for the fairy tales and fireside stories of old. Their rods are utilitarian, functional, and prosaic. They are yard-sticks used to measure height, width and depth of archaeological 'features'. They appear in photographs to show scale. There is no Elcmar here, holding court in the *Síd*, no Oengus Óg to bewitch him with cunning. There is only the 'material evidence', the one thing so treasured by the archaeologist.

During the excavation of Newgrange, Professor Michael O'Kelly decided that a spring of water that emerged from between two orthostats in the passage should be piped underground. It wouldn't be

*Síd in Broga (Newgrange), where the magician and druid Elcmar
could be seen with his fork of white hazel, according to myth.*

acceptable for tourists to Newgrange to get their feet wet in the process
of visiting the monument. But how do we know the spring was not
an essential element of the monument's design? Was Newgrange built
upon that spring for sacred and ritual purposes? Is that why Elcmar
held a dowsing rod of hazel in his hand?[8]

'The trouble with archaeologists,' the late Boyne valley folklorist
Bean Uí Chairbre would say, 'is that they have no imagination.'[9]

'The trouble with archaeologists,' the ever-living Elcmar might say,
'is that they do not possess the art of divination.'

Lacking a divining rod, or eschewing it completely, the archaeologist has come to Newgrange only with a spade, to dig – a greater
weapon than anyone possessed on that Samhain day when Oengus Óg
came to Brug na Bóinne to challenge Elcmar. 'Heed not the stories of
fairies and otherworldly folk,' the archaeologist might say. 'Bring the
spades, and trowels, and yard-sticks, and we shall dig it up, measure
it, and know its secrets.'

Are its secrets yet revealed?

Ironically, there is one similarity between the measuring instruments of the archaeologists and the white fork of hazel brandished by Elcmar. Both are ground-penetrating implements used to reveal things that are hidden. Elcmar divines for water, among other things. The archaeologist divines for features using resistivity and gradiometry. Here, it seems, the similarities between the archaeologists and the archetypal magician of Newgrange end. The diviner lives beyond the confines of rationality, analysis and conformance to dogma. He inhabits mystical realms.

'Newgrange is a tomb, a dead thing,' the archaeologists declare.

'Síd in Broga is a living thing, and the spirits of the ancestors come hither from the Land of Promise, to remind us of its true purpose,' cries out Elcmar in retort.

The fork of white hazel is the symbol that is all too often missing from the modern interpretation of Newgrange. Today, it is called a tomb. It has become a dead thing. The image of Elcmar standing on the mound in all his power reminds us that the creative and intuitive

Sunbeams emerge from behind Síd in Broga on a winter evening.

A rainbow touches the earth near Newgrange.

side of our nature must not give way to the deadening image of the archaeologist's measuring rod. Yes, the archaeological interpretation of Newgrange is hugely important, and we are extremely grateful for all the light that they have shed on these wonderful ancient places. But they do not hold a premium on the interpretation of these sites.

In ancient times, the poet held almost equal court in terms of status with the king. Today, we should allow the druid Elcmar to hold equal standing with the archaeologist. This means accepting that Newgrange has a power beyond what can be measured with a red and white pole. This means empowering aspects of ourselves that are hidden in the darkness of the *sídhe,* and shining that solstice light into the darkness to awaken something latent in us. We must allow our Elcmar nature to stand on the *sídhe* at Samhain. Without that inculcation, that instilling of the wisdom from within, Síd in Broga loses its power, and becomes just the New Grange, that heap of stones that once was a tomb but now is an empty vessel.

The real danger in depriving ourselves of our Elcmar image is that everything thus follows the same path – everything becomes inanimate and materialistic and our view becomes perhaps even nihilistic. Why are we here at all? Our Elcmar image allows us to stand in the power of our presence, in all that it encompasses – scientific and spiritual, awesome and terrible – and to engage fully with the journey of life. Thus, the childlike initiate becomes the supreme poet of the Boyne, the one who has tasted the Salmon of Knowledge. To the rationalist, the monument is called Newgrange, and it is a pile of stones from the past – the corpse of something it once was. To the poet, the monument is called Síd in Broga, and it is a crystal bower, a place where the sun eternally shines.

7.

Cosmology

7.1

The Milky Way in Irish mythology and cosmogony

The Milky Way has been known by several names and phrases in Irish mythology and folklore. Principal among its names seems to have been *Bealach na Bó Finne*, which means the Way of the White Cow. In this respect, it seems to have been regarded as a heavenly reflection of the River Boyne. A variant of this is *Bóthar na Bó Finne*, the Road of the White Cow.

> Many cultures have connected the Milky Way with the concept of a river or road. The ancient Akkadians called it... 'the River of the Divine Lady'.[1]

The goddess Bóinn's name is from *Bó* and *Find*, together meaning 'White Cow'. In the Dindshenchas, we are told that the Boyne river was formed when Bóinn approached Nechtain's Well and it overflowed, washing her along the river, mutilating her, and finally carrying her out to sea where she was drowned.[2] There, we are told, her lapdog Dabilla was turned into the Rockabill Islands. This is undoubtedly a creation myth.

A feature of some Indo-European cosmogonic mythology is the dismemberment or mutilation of a deity or giant or a monster in legends about origins or the naming of landscape features.[3] In fact, this dismemberment in creation myth features in other parts of the world too:

272

*Heaven's mirror: the Milky Way (Bealach na Bó Finne) reflected
in the River Boyne (Abhainn na Bó Finne) near Newgrange.*

> The shamanistic aspect of the religion of the Stone Age hunter
> societies presupposes…the dismemberment and/or sacrifice
> of a primordial deity.[4]

Other creation myths in which a female deity are ripped apart include the Mesoamerican story of Coatlicue, who is torn to pieces to form the earth and sky, and the Babylonian myth of Tiamat, who is dismembered by the god Marduk.[5] In Norse myth, the primordial deity Ymir (who is male) is killed, and heaven is created from his skull and mountains from his ribs.[6]

While the story of Bóinn's destructive approach to Nechtain's Well has always been considered a myth about how the Boyne river was formed, it could be a creation myth relating equally to the earth and the sky. There is at least one other Irish creation myth relating to the origin of the Milky Way, as we will see.

One fascinating possibility, drawn from the studies of world mythology by E.J. Witzel, is that the myth of Bóinn and Nechtain's Well might have its origins in pre-agricultural Ireland and, consequently, this myth would predate Newgrange and the other great monuments of Brú na Bóinne. Witzel says that the killing and dismemberment of the primordial giant was substituted in Neolithic and later societies by the killing and offering of domesticated local animals.[7]

There are other Irish names and phrases for the Milky Way. These include:

Ceann Síne

Síne is 'chain', and *ceann* is 'head' or 'chief', perhaps even an 'end point'. An end point would be interesting with regards to the movement of the sun, moon and planets along the ecliptic, which intersects the Milky Way at two points in the sky. Perhaps one of these points was considered the place where the heavenly cycles began and ended?

Síog na Spéire

The Streak or Stripe of the Sky.

Earball na Lárach Báine

The Tail of the White Mare. The *Láir Bhán* (white mare) is considered by some to be an ancient sovereignty goddess. Fascinatingly, Ronald Hicks says that, in Irish tradition, 'the moon was referred to as *an lair bhán*, 'the white mare'.'[8] This idea is similar in some respects to the idea of the moon as a white cow, *bó fhinne*.[9] One old Samhain custom in Ireland involved the procession of the *Láir Bhán* (White Mare) from house to house. People would blow on cows' horns and the party was headed by a person dressed in a white robe or sheet who was known as the 'White Mare'.[10]

There is a place in Scotland called Larach Na Ba Baine, which means the 'place of the white cow'. The story associated with this place says that it was the spot where the cow first lay down to rest.[11]

There is a famous, or rather infamous, account of a bizarre inauguration ritual involving a white mare in which the Cenél Conaill, a northern sept of the Uí Néill dynasty in Donegal, participated.

The Milky Way over the Boyne at Oldbridge.

The account was given by a twelfth century Welsh scholar, Giraldus Cambrensis, whose writings about Ireland have been described as a 'hatchet job'.[12] Nonetheless, the ritual has echoes in the Hindu *as-va-medha* (horse sacrifice)[13] and is worth recounting in summarised form. The one to be inaugurated embraces a white mare, ('professing himself to be a beast also'[14]). The mare is killed, chopped into pieces and boiled in water. A bath is then made from the same water and the man sits in this bath surrounded by all his people. Together, they eat the meat of the white mare that has been killed. The man drinks from the water of the bloody bath in which he is immersed by dipping his mouth into the water. 'When this unrighteous rite has been carried out, his kingship and dominion has been conferred.'[15]

Mór-Chuing Argait

This is a name given for the Boyne in the Dinshenchas, meaning 'Great Silver Yoke',[16] which might also have been a description of the Milky Way. Several times in Irish mythology, swans are described as having a silver chain linking them. For instance, in Aislinge Oengusso the swans have silver chains around them and even when in human form the women at the lake are linked in pairs by silver chains.[17]

Another story involving swans, chains and Newgrange (Síd in Bróga) is the tale from the Táin Bó Cuailnge of how Sétanta (Cúchulainn) was born. Deichtine was driving a chariot with her brother Conchobhar, who was the king of Ulster. A troublesome flock of birds was eating all the plants and grasses at Emain Plain, so the men of Ulster got their chariots together to chase them away. They chased the birds southwards over Sliab Fuait and Breg Plain.

> There were nine scores of birds with a silver chain between each couple. Each score went in its own flight, nine flights altogether, and two birds out in front of each flight with a yoke of silver between them.[18]

Smir Find Fedlimthi

The White Marrow of Fedlimid, also from the Dindshenchas (poem Boand I)[19]. The idea of the Milky Way representing marrow is a curious and perhaps obscure notion. In the Táin Bó Cuailnge we encounter the *smirammair,* or *smirchomairt,* a 'marrow-tub'[20] which is, in effect, a bath made from marrow and crushed bones used in the treatment of wounded warriors.[21] There are obvious similarities here with the bath made from the cut-up remains and blood from the white mare, in which the king must bathe and eat and drink in order to be confirmed as king.

Claí Mór na Réaltaí

The Great Fence/Ditch/Dyke of the Stars. This is fascinating, not least because of its possible connections with several Irish creation myths. Of particular interest here are the stories about the Black Pig's Dyke and the dismemberment of the monster called the Mata. A prominent tale abounds in several parts of Ireland about a mysterious black pig which is said to have run through the landscape, following a route often called 'The Valley of the Black Pig'[22] or the 'Black Pig's Race'. A linear earthwork known as the Black Pig's Dyke is found, incomplete, in nine different counties, stretching from Sligo in the northwest of Ireland to Armagh, in the northeast.[23]

> The names attached to the earthwork are strange. 'The Black Pig's Race', or 'Rut', or 'Valley' (*Gleann na Muice Duibhe*), and the 'Worm Ditch' or 'Dyke'. The legends attached to the former name are very grotesque; and their main drift is that a magical pig, originally from Meath, raged westward through Ireland, and tore up this deep furrow with its snout.[24]

The folklore attests that when this mystery pig runs again, the end of the world will come, or some great war involving particularly great slaughter for those living in the Valley of the Black Pig, but that the slaughter will end when the pig is killed.[25]

The Milky Way is seen as a bright ribbon of countless stars, stretching across the sky. It is actually a complete circle, but the entire ring of stars cannot be seen at any one time. Running through the Milky Way is a murky band known as the Dark Rift or Great Rift. Is it possible that the story of the Black Pig tearing up a furrow across the land is a creation myth, but one pertaining to both sky and ground?

*The author contemplates the vastness of the cosmos and the beauty
of the 'Great Silver Yoke' at the beach near Clogherhead.*

In the Táin Bó Cuailnge, 'the bull paws up the earth, or perhaps digs a trench'.[26] At the conclusion of the Táin, the white bull Finnbennach is torn to pieces (dismembered) by the brown bull, Donn Cuailnge, and its remains are scattered across Ireland, forming different landscape features.[27] This is reminiscent of the story of Bóinn and Nechtain's Well, in which the dismemberment of Bóinn leads to the formation of the River Boyne (Milky Way). Are these two stories different versions of a similar (and possibly very ancient) creation myth? In one, the destruction of a white bull leads to the creation of new landscape features. In the other, the goddess is the white cow, and her destruction leads to the formation of the Boyne, which we have seen has obvious connections with the Milky Way.

The earthwork known as the Black Pig's Dyke is also sometimes referred to as the 'Worm Ditch' or 'Dyke'.[28] We are told that 'the worm or *peist* was a dragon whose folds left the sinuous track over hill and dale...'[29] There was a strange creature in the Irish oral tradition called the *Oillphéist,* a fabulous reptile or dragon-like monster which was said to have cut out the route of the River Shannon.[30] This beast has obvious parallels with another mysterious creature known as The Mata, the monster that was dismembered, torn limb from limb at Brú na Bóinne and tossed piece by piece into the River Boyne, after which his various limbs and bodily portions created new parts of the landscape, including the ford of the River Liffey.[31] But before he had been killed by the men of Erin, the Mata had first 'licked up Boyne till it became a valley'.[32]

Is it a stretch of the imagination to suggest that the myths about the Valley of the Black Pig, the *Oillphéist* and the Mata might be connected with the Dark Rift of the Milky Way? Certainly if the Mata licked up the Boyne this suggests that the river was there in the first instance and that the monster was responsible for removing its water, as if gouging out the Dark Rift from the river of the sky. Here again, in the Mata myth, we encounter the theme of dismemberment leading to the creation of something. The monster's ribs (*cliath,* 'hurdle of its frame', ie its breast[33]) reach the ford of the Liffey in Dublin, 'whence Áth Cliath is said'.[34] Fascinatingly, there is a connection here with the *Claí Mór na Réaltaí.* In the Metrical Dindshenchas version of the tale, there is a mysterious quatrain about a palisade (fence) in the ford:

Who was the wright that planted the palisade ?
in its great size he set it in the ford :
what is this palisade, we wonder?
it shall abide in the pool till Doomsday.[35]

The bull pawing up the earth or creating a furrow in the Táin could also be connected to the Milky Way. The bull of the sky, Taurus, is above Orion with its horns immersed in the bright river of the sky. The story of Donn Cuailnge scattering Finnbennach's remains is unquestionably a creation myth, but can we now also assume that it possibly relates to the Milky Way? There are three stories here which share common themes. The dismemberment of a goddess (the white cow) leads to the formation of the Boyne/Milky Way. The Mata licks up the Boyne/Milky Way (forming the Dark Rift?) before being dismembered, and one part of him – his ribs or the frame of his chest – reach the ford of the River Liffey in Dublin, forming a mysterious fence or palisade. And the Finnbennach (white bull) is torn to pieces, its bits scattered around the place to make new landscape features, including, significantly, two river fords – at Athlone and Trim (Áth Troim). Even more significant is the relating, in Joseph Dunn's translation of the Táin, the fact that Donn Cuailnge 'sent its [Finnben-

Sgríob Chlann Uisnich (the Milky Way) over Dowth.

280

nach's] ribs (*clíathac*) from him to Dublin, which is called Áth Cliath'.[36] There's a white theme also – the white cow is dismembered, as is the white mare (the Láir Bhán) and the white bull (Finnbennach).

One more possible link to the Dark Rift is present in the *Cath Maige Tuired,* the Battle of Moytura, which refers to a large track, big enough to be the boundary ditch of a province, which is called 'The Track of the Dagda's Club'.[37] This is, we are told, created when the Dagda (the chief of the Tuatha Dé Danann and original owner of Newgrange in some of the myths) drags his giant club along the ground.[38]

Slabhra Lugh

Lugh's Chain. One of the chief Tuatha Dé Danann deities, Lugh Lamhfada (Lugh of the Long Arm), is said to have worn the Milky Way around his neck.

> It was claimed of Lugh, the Superman of these wonder-tales, that on a morning when he stood on the rampart of Tara, people thought the sun had risen in the west, so bright did his countenance shine. The Milky Way he wore as a silver chain around his neck ...[39]

This description of Lugh, with his long arm and an ability to hurl a weapon over a long distance, suggests an underlying cosmological aspect as the constellation we know today as Orion:

> It is this image, of a huge god-like figure casting weapons from his powerful arm, which brings to mind the constellation Orion, which in one form could be seen as a giant warrior with his upraised arm appearing to 'throw' the sun, moon and planets along the zodiac.[40]

Sgríob Chlann Uisnich

Track[41] of the Children of Uisneach. This last one is contained in a beautiful folk memory, recalled in Scotland and in Nova Scotia[42] but relating to an Irish myth (Deidre and the Sons of Uisneach) which appears to be the recounting of an ancient creation myth about the Milky Way. In this story, the Milky Way is known as *Sgríob Chlann Uisnich.*

In Uist the Milky Way was known as *'Slighe Chlann Uisne,'* the way of the Clan Uisne, or *'Sliabh Chlann Uisne,'* declivity of the Clan Uisne.[43]

> Sliabh Chlann Uisne
> Nan cursair geala,
> Is caoine beus
> *Na gleus na h-eala.*
> Declivity of the Clan Uisne
> Of the white coursers,
> Of fairer carriage
> Than the graceful swan.

It is not surprising to see the Milky Way described in conjunction with the swan. The constellation we know today as Cygnus may have been important to Stone Age astronomers and it appears to fly along the heavenly river.

In the Nova Scotia version of Deirdre and the Sons of Uisneach, 'the origin of the Milky Way galaxy is depicted as emerging from two trees separated by a loch, as if to complete an arch between them'.[44] This episode is placed in the well-known Ulster tale of Deirdre, whose lover, Noíse, is one of the Children of Uisneach.

> ... the sons of Uisneach are killed in a great, unnamed battle, after which Deidire falls into the grave with the men. The bodies of the two lovers are exhumed and reburied on either side of the burial mound. Soon a tree grows from each grave and rises until the two join. This arouses a great deal of vengeful malice in an unnamed king, who orders that the trees be cut down. Soon another pair of trees grows and joins until the king has them cut down as well. This sequence of events recurs repeatedly until the king decides to have the bodies placed on either side of a loch, a distance too great for the trees to span. Between the trees a cluster of stars gathers in a light trail, *Sgríob Chlann Uisnich* [track of the Children of Uisneach].[45]

7.2

Watching the northerly march
of the sun near midsummer

In recent years, during the summer, I've been tracking the northerly progress of the sunsets as we march inevitably towards summer solstice and the longest days of the year. As much as I love the approach of midsummer, watching the sunsets is always tinged with sadness for me.

It is difficult to live at any latitude so removed from the equator that the difference in the length of day from midwinter to midsummer is enormous. It's not so difficult to live in Ireland in summer, when the days are long and there is a great spurt of life and growth. Winter is a very different story. The days are short, and are often shortened further by a darkness that is creeping and all-encompassing. Immersed in this darkness, all you can do is accept it, and perhaps embrace it, and wait for the days to lengthen.

Summer then arrives rather abruptly. In late March, the clocks go forward by an hour. Where previously the sun was setting around 6.00 pm, now it sets at 7.00 pm, and it doesn't get dark until nearly 8.00. Because it's the time of equinox, the sun's rising and setting positions on the eastern and western horizons are moving at their greatest speed. The days are rapidly getting longer from Imbolc (the ancient Celtic spring festival of early February), through spring equinox, and on towards Bealtaine (early May). Before Daylight Saving Time kicks in, you are probably driving to and from work in the dark (if you work

A dramatic sunset viewed from Millmount in Drogheda in early June,
a few weeks before summer solstice.

regular hours), and find that the only daylight activities you can par-take in (apart from whatever work you do) are at weekends, when you try to cram it all in.

From late March onward, you can start to enjoy the 'stretch in the evenings', as it is commonly referred to here in Ireland. And very quickly, within a month, you've gone from driving home in the dark to enjoying brightness until well after 9pm.

Approaching midsummer, the sunsets occur quite late in the day. In late May, the sun sets at about 9.30 pm. By Midsummer's Day, the sunset is around 9.50 pm. And by that time, the nights do not get fully dark.

I love the height of summer. And I love the long evenings. I enjoy the extra light. It invigorates my spirit. There is something about the lingering of the light that I have always connected with hope, and vi-tality. I suppose there's probably nothing unusual about that.

However, part of the sadness that I feel, even at this time of year, stems from the realisation that inevitably the sun will reach a certain maximum setting azimuth and, after halting there for a few days, will begin to start heading south again. No sooner do the glorious days of summer arrive and suddenly the pendulum swings against us.

Midsummer brings some glorious days in the Boyne Valley. They are warm and sunny and the whole valley comes alive with the business of summer. People are out in droves, walking, playing, relaxing. On days like those, you might say to yourself, 'if it was like this all the time you'd never want to leave'.

But some of us are so married to the place – despite the sometimes endless rain, and the short cold days of winter – that we never leave it anyway.

The swifts and swallows and house martins, having recently arrived back from their faraway wintering grounds in Africa, perhaps conversely remind us of our own rooting to place, our connection to home, something that, until the invention of powered flight, was largely intrinsic to our lives as humans. We might have ventured across the globe as a species, but locally, once we find home, we tend to stay there. And sometimes, bound to that spot on the earth by our sense of belonging, and perhaps reinforced by our sense of community, we might wish that, like the swallow, we could just alight into the great air and fly off somewhere else for the winter, leaving the harsh chill behind.

One of the other things that makes me sad, even on those lovely long evenings of summer, is the fact that the relentless movement of the sun, and the consequent brightening and darkening of the days, is an eternal reminder of the fleeting and changing nature of our own lives. There, reflected in the everyday movements of that golden ball upon which we depend for so much, we see in vivid reality the corruptible nature of our own carnal selves. Just as the day rises tentatively in the east, and the noon comes brightly to strengthen the day, the evening arrives all too swiftly and the day is spent. All this is extended and magnified in the great drama of the seasons, and all too quickly

Sunset near the Hill of Slane, viewed from Dowth.

the autumn arrives, with its fallen leaves and drooping spirits ushering in the harsh winter.

So even as we watch the sun dropping down onto the far green-grey hills in the warm evening, we contemplate the relentless march of time, and of season, and how the winters and summers rise and fall with alarming haste. And we think back, perhaps, to the metaphorical dark and bright seasons in our own lives – times when we might have enjoyed a fulsome vitality, or times when maybe there was darkness or a lack of light. We might think of people – friends, relatives or acquaintances – upon whose lives the sun set all too soon.

All of this gives us good reason to enjoy, as much as possible, while we have the time, and while we might be able to, the glorious coming of the long evenings of summer.

And perhaps, as we watch that sinking red orb strike the horizon, we might remember also the ancient ancestors who possibly stood at the same spot and watched that same sun disappear into the earth.

7.3

Orion carries the summer solstice sun across the sky

I wrote this on midsummer's day.

The longest days of the year have arrived. The sun's rising and setting positions have reached their most northerly points along the horizon and these rising points are now 'standing still' - hence the word solstice, or in Irish *grianstad*, meaning, literally, 'stopped sun'.

The further north you are located from the equator, the longer the days in summer, and the shorter in winter. Here in Ireland, in the Boyne Valley, the sun rises before 5.00 am on summer solstice and sets around 10.00 pm. Even in the middle of the night, there is no real darkness as the whole northern horizon remains bathed in light. This is a result of the fact that the sun does not go far enough below the horizon at midsummer for Astronomical Twilight to end.

Something else that's really interesting is happening right now as the sun crosses the sky on these, the longest days. If you could somehow darken the sun, mimicking what happens in a total eclipse, you'd see that the sun is currently positioned directly above Orion. In fact, at summer solstice in this modern epoch, the sun appears to be 'carried' across the sky by this great anthropomorphic warrior/god/hunter constellation, in his hand, at the top of his upraised arm. Further to this is the fact that the sun is currently located in one of the two positions where it appears to 'cross' the Milky Way. Astronomers today call the sun's path the ecliptic. This imaginary ring through the sky intersects

Orion, Sirius and the moon over the Boyne near Drogheda.

the Milky Way in two places – one above Orion and the other beneath Ophiuchus, between Sagittarius and Scorpius. It just so happens that in our lifetime, these positions correspond with the location of the summer solstice and winter solstice sun, respectively.

It is fascinating that the Boyne river, along which the greatest megalithic passage-tombs in Europe were built, has a name that is the same as the old Irish name for the Milky Way – *Bealach na Bó Finne,* the Way of the White Cow.

In mythology, there are many gods and warriors, but some particularly interesting ones which might be candidates for an early Irish Orion. One of these is Lugh Lamhfada, Lugh of the Long Arm (or the long throw, perhaps). In the ancient mind, was it perhaps Lugh who was seen to 'throw' the sun, moon and planets from his upraised hand?

There are other characters of mythology that are interesting. Amergin, leader of the Milesians, was known as Amergin of the Bright Knee. The star that we know today as Rigel has an Arabic name which means 'bright knee'. Amergin asked 'who but I knows the place where the sun sets, who but I knows the ages of the moon?'[1] The Annals of the Four Masters says the Milesians arrived in Ireland at Bealtaine in 1694 BC.[2] On that date, the sun was above Orion, being carried across the sky. Because of an effect of the wobble of the earth's axis called Precession of the Equinoxes, the sun's position on the ecliptic on a specific day of the year (for example, on the solstices and equinoxes) is slowly moving westwards through the ecliptic. When the Milesians arrived in 1694BC, their bright-kneed leader set foot on the shore of the Boyne river at the moment the sun was being carried by the constellation Orion – a grouping of stars that might have been known then as Amergin. Nowadays, the sun's position at Bealtaine has moved so that it is beneath Aries. It is on summer solstice now that Orion/Amergin/Lugh appears to carry the sun across the sky.

And then there's Cúchulainn, the warrior hero of the Táin Bó Cuailnge, who battles in ford water – a ford being the crossing point of a river. Was he guarding the ford of the sky, where the track of the cattle crossed the *áth* of the *Bealach na Bó Finne*, as hinted in the Táin?

> a fair man facing your foes
> in the starlit ford of night.[3]

It is no mere coincidence that Cúchulainn is a son of Lugh. The Milky Way was known as Lugh's Chain and Lugh used a weapon called the Tathlum, which is described as a concrete ball – made of his enemies' brains hardened with lime. Could this be the moon?

> To the hero Lugh was given
> This concrete ball – no soft missile –
> In Mag Tuireadh of shrieking wails,
> From his hand he threw the tathlum.[4]

Fionn Mac Cumhaill was said to have thrown standing stones into the landscape from places like Hill of Tara and Slieve Gullion. I wonder if this myth/folk tale perhaps connects Orion with the solstices – it's possible that some standing stones have alignments towards the

An illustration from the Stellarium software showing the position of the sun in the hand of Orion on summer solstice.

sun's solstices or the lunar standstills. If Fionn threw the stones, perhaps this is a reference to the alignment with such astronomical events seen to be controlled by this illustrious man in the sky. Fionn's name translates as 'Bright Son of the Hazel' or 'Starry Son of the Hazel'.[5]

An equally illustrious character from the early Irish myths is Nuadu of the Silver Arm, King of the Tuatha Dé Danann, whose arm was chopped off in the first battle of Moytura. He had a new silver arm made for him by the Tuatha Dé Danann healer, Dian Cecht. Thus he was able to take part in the second battle of Moytura (Mag Tuired) in which the Dananns were victorious against the Fomorians. This myth inspired the famous scene in the Star Wars movies where Luke Skywalker (Orion is perhaps seen to walk through the sky) confronts the evil Darth Vader, who chops off his arm with a light sabre. Towards the end of the movie, we see that Luke is given a metal, robotic prosthesis, similar perhaps to Nuadu's new 'silver' arm.

On the next summer solstice, as you watch the sun make its way across the sky, it would be nice to reflect upon the powerful imagery. The god of light has the sun in his hand.

7.4

Easter Sunday and controlling time at Brug na Bóinne

This was written on Easter Sunday 2016.

I suppose it's fitting that I should come to Newgrange on Easter Sunday, as the country remembers the events of a century ago, events that gave birth to a new nation. It's fitting in many ways. It's fitting because of the rebirth that Newgrange represents – the rebirth of the sun, and of new life, and perhaps also the rebirth of the soul.

I've come here for a short time to get away from the distractions of home, and to perhaps clear the mind a little, to allow the whispers of the gods to be heard among the chill winds of this bright but showery March evening.

What an auspicious day, Easter Sunday; a time when we think of resurrection, of the rebirth of dreams long forgotten in the shadow of winter. Jesus, remember me, when you come into your kingdom. Oengus, remember me, when you come into your kingdom. Just as I write that, I can hear the spring lambs bleating here on the grassy slopes in front of Newgrange. Oh lamb, why is it that you had to be sacrificed? What is it within us that believes something good will come of something so foul? Why do we feel we have to destroy life in order that life may flourish?

Perhaps those who were executed after the Easter Rising were the sacrificial lambs who had to be slaughtered in order for new life to

Easter Sunday sunset at Newgrange.

thrive. But I don't know why that should be. I doubt I will ever understand it. Live and let live.

The sun comes now, beneath the cumulonimbus to the west, high above Rosnaree. Knowth reopens to the public after the winter at Easter. That is highly fortuitous, given that ancient Knowth was a site seemingly designed with finding Easter in mind.[1] Ironically, the only time Newgrange closes is at Christmas, the modern winter solstice festival.

At Knowth, at Easter, let us put Jesus into the eastern tomb at dawn, and perhaps at dusk we will find him emerging from the western tomb, facing Slane, awaiting the lighting of the Paschal Fire. In doing so, we might be putting him on the cross again, for the eastern tomb is cruciform, and the western tomb is not. He will shed his cross in order to come out the other side. Who knows what miracles might have been wrought in the depths of Buí's hill, overlooking the mighty Boyne?

Here at Newgrange, on the solstice, we will watch as god himself is born in man, a miracle of light in the darkness.

What we should not do is to try to control time. The Dagda tried to control time at Newgrange, so that he could lie with Bóinn for the conception of the new miracle son, Oengus Óg, the son of god. But the plan came to nought because the Milesians arrived and sent them all underground.

Bressail Bó Dibad tried to control time at Dowth, so that his ego could be raised to greater heights using a new tower of Babylon. But his plan came to nought when he lay with his sister, and the tower remained unfinished.

Today, on Easter Sunday, the period known as Daylight Saving Time began. At 1.00 am this morning, the clocks went forward by an hour. Yet again, we are trying to control time. But the bleating lambs don't notice. The blackbirds in the hedgerows don't notice. The Dagda himself, in silent slumber somewhere in a realm known as the *sídhe,* doesn't notice. Today, we've fooled ourselves into thinking that the newly risen Jesus will tarry an extra hour at the doorway of Knowth.

Now that we think we have mastered time, what will become of us? Will our Milesians come, to banish us to another realm? Will darkness fall on our rush to build that tower to reach heaven – that new tower of Babylon, the one with which we will climb to heaven and converse with the gods themselves?

The sun strikes the milky quartz on the western limb of New-grange's great wall. The shadows from the Great Circle stones are much the same as they were yesterday. The lone crow riding the wind above the great mound does not see an extra hour of daylight. The sun sets when the sun sets. He does not put a number on it.

But I will delay a while longer, here at Newgrange on Easter Sunday, in the hope that, as Lady Gregory might have wished, Oengus Óg will come out from the Brug and let himself be seen on the earth.

The setting sun on Easter Sunday at Newgrange.

There are other people now. I gather by their accents that they are foreign. Sure weren't we all foreign once? Didn't we all come to this enchanted isle from across nine waves? We all come to Newgrange as foreigners. And we all leave as if leaving home. That is the power of the Brug. You leave it feeling that you are just a speck of dust on the master's table.

We cannot control time. It is futile. We can count it, and doubtless the builders of the great monuments did just that. And in counting it, and measuring it, and putting numbers on it, can we get any sense of beginnings and origins, of endings and destinies? This is one of the key questions that preoccupied the masterful builders of the great monuments: Where did we come from?

Tied up with that question, bound inevitably to it. is the second part: Where are we going, and what will happen to us?

There are few who can answer. But we might wish for a moment to see Elcmar, the magician and druid of Síd in Broga, standing in all his power on the top of the mighty mound, his forked branch of white hazel in hand, divining an answer for us.

The Milky Way and the planet Venus over Newgrange in winter.

Epilogue

Ancestral time;
A return to the Brugh

There's a reason I've been going to Newgrange all these years. I've been trying to remember.

Trying to remember something that I'd never forgotten – rather, I just put it away, in its place, ready to be retrieved when the time was right. A time for everything and everything in its time. A place for everything and everything in its place.

Time at the *Brú* – the *Breo* Park, the *Brug* of *Elcmar*, the *Síd Mac Ind Oc* – is ancestral time. A time to get in touch with ancestors, to bring them back to the living sphere, so that they can tell of the things that they never forgot; things that I shouldn't have forgotten.

'Did you forget?' they ask.

'No, I did not forget anything,' I reply. 'I just put these things away. A time for everything.'

But I did forget something. I forgot that I come from them. And so I forgot them. Now, in the cold light of mature memory, I wonder if that's why I've often felt like I'm living in the wrong time. I don't quite fit in here. (Hardly a unique scenario for an anxiety-ridden guest in the unfathomable world at any time, never mind today). Do I wish to live in another time?

This is my time. This is the time I've been given. It's not that I'm living in the wrong time at all, for you can only live in the time in which you are present. What I have failed to do is to live in ancestral

The doorway of the Brug, looking out towards winter solstice sunrise.

time – that time that transcends reckoning by hours, or clock hands, or sunsets, or new moons, or solstices. For ancestral time is all of time. It does not know of any beginning, or end, or any counting of the days.

I forgot to live in the forever, choosing instead to live in the now, but often times living in the past, or in the future. To live in the forever is what Síd in Broga represents. It's what Tír na nÓg really means. When you step out of 'now' time, and thinking time, and fretting time, and regretting time, and anxious time, you are in ancestral time.

The ancestors brought you here, to this moment, to this place.

On a visit to the Anubis Cave in Oklahoma on March 20, 2007 – the Spring Equinox – the writer and artist Martin Brennan said something which seemed recondite and almost kitsch when I first heard it in a video posted to YouTube. It was clear that he was excited by his visit to that special place. He said:

'I love to get in touch with my eternal self – that which doesn't move.'

What could he possibly have meant? I really did not know, initially, but guessed that he might be playing to some kind of New Age audience that likes to hear enigmatic esoteric bluff. But that was my ego talking, because my spirit did not yet understand. Brennan was experiencing ancestral time.

If you step out of this moment, and look upon it from another viewpoint, perhaps you will see, with ancestral eyes, the futility, and the incongruousness, of the idea of today, and now, and yesterday, and tomorrow. I had forgotten to live in ancestral time. I had forgotten to live in forever time.

And now, with 43 journeys around the sun completed, I think back to when I was a boy, and I used to stare longingly, in complete awe, at the stars of night. And at those times I felt a mighty yearning in my heart, a hankering for something, a pining, something I could never explain in words, or properly understand. It felt like something was missing, or something was lost. I know now that I was living in ancestral time – existing in a forever that knew no boundaries of time or measurement.

If myth can live so long – through centuries and countless generations of ancestors – then why not some greater memory, some intimate inculcation, wrought out of the vague vestiges of ancestral retrospection? By living – even fleetingly – in ancestral time, is it possible to see through the eyes of the ancestor? Do we 'become' the ancestor when we get in touch with our eternal selves, that which does not move? Unsurprisingly, Brennan seemingly felt that he had entered ancestral time when visiting a place that was sacred in the past. Anubis cave had, at some point in measureable time, been a focal point of ancestral energy. But we can probably say that Anubis cave *is* a focal point of ancestral energy, now and always, and never. As an artist with a considerable track record of noticing things, he noticed that the cave resembled a skull. He had gone there to die, or at least to allow the ego to die and the spirit to soar. He was living in the forever. That's what the ancestors had probably done too. Sitting in the eye sockets of a stone skull, they had gone to witness the death of the ego, and the glorious ascension of the spirit. There isn't much room for the ego in ancestral time.

And in many of my anxious hours as a youth, I forgot to live in ancestral time. But somehow, gazing at the stars brought it all back to me, even if I did not know it at the time. Orion, won't you hunt with your dogs across the skies of forever, and never set on me again. Pegasus, won't you fly with your great wings upon gossamer skies in the myths of eternity. Sagittarius, won't you come forth a little, and tarry awhile above your lowly horizon, so that I might glare upon your teapot shape in the never-ending summer.

As I write this, I can see the veiled sun, behind some thin cloud. As I stare, I wonder if I haven't entered the realm of ancestral time, which isn't a real place or a discernible thing at all, but rather the indescribable *sídhe*, that which has no translation.

Samhain sun beams over Síd in Broga.

Unsurprisingly, we find that Síd in Broga encompasses the duality of countable, calendrical time, and also the notion of eternity, something beyond time. Around its border are giant slabs of shale, forming a huge ring around the base of the cairn, like a belt keeping everything in place. Walking around the cairn – *deiseal,* or sunwise, not widdershins – we count stones, like counting months, or lunations, reckoning time by three-tonne monoliths. Maybe there is supposed to be an incantation, some utterance or prayer or petition, at each stone on the round. I make no such utterance. I prefer not to process in a processional way, but rather to lose count, or not to count at all. And, becoming distracted by ancient artwork, I wonder if, with the wobbling of the earth's axis and the slowly changing positions of the stars, I should rather be processing in a precessional way, and not a processional way. Either way, Newgrange is not a giant set of rosary beads.

Do not impart the repetitive strains of a contrived prayer at the kerb side at the Síd of Mac Ind Oc. Oengus Óg does not want to hear your monotonous utterances. He wants you to follow the stones, to see where they lead. Some of you will find that they lead nowhere. Perhaps some of you will find that they lead everywhere. Some of you will find yourselves, as I have done, going around in circles. And in doing so, a whole year might feel like just one day, or, as in the story of the begetting of Oengus, maybe nine months will seem like a single day. Be careful if you are counting stones to make sure you don't get the same number the second time…. that's one of the secrets of the stones.

In the counting of time, it's interesting that the kerb of stones around Newgrange is unbroken. It could be said that the kerb is unending. If you walk *deiseal* around Newgrange, where do you start, and where do you end? If you process, and progress, processionally around Newgrange, you merge calendrical, countable time with eternity. You can count stones as days, or weeks, or lunations, or years, but unless you choose a starting stone and a finishing stone, you are walking towards eternity.

The sun sets into Síd in Broga (Newgrange) in early June,
viewed from the southern bank of the Boyne.

I once met an elderly woman in a library. I was researching old myths and place names. We ended up sitting at the same table, and we got talking. After a while, when we realised we had mutual interests, the lady told me about an interesting word in Irish, a word that I cannot now remember. She said that the word represented a point on a circle. It was typical of one of those Irish words that does not translate easily into English.

A point on a circle.

Surely there is no such thing as a point on a circle? A circle is a continuous loop, a never-beginning and never-ending thing.

We discussed this 'point on a circle'.

Perhaps it was a beginning and/or an ending point? Maybe it was a counting aid? Perhaps it was just a decorative item, like a diamond on an engagement ring. Maybe the entrance kerb stone at Newgrange, with its lavish designs, is the diamond on the engagement ring of Síd in Broga.

In the library, this old lady and I agreed that there were some ancient ideas and customs that were not easily explained or understood. The point on a circle was just such a notion.

Years later, with the benefit of many journeys around the kerb-belt of Newgrange, I now know that the point on a circle is a concept that encompasses both countable time and eternity. It's a pity I cannot recount that word.

For the sake of discussion, let us suppose that the kerb stone situated immediately outside the entrance to the passage of Newgrange, the one inconsiderately labelled Kerb 1, is the point on the circle of the belt-kerb. That is the point at which a visitor is likely to begin a complete journey around the kerb. It is, fascinatingly, the point where the 'circle' of the kerb (it's really more like a flattened egg, or even a heart) meets the cross of the passage and chamber. It is a sacred point; a liminal zone; a remarkable junction. It is where the calendar meets eternity. It is now and it is forever.

Perhaps that's why it appears to present a challenge to the visitor who wants to enter Newgrange. To get to the doorway of the Brugh, one must climb over the kerb. Today, there are wooden steps to make it easier. But in the old days, before the excavation, a little bit of nimble dexterity was involved. If you wished to knock on the door of the Brugh, first you must cross over the kerb, at that point on the circle where now meets eternity.

And if you could knock on the door of Newgrange, and if Oengus Óg answered, what would you ask him?

Definitely don't ask him where the treasure of Newgrange lies. If you do that, he will laugh at you, and point you towards Dowth, with its giant crater – a gaping mouth-hole that shouts 'there is no treasure'. For the treasure of Newgrange is no mere gold trinket, or Roman coin.

I might ask Oengus if it's okay to walk widdershins around the kerb, and to come to the door against the path of the sun. Might I be washed out to sea if I come widdershins around the Brugh? No. the spirals tell me otherwise. For they are wound inwards and outwards. There are *deiseal* spirals and there are widdershins spirals. The only wrong way to approach the doorway of Newgrange is the preconceived way. If you pretend you know what it's about, you will never arrive at the doorway of the *sídhe*. You will come to the entrance, but Oengus will not be there to greet you.

So even today, when I approach the *geata na sídhe* (the gateway of an untranslatable concept), I sometimes admit that I haven't a clue what Newgrange is about. And when that happens, Oengus invites me in.

'Did you process processionally around the mound?' he asks me.

'No,' I answer. 'I precessed. I regressed. I digressed. I came to the doorway of the Brugh by paths unknown, the lone pilgrim who was lost at Cleitech, and somehow found the salmon in the pool beneath Rosnaree.'

'Did you ford the Boyne?' he asks.

'I did. I managed, through means that are perhaps Damascene, to do what King Cormac could not. I crossed the Boyne at Rosnaree, and conquered all my fears. I was converted on the road to *Síd in Broga*.'

'Converted?'

'Deconverted actually. As I said, I regressed and I digressed. I left the Christian side and waded across into realms unknown. I wanted to go back to the ways of the ancestors.'

'And who did you meet, when you got to the other side?'

'I met the house keeper – the keeper of the House of Broe, above the ford on the Boyne, the ancient M1 motorway, where many a lost pilgrim crossed from the Wood of the King and found their ancestors.'

'And what did the house keeper ask you?'

'He asked me the secret to crossing the river safely.'

'And?'

'I told him that Bóinn's course from source to sea is *deiseal*.'

Oengus jumps up, half in surprise and half in joy.

'I told him that Bóinn follows sun-wise from the Well of Segais to Inbher Colpa. She might have walked widdershins around the well, but her greater journey followed the round of the sun. With Bóinn flowing *deiseal*, there would be no flood at Rosnaree.'

No flood of water. No flood of dreams. No flood of nightmares. Today, there will only be a flood of memories – memories from old days, memories from today and memories from the future; memories of Diarmuid, and memories of Fionn, and memories of Cormac, buried there at Cleitech, beneath lofty Rosnaree. Today, I will remember the ancestors of the past and the ancestors of the future. I will not drown in a flood of Bóinn's tears.

And when I come to the doorway of the Brug, I will ask a question of Oengus, the young son, who knows no age. I will ask him how the Tuatha Dé Danann first encountered ancestor time. When did they learn to stand at the point in the circle and to enter infinity?

Was it when he, Oengus the Young, Oengus the Innocent, Oengus the Initiate, asked his dad for a loan of Newgrange, for just a night and a day?

> Give us your house,
> For a night and a day,
> I'll give it a try,
> But I will not stay.

Dagda agreed.

And just like Dagda had sent Elcmar off – to count stones, or to process processionally around the kerb; to lose track of time, in the many journeys past the point in the circle, the point where now meets forever – maybe Oengus sent Dagda on a similar journey.

Elcmar left Síd in Broga, not knowing that things would never be the same again. Dagda left Síd in Broga, not knowing that things would never be the same again.

The Boyne at Roughgrange on a misty spring morning.

Elcmar returned to the Brug to find there was a young son, Oengus Óg, who had not been there before.

Dagda returned to Síd in Broga to find that it was no longer Síd in Broga – it was now Síd Mac Ind Óc.

Once Elcmar left the Brug, it didn't matter how he returned, whether he approached from the south or the north, the west or the east. It mattered not whether he brought quartz or granodiorite or greywacke stones to place on the cairn. It mattered not if he came around it *deiseal* or widdershins. In his absence, the Young Son/Sun had arrived, the one who is forever young, the one who tarries on the edge of eternity. Bereft of his fork of white hazel, Elcmar could not find the point on the circle, the doorway to forever. He would have to find a different *sídhe.*

When Dagda left the Brug, it didn't matter how he returned. For all of time is made up of day and night, and no matter how he might argue with his son, he could not win. He gave it away for a night and a day; he gave it away for all of time.

And so the Tuatha Dé Danann learned about ancestor time. They learned that there is no today, and no yesterday, and no tomorrow. There is only all of time, and no time. And that's how they won the wars with the Fomorians and the Milesians. Win, lose or draw, they could live in forever time, so that they are just as present today as they were in those mystical horizons of time in the distant past.

Outside Newgrange, there is the known, measurable, calendrical time.

Inside, there is no time. There is only forever.

Dagda gave Newgrange to Oengus for a night and a day.
Oengus insisted that this equated to eternity.

Endnotes

Prologue

1. Franz (1975), p. 131.
2. Jung (1990), p. 12.
3. Nilan (2014), p. 46.
4. D'Alton (1828), p. 28.
5. See Moriarty (2006).

1.1 Summer solstice sunrise at Newgrange

1. One of the ancient names of Newgrange.

1.2 Science and mysticism: The genius of the Stone Age

1. Freund (2003), p. 282.
2. Campbell (2004), p. 91.
3. Ibid., p. 92.
4. The otherworld mounds.

1.3 Do the myths about the mounds offer an insight into their function?

1. Mallory (2016), p. 73.
2. Waddell (2015), p. xi.
3. In particular, see Murphy (2013), pp. 67-76.
4. Campbell (1991), p. 431.
5. Prendergast (1991), p. 11.
6. See 1.4 infra.
7. Carey (1990).
8. Ibid., p. 27.
9. Ibid., p. 25.
10. For further discussion of this theory, see Murphy and Moore (2008), chapter 6.
11. Murphy and Moore (2008).
12. Hicks (2009a), p. 116.
13. Rolleston (1998), p. 156.
14. Hicks, op. cit., p. 123.

15. MacKillop (2000), p. 195.
16. Hicks, op. cit., p. 116.

1.4 Folk memory: 1938 knowledge foreshadowed excavation findings

1. Briody (2007), *The Irish Folklore Commission 1935-1970, History, ideology, methodology*, Finnish Literature Society, p. 270.
2. For instance, there are 151 recorded souterrains in County Louth and a further 139 possible examples. See Buckley and Sweetman (1991), p. 100.
3. Hensey (2015), *First Light: The Origins of Newgrange*, Oxbow Books, p. 84.
4. Murphy (2012), p. 49.
5. Borlase (1897), p. 357.
6. Coffey (1977), p. 31.

1.5 The archaeologist who unwisely dismissed Newgrange folklore

1. Ó Ríordáin and Daniel (1964).
2. Which he incorrectly asserts is 'the cave of Grainnè' (p. 16) , rather than 'the cave of the sun' which is likely the better translation of *greinè*. He goes on to say that Grainnè is a 'mythological Irish figure who made a tour of Ireland in a year and a day and carried large stones in her apron that were sometimes thrown down to make her bed'. I suspect he read the foregoing in Borlase's *The Dolmens of Ireland* (Vol. III), as it appears to be largely a repetition of same, but I might add that Borlase suggests that Grainnè is a personification of the sun.
3. Ó Ríordáin and Daniel, op. cit., p. 19.
4. Ibid.
5. Ibid., pp. 19-20.
6. Murphy (2012), p. 114.
7. Indeed, Carnbawn/Carnbane is mentioned in Daniel's book in the section about Loughcrew on pp. 100-101.
8. Murphy (2012), p. 170.
9. Campbell (1959), p. 431.
10. MacKillop (1998), p. 47.
11. Ó hÓgáin (2006), p. 386.
12. O'Kelly, (1982), p. 47.
13. Ó Ríordáin and Daniel (1964), p. 20.
14. http://www.rte.ie/archives/2017/0727/893320-new-discoveries-at-newgrange/ Extracted 17 September 2017.

1.6 The collapse of Mellifont and the renaming of Síd in Broga

1. For the history of Mellifont, see Colmcille (1958).
2. Stout (2002), *Newgrange and the Bend of the Boyne*, Cork University Press, p. 86.
3. eDIL s.v. 1 síd , síth (dil.ie/37441).

4. eDIL s.v. bruig (dil.ie/7102).
5. This is related in the tale *De Gabáil int Síde* ('The Taking of the Otherworld Mound').
6. O'Kelly (1982), p. 25.
7. Magan, Monchán, 'Collops and fíbíns: The lost language of Ireland's landscape', *The Irish Times*, Saturday, 29 July 2017.
8. For more information, see the website http://www.mellifontabbey.ie/.
9. Borlase (1897), p. 346. The original O'Laverty correspondence about the matter is contained in the section titled 'Miscellanea' in *The Journal of the Royal Society of Antiquaries of Ireland*, Vol. II, Vol. XXII (1892), p. 430.

1.7 Newgrange and the return of the Tuatha Dé Danann

1. Jones (2007), p. 156, says: 'The widespread use of entoptic design elements in megalithic art suggests that an important part of passage tomb ritual involved hallucinations. How were these hallucinations induced? Certainly the sensory deprivation produced by being deep inside the tomb might help as would flickering light, rhythmic drumming, fasting and sleep deprivation.' He further suggests that a variety of psilocybin mushrooms commonly found in Ireland, known as the 'Liberty Cap', might have also been involved.
2. See Murphy (2012), chapter 9, 'Cave Myths'.
3. See, for example, Murphy and Moore (2008), p. 274.
4. Nilan (2014), p. 15.
5. It should be said here that the mythology of the Tuatha Dé Danann is not all filled with goodness. There are battles, and murders, and there is retribution (for example, the Fate of the Sons of Tuireann). However, in a broad sense, the Tuatha Dé Danann are seen as beings of light, and because of the complexity of themes in their story, especially those involving retreat and hibernation for some future awakening, we judge them as the best representation of our hopes for the re-emergence of goodness within us.
6. Campbell (1991a), p. 46.
7. These Fomorian forces, in the Jungian analysis, are aspects of the shadow that must be integrated, rather than suppressed or ignored.

1.8 Lecc Benn: The stone on which the monster was killed

1. Stokes (1894), p. 293.
2. There are several mentions of the Mata in the Dindshenchas. Reference to the beast can be found in the Metrical Dindshenchas in 'Brug na Bóinde II' and 'Áth Clíath Cúalann' (Gwynn (1913)) and in the Rennes Dindshenchas in 'Dindgnai in Broga' (the mounds or monuments of the Brug, viz the Bend of the Boyne) and 'Áth Cliath Cualann' (Stokes (1894).
3. In section 7.1, infra.
4. Gwynn (1913), p. 101.

5. Ibid.
6. Stokes, op. cit., p. 293.
7. Gregory (2014), p. 64.
8. Gwynn (1906), p. 23.
9. Gwynn (1913), p. 101.
10. Thompson, Chris (2014), The Dindshenchas of Brug na Bóinde, Boyne Valley, County Meath, https://storyarchaeology.com/the-dindshenchas-of-brug-na-boinde-boyne-valley-co-meath/ (Extracted 11 September 2017).
11. Ibid.
12. See Freund (2003), Chapter 6: 'Out of the Monster'.
13. Stokes, op. cit., p. 329.
14. Squire (1998), p. 54.
15. Gregory (2004), p. 354.
16. Macalister (1919), p. 242.
17. eDIL s.v. lecc (dil.ie/29691).
18. eDIL s.v. benn (dil.ie/5654).
19. Macalister, op. cit., p. 242.
20. Gwynn (1906), p. 25.
21. Thompson, op. cit.
22. Gwynn (1906), p. 25.
23. Witzel (2012), p. 153.
24. Stout (2002), p. 66.
25. Ibid.
26. Murphy (2012), p. 82.
27. Gibbons and Gibbons (2016), p. 68.
28. McGuinness (1996), p. 63. See also Wilde (2003), pp. 191-192.
29. The drawing is part of the Stowe collection in the British Library (Stowe. 1024 f127). It has been printed in Smyth (2009) p. 11, and also in Ó Ríordáin and Daniel (1964), p. 37.
30. Gibbons and Gibbons, op. cit., p. 69.
31. Ibid.
32. Murphy (2012), p. 87.
33. Murphy and Moore (2008), p. 153.

2.1 What is the meaning of Knowth's pillar stones?

1. Brennan (1983), p. 101.

2.2 Dowth and the story of hunger

1. Slavin (2005), p. 37; Gwynn (1935), p. 3.
2. Ó hÓgáin (1991), p. 55.
3. Gwynn (1913), p. 45.
4. Ibid.
5. Ibid.
6. Murphy and Moore (2008), pp. 118-9.

7. Gwynn (1924), p. 273.
8. Gwynn (1924), p. 271.
9. See Harbison (2007).
10. *Drogheda Conservative*, 5 July 1856.
11. O'Kelly (1982), p. 36.
12. Ibid.
13. Ibid., pp. 36-7.
14. Murphy (2012), p. 103.
15. Gwynn (1913), p. 47.

2.3 Heaven's mirror: As above, so below at Knowth

1. Brennan (1983).
2. Streit (1984), p. 125.
3. Gregory (2004), p. 66.

2.4 Winter sunlight at Dowth

1. Moroney (1999).
2. Brennan (1980), p. 47.
3. Gwynn (1924), pp. 271-273.

2.5 Buí and Englec: The ancient goddesses of Cnogba

1. Monaghan (2003), pp. 28, 39.
2. Carmody, Isolde, Brú na Bóinne and Cnogba – the Boyne Valley in the Metrical Dindshenchas, a translation of the Metrical Dindshenchas based on the work of Edward Gwynn. Accessed 10 August 2017. http://storyarchaeology.com/bru-na-boinne-and-cnogba-the-boyne-valley-in-the-metrical-dindshenchas/
3. The 'two paps of the Morrígain', in Dindgnai in Broga, in Stokes (1894), p. 293.
4. Gwynn (1913), pp. 41-43.
5. Carmody, op. cit.
6. O'Cathasaigh, Tomás, Knowth - The Epynom of Cnogba, http://www.carrowkeel.com/sites/boyne/knowth2a.html. (Extracted 18 September 2017).

3.2 Sunrise at Cairn U

1. Brennan (1994), p. 116.
2. Ibid., pp. 110-111.
3. You can see some of Ken's beautiful photography on his website http://www.shadowsandstone.com/
4. Ken Williams, personal communication.
5. Murphy and Moore (2008), p. 54.
6. See Murphy (2012), pp. 89-91.
7. Thom (1971), p. 23.

3.3 The Hag's Chair at Loughcrew: The throne of an ancient queen of the sky and the land

1. Conwell (1864), p. 357.
2. See, for instance, The Schools' Collection, Volume 0998, Page 400. https://www.duchas.ie/en/cbes/5070784/5063151/5095468 – viewed 10 August 2017.
3. O'Donovan (2001), p. 38.
4. eDIL s.v. 1 bert (dil.ie/5735). Dinneen (1927), p. 90, says *beart* is 'a bunch or heap; a bundle chiefly carried on the back or shoulders'.
5. Murphy and Moore (2008), p. 167.
6. Murphy and Moore, op. cit., p. 17.

3.4 The story of the Cailleach of Loughcrew and its meaning

1. For a beautiful guide to the Loughcrew monuments and landscape, see Hand et al (2016).
2. McMann (1993), p. 9.
3. Ibid., p. 10.
4. Ibid., p. 16.
5. The Schools' Collection, Volume 0716, Page 097. https://www.duchas.ie/en/cbes/5009014/4977219. Extracted 12 August 2017.
6. Conwell (1864), pp. 356-357.
7. McMann (1993), p. 20.
8. It is labelled as such on the early Ordnance Survey maps.
9. McMann (1993), p. 20.
10. Dames (2000), p. 207.
11. Gimbutas (1991), p. 223.
12. Murphy and Moore (2008), pp. 16-17.
13. For a good summary of this, and a discussion of the work of Margaret Curtis, see http://www.laurelkallenbach.com/lkblog/uncovering-callanishs-secrets-an-archaeological-tour/ . Extracted 12 August 2017.
14. Murphy and Moore (2008), chapter 6 – Dowth: The Darkening of the Sky.
15. McMann (1993), p. 19.
16. The major and minor standstills were terms coined by Alexander Thom. See Thom (1971), p. 18.

3.5 A glorious dawn announces the beginning of winter at Cairn L

1. For more about Red Mountain, see the next chapter.
2. Borlase (1897), Vol. III, p. 761.
3. Brennan (1994).
4. For a discussion of the ancient festival of Samhain, see Gilroy (2000), chapter 16.
5. Prendergast, Frank (2013), Tomb L, Carnbane West, Loughcrew Hills, County Meath – an archaeoastronomical assessment, http://www.newgrange.com/pdf/loughcrew-cairnl.pdf. (Extracted 18 September 2017).

6. Ibid., p. 5.
7. Ibid., pp. 5-6.
8. Ibid., p. 7.
9. See 3.6, infra.
10. Conwell (1864), p. 358.
11. Ibid.
12. Gimbutas (2001), p. 5.

3.6 Why Carrigbrack is also called Red Mountain

1. The four hills of Loughcrew are Carnbane (better known today as Carnbane West), Carrigbrack (Sliabh Rua), Slieve na Calliagh (better known today as Carnbane East) and Patrickstown Hill (the ancient name of which has been lost). In some versions of the creation myth, the Cailleach is said to have jumped on three hills, dropping stones from her apron, and in these versions it would appear Sliabh Rua is omitted. It's not clear why this is. In an old poem, in which the Cailleach is called the Garvoge, the hills are called Carnmore, Loar and Carnbeg.
2. McMann (1993), p. 34.
3. Meehan (2012), 7. 'The Long Steps of the Hag: A mythic narrative'.
4. Murphy and Moore (2008), p. 140.

4.1 Neolithic passage-tomb construction: Cooperation or enforced labour?

1. Murphy (2012), p. 56.
2. Mallory (2013), pp. 76-77.
3. Ibid., p. 74.
4. From 'Sláine' in the Metrical Dindshenchas. Gwynn (1924), p. 271.
5. From 'Mac mBreg' in the Rennes Dindshenchas. Stokes (1894), p. 62.
6. Mallory (2013), p. 77.
7. Ibid.
8. Ibid.
9. Hensey (2015), p. 29.
10. Ibid.
11. eDIL s.v. díth (dil.ie/16842)
12. Gywnn (1913), p. 43.
13. Hensey (2015), p. 29.
14. Gywnn (1924), p. 273.
15. Gwynn (1913), p. 45.
16. Gantz (1981), p. 39.
17. Gregory, Lady Isabella Augusta (2004), p. 64.
18. Gwynn (1924), p. 105.
19. MacKillop (2000), p. 125.
20. Ó hÓgáin (1991), p. 146.
21. Gwynn (1924), p. 295.

22. Ibid.
23. See chapter 7.1.
24. Gregory (2004), p. 64.
25. Gwynn (1924), p. 294.
26. eDIL s.v. seilche. (dil.ie/36903 extracted 14 August 2017).
27. Ó hÓgáin (1991), p. 146.
28. Witzel (2012), p. 154, suggests that the motif of killing a dragon and releasing the light of the sun are old motifs that can be dated to well before 20,000 years ago.
29. Hancock (2001), p. 208.
30. Waddell (2015), p. 80, quoted from Kock and Carey, *The Celtic Hero Age*, p. 145.
31. Murphy and Moore (2008).
32. See Hicks (2009a).
33. Hensey (2015), p. 118.

4.2 Ceremonial dismemberment and excarnation in prehistoric Ireland

1. O'Kelly (1982), p. 197.
2. Cooney (2000), p. 109.
3. Ancient Irish burial rites fleshed out, *Sunday Times*, July 27th 2003. https://www.thetimes.co.uk/article/ancient-irish-burial-rites-fleshed-out-c9jwdggcxmp (Extracted 18th September 2017).
4. Ibid.
5. Ibid.
6. Ibid.
7. Excarnation can also involve burying a body until only a skeleton remains. See Geber et al. (2017), p. 11.
8. Evidence for prehistoric human dismemberment found at Carrowkeel. http://irisharchaeology.ie/2017/09/evidence-for-prehistoric-human-dismemberment-found-at-carrowkeel/ (Extracted 18th September 2017).
9. Geber et al (2017), Abstract.
10. http://irisharchaeology.ie, op. cit.
11. Ibid.
12. Brennan, Colin, Archaeologists found bones of a Stone Age child and an adult in tiny cave, http://www.irishmirror.ie/news/irish-news/archaeologists-sligo-found-bones-stone-3193318 (Extracted 14 August 2017).
13. Dowd (2015), p. 106.
14. Were the monuments themselves used for the purposes of cave excarnation? At Newgrange, a body could have been deposited in the chamber and the giant 'door' slab moved into place against the passage entrance, preventing human access. But animals and birds would still have been able to enter the 'cave' via the roof box above the entrance.

15. Roy, David, 'The Irish wake is the best way to deal with death', https://www.irishnews.com/arts/2017/09/14/news/journalist-kevin-toolis-on-celebrating-the-irish-way-of-death-1134776/ (Extracted 18th September 2017).
16. Toolis (2017), p. 37.

4.3 Climbing Slieve Gullion to see the highest passage-tomb on the island of Ireland

1. https://www.ringofgullion.org/stories/the-calliagh-berras-lake/ Extracted 18 August 2017.
2. For instance, the house or tomb of the Calliagh Vera, or Birra, at Monasterboice. See Ferguson (1872), pp. 230-231.

4.4 The huge monoliths of Ireland's Stonehenge were buried

1. And published in his book *Louthiana* in 1748.
2. Wright, Thomas (1748).
3. Morris (1907), p. 61.
4. Ibid.
5. Bonwick (1986), p. 6.
6. Hodgson (1824), p. 439.
7. King (1799), p. 250.
8. Wright (1748), Plate III and IV. The townland Raskeagh is from the Irish *Ráth Sciach*, the 'fort of the thorns'. (https://www.logainm.ie/33795.aspx - Extracted 19 August 2017). An alternative derivation is suggested in CLAJ Vol. 2 No.1 (1908), where it is proposed that Roskeagh might signify 'The Wood of the Thorn Tree'. (p. 89). It is there suggested that 'Wright's "Russkugh" looks as awkward as, no doubt, the sound seemed to his locally untutored ear'.
9. Wright (1748), Plate III.
10. The cairn was also described in Wright's *Louthiana*, separately to the stonehenge and the fort at Raskeagh.
11. Joyce (1910), p. 174.
12. Joyce (1869), p. 523.
13. https://sites.google.com/site/gapothenorth/the-townlands/kieran-murphy-1. Extracted 19 August 2017.
14. Hicks (2009b), pp. 36, 41.
15. Ibid., p. 36.
16. Ibid., p. 40.
17. Ibid., p. 36.
18. Ibid.
19. Hicks, Ronald, personal communication.
20. Ibid.
21. The road is not shown on a map dating from 1737, but appears a map in 1754. I am grateful to Sharon Oddie Brown for this informat See:

http://www.thesilverbowl.com/maps/Carn Beg/Carn Beg-history&maps. html (Extracted 5 September 2017).

22. Bonwick (1880), p. 10.
23. For much more information, and sources, see Murphy and Moore (2008), chapter 5, 'The Giant Rings'.
24. Murphy and Moore (2008), p. 103.
25. Basset (1886), p. 9.
26. Ibid.
27. Hicks, Ronald, pers. comm., September 2017.
28. Nelson and Probert (1994), p. 5.
29. Buckley (1909), p. 166.
30. Ibid., p. 182.
31. Ibid.
32. Nelson and Probert (1994), p. 9.
33. Ibid., pp. 13-14.
34. Bassett explicitly refers to a 'tenant', suggesting it was more likely to have been Coulter than Limerick, but the truth of the matter is likely never to be known and we can only speculate.
35. This was related in correspondence to Sharon Oddie Brown, who had asked Mr. Nelson about the matter on my behalf.
36. Personal communication from Sharon Oddie Brown, November 2008.

4.5 Only the guardian of Fourknocks knows its true name

1. Half-spirals actually. But to represent the sun's movement from solstice to solstice, the spiral is an apt and convenient symbol.
2. Cooney (2000), p. 109.
3. Ibid., p. 108.
4. It is also, in fairness, a very insightful process, but the large-scale excavation of ancient monuments can now be considered a thing of the past as new archaeological instrumentation and techniques are developed.
5. https://www.irishtimes.com/news/keeping-the-past-alive-1.310020 (Extracted 22 August 2017).
6. Byrne, Excavations at Knowth PRIA 66C4 p. 396.
7. See Murphy and Moore (2008), Chapter 7: Newgrange: The Cygnus Enigma.

4.6 An investigation of the alignment of the passage of Fourknocks

1. Murphy and Moore (2008), chapter 7, 'The Cygnus Enigma'.
2. According to my measurements using Google Earth.
3. Murphy and Moore (2008), pp. 147, 316.
4. Ibid., p. 22.
5. Monument ref. (ME027-034----) in the Sites and Monuments Record.
6. It's really an arc, because it's following the curvature of the earth, but for the purpose of simplicity we are thinking in two dimensions here.

7. Murphy (2012), p. 48.
8. Ibid., p. 53.
9. Ibid., p. 49.
10. Hensey (2015), p. 84.
11. Ibid.
12. Murphy and Moore (2008), chapter 1.
13. Murphy and Moore (2008), chapter 7.
14. There is no current evidence that this author is aware of to suggest there was stone age activity at Mullaghtellin.

5.1 Cleitech, Rosnaree and the ancient ford of the Boyne

1. This was erected in the 1990s.
2. Holten (2016), p. 527. See also Hickey (1966), p. 9.
3. Hickey (2000), p. 9.
4. The journey from that landing spot across land up to Newgrange must have been an arduous one. The stones had to be hauled a distance of one kilometre, up an incline of 60 metres. See Murphy (2012), chapter 3, 'Community Effort'.
5. Hickey, op. cit., p. 9.
6. The present owners of the old mill house, the Heise family, showed me the location of these rocks in the spring of 2017.
7. Stout (2002), p. 70.
8. Wilde (2003), p. 116.
9. O'Donovan (1854), pp. 115-116.
10. Hickey, op. cit., p.65.
11. Ibid, pp. 65-66.
12. This is speculation on my part.
13. Stout (2002), p. 68.
14. Gregory (2004), p. 355.
15. Mallory (2013), pp. 44-45.
16. O'Kelly, (1982), p. 43. This is cited from Ni Sheaghdha, N. (1967), *Tóruigheacht Dhiarmada agus Ghráinne*.
17. Shaw (1780).
18. Hickey, op. cit., p.68. Hickey was here speaking with the then owner of Rosnaree House.

5.2 Up close with the Rosnaree Sheela-na-gig

1. Sheela-na-gig theories by Tara McLoughlin. http://www.members.tripod.com/~taramc/myths.html (Extracted 22 August 2017).
2. McMahon and Roberts (2001), p. 11.
3. For instance, Dineen (1927), p. 1027.
4. http://webgis.archaeology.ie/historicenvironment/ (Extracted 22 August 2017).
5. Ralph Riegel (March 16th 2017), Revealed: St Patrick had a wife...and his name day was extended for another 24 hours to 'honour' her. http://www.

independent.ie/irish-news/revealed-st-patrick-had-a-wifeand-his-name-day-was-extended-for-another-24-hours-to-honour-her-35536627.html (Extracted 18th September 2017).

6. Monaghan (2003), p. 33.

5.3 The remarkable geological secret of the Newgrange kerb stones

1. Power (2014), p. 256.
2. Ibid.
3. Ibid.
4. Vaughan and Johnston (1992), abstract.
5. Mulvihill (2002), p. 121.
6. http://www.ingeniousirelandonline.ie/en/stories/st0003.xml?page=3 (Extracted 23 August 2017).
7. See Hensey (2015), p. 86 and Stout and Stout (2008), pp. 10-11.

5.4 On the quest for the Cailleach of Clogherhead

1. Murphy and Moore (2008) pp. 89-90.
2. http://www.termonfeckinhistory.ie/townlands_and_placenames_11.html (Extracted 25 August 2017).
3. For Buí/Boí, see Ó hÓgáin (2006), p. 58.
4. Murphy and Moore, op. cit., p. 106.
5. Du Noyer (1866), pp. 497-500.
6. Murphy and Moore (2008).
7. Ó Crualaoich (2007), pp. 83-86.
8. 'Ancient Parish of Clogher and Kilclogher', Clogherhead Development Group website, www.clogherhead.com. (Extracted 19 June 2013).
9. Ibid.
10. Logainm.ie.
11. Dinneen (1927), p. 148.
12. Ibid.
13. Mac Cionnaith, p. 250.
14. Dinneen, op. cit., p. 148.
15. http://www.termonfeckinhistory.ie/townlands_and_placenames_11.html (Extracted 25 August 2017).

5.5 The Tara Brooch: Ireland's finest piece of jewellery

1. Wheeler (1950), pp. 155-158.
2. Ibid.
3. https://www.irishcentral.com/roots/the-tara-brooch-one-of-irelands-greatest-treasures-explained (Extracted 23 August 2017).
4. Ibid.
5. http://www.museum.ie/Archaeology/Exhibitions/Current-Exhibitions/The-Treasury/Gallery-1-Iron-Age-to-12th-Century/Tara-Brooch-(1) (Extracted 23 August 2017).

5.6 Tracing the goddess of the Boyne river

1. Franz (1975).
2. Van Der Post (1978).
3. Lavrin (1971).
4. Van Der Post (1978), pp. 66-67.
5. Ibid., p. 67.
6. Ibid. pp. 23-24.
7. Moriarty (2006), p. 42.
8. From Ledwidge's poem 'The Dead Kings'.
9. O'Reilly and Tuite (1994), p. 9.
10. Van der Post (1978), p. 68.

5.7 Some old names for the town of Drogheda

1. The word *drochet* can refer to a causeway as well as a bridge. eDIL s.v. drochet (dil.ie/18757).
2. Stout (2002), p. 70.
3. Murphy and Moore (2008), p. 18.
4. Shaw (1780) and Murphy (2012), p. 92.
5. Murphy (2012), p. 92.
6. Murphy and Moore (2008), pp. 26-27.
7. Cross and Slover (1996), p. 459.
8. Shaw (1780), p. 358.
9. Nagy (1997), p. 319.
10. Murphy and Moore (2008), chapter 2.
11. Louth Ordnance Survey Letters, Co. Louth Archaeological Journal Vols. IV, V & VI, p.92.
12. With further possibilities thus: 'The Ford of the Fort of Redness' and 'The Fort of Dark-redness'.

5.8 The Hill of Slane: Where Christianity met prehistory

1. Murphy and Moore (2008), pp. 50-51.
2. Seaver and Brady (2011).
3. Ibid.
4. Murphy and Moore (2008), pp. 209-214.
5. Ibid., pp. 214-215.
6. See picture in Murphy and Moore (2008), p. 219.

6.1 All the dead kings came to me

1. http://www.francisledwidge.com/francis-ledwidge-biography.php (Extracted 23 August 2017).
2. Used with the kind permission of the Francis Ledwidge Museum, Slane, County Meath.
3. Ledwidge (2017).

4. Murphy and Moore (2008), pp. 273-274.
5. Marsh (2013), p. 164. A similar version, from the same original source (Johnny Murray) can be found in The Schools' Collection, Volume 0687, Page 123. http://www.duchas.ie/en/cbes/5008912/4966251/5106184. (Extracted 23 August 2017.)
6. Murphy and Moore (2008), p. 274.
7. https://www.counter-currents.com/2011/08/the-mountain-kings/ (Extracted 23 August 2017).
8. https://www.logainm.ie/en/38699?s=Rossnaree (Extracted 23 August 2017).
9. http://www.francisledwidge.com/francis-ledwidge-biography.php

6.2 Kissing the Cailleach: The sovereignty dream of Ireland

1. The quote is widely attributed to Campbell on the internet, but it might be that it is merely a summary of some things he said or wrote. See https://quoteinvestigator.com/2013/05/23/campbell-treasure/ (Extracted 3 September 2017).
2. Osbon (1991), pp 8, 24.
3. Gwynn (1913), p. 29.
4. Jung (1990), p. 17.
5. Ibid., p. 20.
6. Ibid., p. 23.
7. Gwynn, op. cit. See Boand I, pp. 26-32. Undoubtedly the story of Bóinn and Nechtain's Well is a creation or origin myth.
8. Jung, op. cit., p. 22.
9. Ibid.
10. Ibid., p. 21.
11. Campbell (2008), p. 84.
12. Along with Conn of the Hundred Battles and Cormac Mac Airt.
13. MacKillop (2000), p. 169.
14. Ibid.
15. Franz (1975), p. 100.
16. Ibid.

6.4 The Dawning of the Day

1. 'Déalradh Án Lae: The Co. Louth Original of Mangan's Famous Poem', CLAJ No. 2, Vol. V, 1922, p. 109.
2. Ibid.
3. Ó Síocháin, pp. 147-148.
4. Murphy (2012), p. 159.

6.5 Awaiting my salvation in Fiacc's Pool beneath Rosnaree

1. Jung (1990), p. 18.
2. Ibid.

3. Gregory (2004), p. 119.
4. Mallory (2013), pp. 44-46.
5. MacKillop (2000), p. 61.

6.6 The synchronicity of the swans

1. A remarkable synchronicity is detailed in Murphy and Moore (2008), pp. 93-95.
2. http://www.independent.co.uk/news/obituaries/philip-freund-writer-and-theatre-historian-774882.html (Extracted 1 September 2017).
3. Freund (2003), p. 280.
4. See Murphy and Moore (2008), Chapter 7 – Newgrange: The Cygnus Enigma.

6.7 Rekindling the powerful image of the druid Elcmar

1. Carey (1990), p. 29.
2. One presumes he is *on* the mound, and not inside it, because he is described as 'watching three fifties of youths at play on the playing field'. See Gantz (1981), p. 41.
3. MacKillop (2006), p. 97.
4. Mac Coitir (2003), p. 74.
5. Ibid., p. 75.
6. MacKillop (2000), p. 376.
7. Mac Coitir, op. cit., p. 74.
8. For some discussion around water and its possible role in ceremonies in Newgrange, see Garnett (2005), Chapter 3, 'An Immemorial Well'.
9. Stout and Stout (2008), p. 103. Ó Gibne (2012).

7.1 The Milky Way in Irish mythology and cosmogony

1. Davidson (1986), p. 161.
2. Murphy and Moore (2008), pp. 16-17.
3. Waddell (2015), p. 36.
4. Witzel (2012), p. 394.
5. Leeming (2005), p. 105.
6. Witzel, op. cit., p. 117.
7. Witzel, op. cit., p. 401.
8. Hicks (2009), p. 116.
9. Murphy and Moore (2008), p.198.
10. Paice MacLeod, Sharon (2012), p.175.
11. Murphy and Moore (2008), p. 319.
12. Mallory (2016), p. 24.
13. Waddell (2015), p. 102.
14. Ibid.
15. Ibid.
16. Gwynn (1913), p. 27.

17. See the chapter about Aislinge Oengusso.
18. Kinsella (1969), p. 22.
19. Gwynn, op. cit., p. 27.
20. eDIL s.v. smirammair (dil.ie/38063 – extracted 10 September 2017).
21. Carson (2007), p. 168. Kinsella (1969), p. 212.
22. Leenane (2014), p. 93.
23. A good website exploring this earthwork is www.blackpigsdyke.ie.
24. Marsh (2013), p. 36.
25. Campbell et al. (2014), pp. 349-350.
26. Leenane, op. cit., p. 90.
27. Kinsella (1969), p. 252.
28. Marsh, op. cit., p. 36.
29. Ibid.
30. MacKillop (2000), p. 354.
31. Stokes (1894), p. 329.
32. Gwynn (1913), p. 101.
33. Stokes, op. cit.
34. Ibid.
35. Gwynn, op. cit., p. 101.
36. Dunn (1914), 29. 'The Account of The Brown Bull of Cualnge'.
37. Leenane, op. cit., p. 94.
38. Ibid.
39. Slavin (1996), p. 19.
40. Murphy and Moore (2008), p. 238.
41. Dinneen (1927), p. 988, gives *scríob* as 'a track, line, furrow, mark or limit'. Mostly by Gaelic-speaking Highlanders who had settled there from the late eighteenth century through to the middle of the nineteenth. See MacKillop (2006), p. 291.
42. Carmichael (1914), p. 152.
43. MacKillop, op. cit., p. 292.
44. Ibid.

7.3 Orion carries the summer solstice sun across the sky

1. Murphy and Moore (2008).
2. Ibid., p. 301.
3. Carson (2007), p. 104.
4. This poem is quoted from Eugene O'Curry's Manners and Customs of the Ancient Irish, Lecture XII, p. 252,
5. Cited in Squire (1998), p. 113.
6. Murphy and Moore, op. cit., p. 80.

7.4 Easter Sunday and controlling time at Brug na Bóinne

1. Murphy and Moore (2008), Chapter 9 – Knowth: Secrets of the Sky.

Bibliography

Basset, George Henry (1998) [1886], *Louth County Guide and Directory*, published by County Louth Archaeological and Historical Society and reprinted by Dundalgan Press.

Bonwick, James (1880), *Our Nationalities*, David Bogue, London.

Bonwick, James (1986) [1894], *Irish Druids and Old Irish Religions*, Dorset Press.

Borlase, William C. (1897), *The Dolmens of Ireland, Vols I, II & III*, Chapman & Hall Ltd.

Brennan, Martin (1980), *The Boyne Valley Vision*, The Dolmen Press.

Brennan, Martin (1983), *The Stars and the Stones: Ancient Art and Astronomy in Ireland*, Thames and Hudson.

Brennan, Martin (1994) [1983], *The Stones of Time: Calendars, Sundials, and Stone Chambers of Ancient Ireland*, Inner Traditions International.

Briody, Mícheál (2007), *The Irish Folklore Commission 1935-1970, History, ideology, methodology*, Finnish Literature Society.

Buckley, James (editing) (1909), *The Journal of Thomas Wright. Author of Louthiana (1711-1786)*, CLAJ, Vol II, No. 2, pp. 165-185.

Buckley, Victor M. and Sweetman, P. David (1991), *Archaeological Survey of County Louth*, Government Publications Stationery Office.

Campbell, Eve et al (2014), *The Field Names of County Louth*, published by the Louth Field Names Project (LFNP).

Campbell, Joseph (1991a) [1988], *The Power of Myth*, With Bill Moyers, Anchor Books.

Campbell, Joseph (1991b) [1959], *The Masks of God: Primitive Mythology*, Pengiun Compass.

Campbell, Joseph (2004), *Pathways to Bliss: Mythology and Personal Transformation*, The Joseph Campbell Foundation.

Campbell, Joseph (2008) (1949), *The Hero With a Thousand Faces*, New World Library.

Carey, John (1990), *Time, Memory, and the Boyne Necropolis*, Proceedings of the Harvard Celtic Colloquium, Vol. 10.

Carmichael, Alexander (1914), *Deirdre and the Lay of the Children of Uisne*, Hodges, Figgis & Co.

Carson, Ciaran (2007), *The Táin: A New Translation of the Táin Bó Cúailnge*, Penguin Classics.

Coffey, George (1977) [1912], *New Grange and other incised tumuli in Ireland*, Dolphin Press.

Colmcille, Father O.C.S.O. (1958), *The Story of Mellifont*, M.H. Gill and Son Ltd.

Conwell, Eugene (1864), *On Ancient Sepulchral Cairns on the Loughcrew Hills*, Proceedings of the Royal Irish Academy (1836-1869), Vol. 9.

Cooney, Gabriel (2000), *Landscapes of Neolithic Ireland*, Routledge.

Cross, Tom P., and Slover, Clark Harris (editors) (1996) [1936], *Ancient Irish Tales*, Barnes and Noble.

D'Alton, John (1828), *Essay on the Ancient History, Religion, Learning, Arts, and Government of Ireland*, Transactions of the Royal Irish Academy, Volume 16.

Dames, Michael (2000), *Ireland: a sacred journey*. Element Books Limited.

Davidson, Norman (1986), *Astronomy and the Imagination: A New Approach to Man's Experience of the Stars*, Routledge & Kegan Paul.

Dinneen, Rev. Patrick S. (1927), *Foclóir Gaedhilge agus Béarla: An Irish-English Dictionary*, The Educational Company of Ireland.

Dowd, Marion (2015), *The Archaeology of Caves in Ireland*, Oxbow Books.

Du Noyer, George (1866), *Journal of the Kilkenny & South East of Ireland Archaeological Society*, Volume V, New Series.

Dunn, Joseph (1914), *The Ancient Irish Epic Tale Táin Bó Cúalnge*, David Nutt.

Ferguson, James (1872), *Rude Stone Monuments in All Countries; Their Age and Uses*, John Murray.

Franz, Marie-Louise (1975) [1972], *C.G. Jung: His Myth in Our Time*, Hodder and Stoughton.

Freund, Philip (2003) [1964], *Myths of Creation*, Peter Owen Publishers.

Gantz, Jeffrey (1981), *Early Irish Myths and Sagas*, Penguin Classics.

Garnett, Jacqueline Ingalls (2005), *Newgrange Speaks For Itself: Forty Calved Motifs & Related Site Features*, Trafford Publishing.

Geber, Jonny; Hensey, Robert; Meehan, Pádraig; Moore, Sam and Kador, Thomas (2017), *Facilitating Transitions: Postmortem Processing of the Dead at the Carrowkeel Passage Tomb Complex, Ireland (3500-3000 cal B.C.)*, Bioarchaeology International, Vol. 1.

Gibbons, Michael and Gibbons, Myles (2016), *The Brú: A Hiberno-Roman Cult Site at Newgrange?*, emania 23.

Gilroy, John (2000), *Tlachtga: Celtic Fire Festival*, Pikefield Publications.

Gimbutas, Marija (1991), *The Language of the Goddess: Unearthing the Hidden Symbols of Western Civilisation*, Harper, San Francisco.

Gimbutas, Marija (2001) [1999], *The Living Goddesses*, University of California Press.

Gregory, Lady Isabella Augusta (2004) [1904], *Lady Gregory's Complete Irish Mythology*, Bounty Books.

Gwynn, Edward (1906), *The Metrical Dindshenchas, Part II*, Hodges, Figgis & Co. (Royal Irish Academy Todd Lecture Series Volume IX).

Gwynn, Edward (1913), *The Metrical Dindshenchas, Part III*, Hodges, Figgis & Co. (Royal Irish Academy Todd Lecture Series Volume X).

Gwynn, Edward (1924), *The Metrical Dindshenchas, Part IV*, Hodges, Figgis & Co. (Royal Irish Academy Todd Lecture Series Volume XI).

Gwynn, Edward (1935), *The Metrical Dindshenchas*, Hodges, Figgis & Co. (Royal Irish Academy Todd Lecture Series Volume XII).

Hancock, Graham (2001) [1995], *Fingerprints of the Gods: The Quest Continues*, Century.

Hand, Malachy, Knight, George, Halpin, Tina, Flynn, Susan and Barrett, Siobhán (2016), *Loughcrew Cairns: Sliabh na Caillí*, published by Malachy Hand.

Harbison, Peter (2007), *The Royal Irish Academy's only archaeological excavation: Dowth in the Boyne Valley*, Proceedings of the Royal Irish Academy Vol. 107C, pp. 205-213.

Hensey, Robert (2015), *First Light: The Origins of Newgrange*, Oxbow Books.

Hickey, Elizabeth (2000) [1966], *I Send My Love Along the Boyne*, published by Áine Ni Chairbre, Drogheda.

Hicks, Ronald (2009a), 'Cosmography in Tochmarc Étaíne', *Journal of Indo-European Studies*, Vol. 37.

Hicks, Ronald (2009b), *Some correlations between henge enclosures and oenach sites,* Journal of the Royal Society of Antiquaries of Ireland, Vol. 139 (2009).

Hodgson, Adam (1824), *Letters from North America,* Volume II, Hurst, Robinson & Co and A. Constable & Co.

Holten, Anthony (2016), *The River Boyne: Hidden legacies, history and lore explored on foot and by boat,* published by Anthony Holten.

Jones, Carleton (2007), *Temples of Stone: Exploring the Megalithic Tombs of Ireland,* The Collins Press.

Joyce, P.W. (1869), *The Origin and History of Irish Names of Places, Volume I,* The Educational Co. of Ireland.

Joyce, P.W. (1879), *The Origin and History of Irish Names of Places, Volume II,* The Educational Co. of Ireland.

Joyce, P.W. (1910), *The Origin and History of Irish Names of Places, Volume III,* The Educational Co. of Ireland.

Jung, C.G. (1990) [1959], *The Archetypes and the Collective Unconscious,* Bollingen Series XX, translated by R.F.C. Hull, Princeton University Press.

King, Edward (1799), *Munimenta Antiqua,* Vol. I., W. Bulmer and Co.

Kinsella, Thomas (1969), *The Tain, Translated from the Irish Epic Táin Bó Cuailnge,* Oxford University Press.

Lavrin, Janko (1971), *Nietzsche: A biographical introduction,* Studio Vista London.

Ledwidge, Francis E. (2017), *Legends and Stories of the Boyne Side,* Excel Printing Ltd.

Leeming, David (2005), *The Oxford Companion to World Mythology,* Oxford University Press.

Leenane, Dr. Mary (2014), *The Written and Oral Landscape of the Black Pig's Dyke,* The Black Pig's Dyke Regional Project Report Volume 1 of 2.

Mac Cionnaith, L. (1935), *Foclóir Béarla agus Gaedhilge: English-Irish Dictionary,* Oifig Díolta Foillseacháin Rialtais.

Mac Coitir, Niall (2003), *Irish Trees: Myths, Legends & Folklore,* The Collins Press.

Macalister, RAS (1919), *Temair Breg: A Study of the Remains and Traditions of Tara,* Proceedings of the Royal Irish Academy 34 C.

MacKillop, James (2000), *Oxford Dictionary of Celtic Mythology,* Oxford University Press.

MacKillop, James (2006) [2005], *Myths and Legends of the Celts,* Penguin Books.

Mallory, J.P. (2013), *The Origins of the Irish,* Thames & Hudson.

Mallory, J.P. (2016), *In Search of the Irish Dreamtime: Archaeology & Early Irish Literature,* Thames & Hudson.

Marsh, Richard (2013), *Meath Folk Tales,* The History Press Ireland.

McGuinness, David (1996), *Edward Lhuyd's Contribution to the Study of Irish Megalithic Tombs,* Journal of the Royal Society of Antiquaries of Ireland, Vol. 126, pp. 62-85.

McMahon, Joanne and Roberts, Jack (2001), *The Sheela-na-Gigs of Ireland and Britain: The Divine Hag of the Christian Celts – An Illustrated Guide,* Mercier Press.

McMann, Jean (1993), *Loughcrew: The Cairns, A Guide,* After Hours Books.

Meehan, Pádraig (2012), *A Possible Astronomical Alignment marking Seasonal Transitions at Listoghil, Sligo, Ireland,* Internet Archaeology, Issue 32.

Monaghan, Patricia (2003), *The Red-Haired Girl From the Bog,* New World Library.

Moriarty, John (2006) [2005], *Invoking Ireland: Ailiu Iath n-hErend,* The Lilliput Press.

Moroney, Anne-Marie (1999), *Dowth: Winter Sunsets,* Flax Mill Publications.

Morris, Henry (1907), *"Louthiana: Ancient and Modern",* CLAJ, Vol. 1, No. 4.

Mulvihill, Mary (2002), *Ingenious Ireland: A County-by-County Exploration of the Mysteries and Marvels of the Ingenious Irish,* TownHouse & CountryHouse Ltd.

Murphy, Anthony and Moore, Richard (2008) [2006], *Island of the Setting Sun: In Search of Ireland's Ancient Astronomers,* The Liffey Press.

Murphy, Anthony (2012), *Newgrange: Monument to Immortality,* The Liffey Press.

Murphy, Anthony (2013), *Venus, The Caillichín na Mochóirighe of Newgrange, Ireland,* in The Mythology of Venus: Ancient Calendars and Archaeoastronomy, Benigni, Helen (editing), University Press of America.

Nagy, Joseph Falaky (1997), *Conversing with Angels and Ancients: Literary Myths of Medieval Ireland,* Cornell University Press.

Nelson, E. Charles and Probert, Alan (1994), *A Man Who Can Speak of Plants: Dr Thomas Coulter (1793-1843) of Dundalk in Ireland, Mexico and Alta California.*

Nilan, Judith L. (2014), *A Legacy of Wisdom: The Genius, Power, and Possibility of Ireland's Indigenous Spiritual Heritage,* Home Colony, Washington.

Ó Crualaoich, Gearóid (2007) [2003], *The Book of The Cailleach: Stories of the Wise-Woman healer,* Cork University Press.

O'Donovan, John (translator and editor) (1856), *Annals of the Kingdom of Ireland by the Four Masters*, Vol. I, Hodges, Smith, and Co.

O'Donovan, John, (Herity, Michael editing) (2001) [1836], *Ordnance Survey Letters Meath*, Four Masters Press.

Ó Gibne, Claidhbh (2012), *The Boyne Currach: from beneath the shadows of Newgrange*, Open Air.

Ó hÓgáin, Dáithí (1991), *Myth, Legend & Romance: An Encyclopaedia of the Irish Folk Tradition*, Prentice Hall Press.

Ó hÓgáin, Dáithí (2006), *The Lore of Ireland: An Encyclopaedia of Myth, Legend and Romance*, The Collins Press.

O'Kelly, Michael J. (1982), *Newgrange: Archaeology, Art and Legend*, Thames and Hudson.

O'Reilly, Peggy and Tuite, Breeda (ed) (1994), *The Cry of the Dreamer and Other Poems: John Boyle O'Reilly.*

Ó Ríordáin, Sean P., and Daniel, Glyn (1964), *New Grange and the Bend of the Boyne*, Thames and Hudson.

Ó Síocháin, P.A. (1967), *Ireland – A Journey into Lost Time*, Foilsiúcháin Eireann.

Osbon, Diane K. (editing) (1991), *Reflections on the Art of Living: A Joseph Campbell Companion*, HarperCollins, New York.

Paice MacLeod, Sharon (2012) [1960], *Celtic Myth & Religion: A Study of Traditional Belief, with Newly Translated Prayers, Poems and Songs*, McFarland & Company Inc Publishers.

Power, Dr Siobhan (2014), *The Geology of County Louth*, in Campbell (2014), pp. 256-260.

Prendergast, Frank (1991), *Shadow Casting Phenomena at Newgrange*, Survey Ireland.

Prendergast, Frank (2013), Tomb L, Carnbane West, Loughcrew Hills, County Meath – an archaeoastronomical assessment, http://www.newgrange.com/pdf/loughcrew-cairnl.pdf.

Rolleston, Thomas (1998) [1911], *Myths and Legends of the Celts*, Senate.

Seaver, Matthew and Brady, Conor (2011), *Hill of Slane*, Archaeology Ireland Heritage Guide No. 55.

Shaw, Rev. William (1780), *Galic and English Dictionary*, Volume 1.

Slavin, Michael (1996), *The Book of Tara*, Wolfhound Press.

Slavin, Michael (2005), *The Ancient Books of Ireland*, Wolfhound Press.

Smyth, Jessica (ed) (2009), *Brú na Bóinne World Heritage Site: Research Framework.* The Heritage Council.

Squire, Charles (1998) [1912], *Mythology of the Celtic People,* Senate.

Stokes, Whitley (1894), *The Prose tales in the Rennes Dindshenchas,* Revue Celtique 15, pp. 272-336, 418-484.

Stout, Geraldine (2002), *Newgrange and the Bend of the Boyne,* Cork University Press.

Stout, Geraldine and Stout, Matthew (2008), *Newgrange,* Cork University Press.

Streit, Jakob (1984), *Sun and Cross: From Megalithic Culture to Early Christianity in Ireland,* Floris Books.

Thom, Alexander (1971), *Megalithic Lunar Observatories,* Oxford University Press.

Toolis, Kevin (2017), *My Father's Wake: How the Irish Teach Us to Live, Love and Die,* Weidenfeld & Nicolson.

Van der Post, Laurens (1978) [1976], *Jung and the Story of Our Time,* Penguin Books.

Vaughan, A.P.M. and Johnston, J.D. (1992), *Structural constraints on closure geometry across the Iapetus suture in eastern Ireland,* Journal of the Geological Society, 149, 65-74.

Waddell, John (2015) [2014], *Archaeology and Celtic Myth: An Exploration,* Four Courts Press.

Wheeler, H.A. (1950), *The Tara Brooch: Where Was It Found?,* Journal of the County Louth Archaeological Society, Vol. 12, No. 2.

Wilde, William (2003) [1849], *The Beauties of the Boyne and Blackwater,* Kevin Duffy.

Witzel, E.J. Michael (2012), *The Origins of the World's Mythologies,* Oxford University Press.

Wright, Thomas (2000) [1748], *Louthiana: or, an Introduction to the Antiquities of Ireland,* Dundalgan Press.

Index